READ *Between* THE GRINDS

Cat Collins

THE CURSE OF BETWEEN BOOK ONE

READ BETWEEN THE GRINDS

OTHER BOOKS BY CAT COLLINS

Diminishing Magic Series
(Paranormal romance)

Jewels of Clay

Flames of Gold

Guardian of Whispers

Ripples of Glass – COMING SPRING 2024

Reindeer Games Series
(Paranormal romance)

Fixin' Vixen

Book Two – COMING CHRISTMAS 2024

The Curse of Between Series
(Urban Fantasy)

Read Between the Grinds

Book Two – COMING SUMMER 2024

Dedication

To the staff at Guillermo's Coffee Shop
Little Rock, AR
Thanks for the help & the inspiration.
Also:
Happy Birthday, Harrison!

Content Information

WELCOME TO BETWEEN, NEVADA

WHERE THE RESIDENTS KNOW
THERE ARE TWO SIDES TO EVERY CURSE

This book contains two stories. One light, one dark.
The following is the content you can expect.
Light: rom-com vibes, dirty talk, hot nerd
Dark: some choking, more dirty talk, murder, revenge,
creepy relatives, sex traffic & flashbacks with trauma.
For more specific information, please see my website.
catcollinsbooks.com

FALLON'S
Light Roast

The sudden jerk of the seatbelt or the scent of rubber in the air wasn't the worst part of the wreck. Nope, the worst part was facing the screeching banshee of a woman whom I rammed into when I veered left. She wasn't even out of her car yet, but the stream of unrecognizable curse words coming through her closed window was impressive.

In my defense, I didn't cause the wreck.

It was a bird.

I grabbed my insurance info and license for the cop who was already pulling up on the scene, hoping for lenience or sympathy or something that would get me to work on time. I mean, I was the boss, but so was my sister and she hated when she had to open the shop. She said she preferred roasting the beans in the back, but that was a bald-faced lie because she'd rather sit behind the counter and 'spill the tea' about our customers than prep the coffee.

I just hoped the coffee shop was still standing when I got there. Who knew what she would do?

The officer approached the woman's car first, knocking on her window and motioning for her to get out of the vehicle. I waved my papers at him and gave him a thumbs-up to indicate I wasn't hurt.

Okay, I liked my chances here. He was an older man. Way older than I would expect a police officer to be, but I was new to town, so maybe it was a smallish-town thing. Judging by his graying hair and wrinkles, he probably had kids in their late twenties like me. His eyes were friendly, his posture slack with age.

Most people underestimated me with my long blonde hair and petite frame, but people his age tended to treat me like a kid. And kids don't get tickets.

I leaned against my car, watching the steam billow from the woman's hood. It was a very expensive-looking ride, not that I knew anything about cars. This car was a sporty red sportscar that was going to cost me a lot if the cop didn't cut me a break.

After another lengthy minute in which I contemplated bolting but decided in favor of being mature, the woman finally rolled out of the car.

She pointed her crimson-manicured nails at me. I could feel myself shrinking into my hoodie at the sight of her.

Girlfriend was pissed.

The cop motioned me over with a finger, so I took a breath to steady myself, then marched right over to the woman who was still screaming, hitting more English words now than not, but still, it was hard to get a full read on what she said.

When she finally stopped to intake oxygen, the officer nodded politely, then used a light hand to back her away from me. That was for my protection, not hers. He shot me a rueful smile. "Okay, ma'am the best I can tell she believes that you caused the accident when you swerved into her lane at an advanced speed. My Romani is a little rusty though, so maybe you should tell me what happened."

Right. This was my chance to sway the cop to my side.

"I'll admit I did veer a little more to the left than legally advised, but only because I was startled, no I was petrified, by a huge bird that flew right in front of my windshield. Instinct took over and I may have left my lane for a few seconds."

"Hm." Non-committal.

"She had to have seen the bird. It was the biggest, weirdest bird I'd ever seen. That's why I jerked the wh—I mean, wiggled my steering wheel a little. I was shaken by the bird." I took my chances and stepped closer to the woman. "You saw it, right?"

She looked at me like I was crazy and spat on the ground at my feet, barely missing my sneakers before launching into another tirade that ended in the word "Meesh."

Didn't need to be Romani to know that was a slur.

Ignoring her, the cop scratched his chin. "Bird, you say? What did it look like?"

"I don't know. Flappy wings, pointy jagged beak, freaky claws. All of them ginormous. It came out of nowhere. Fast."

The cop's face and posture morphed in an instant. It was so visible that the woman looked at me to see if I'd noticed. His voice got eerily soft. "What color would you say this bird was, ma'am?"

"You're going to think I'm nuts, but I've never seen a bird like it. It was black and white, with zebra-like stripes."

"The eyes? Were they crystal blue, and human-like?"

"I didn't exactly get my phone out to snap a photo. I don't know. I just saw a blur of black and white stripes, then it swooped toward her car. I shut my eyes and when I opened them, it was gone."

"I see. Shut your eyes, huh? Could you describe the call of the bird?"

This was getting weird. "Shouldn't you be asking me to describe the wreck? Or for my insurance? Or anything else." Dude must have been one of those weekend bird watchers.

"Humor me."

Okay fine. I may as well go all the way in on this. "When I heard it's call, I got chills. Like that feeling, you get when they say someone's walking over your grave. It was creepy."

The cop frowned and then grabbed our insurance information without further bird commentary, walking back to his patrol car to, I assumed, write out our tickets or reports or whatever. I was newish to Nevada, and this was my first run-in with the law.

While we waited, I attempted to make nice with the woman, and also diminish my involvement in her smoking car. "Hey, I'm sorry that bird got between us. That was something, huh?"

She folded her arms over her chest, making her boobs push up to her eyeballs. This woman was the type who drew attention from men just by being alive. She was sexy, well-dressed, with manicured hair and hands, and expensive, tight clothes that hugged all of her many curves. "I don't know what you're talking about. I saw no bird."

There was no way she missed that bird.

Not unless she was texting while driving.

Or, typing a novel while driving. That was not a normal bird. It would be like walking down Sesame Street and not seeing Big Bird.

I was about to call her out when the cop appeared again, handing our papers back, along with issuing me a ticket for reckless driving.

Great. Fanfuckintastic.

"She's not getting a ticket too? We ran into each other."

"Yeeahhh," he dragged out. "Your car is in her lane. It's clear to me you're at fault."

I pressed my lips together in a tight line as I tried to steady my breathing. "How much would you say this is going to set me back?" I asked, my voice trembling. I hated that about myself. My voice and my face always betrayed me. Always.

"Well, if you intend just to pay it, figuring in the costs to fix her car and any damage to yours, Have you already met your deductible?"

Of course not. "No sir."

"Then I'd wager it'll set you back three to four thousand, at least. Her car is foreign."

I swallowed. He may as well have said three to four million.

"But that's not your biggest problem right now."

How could it get any worse? I stared at him waiting for him to finish his dramatic pause. "That wasn't just a random bird. How long have you been in Between?"

"Almost six months."

"I see. Well, consider this your initiation. There's a curse on our town. We call that bird the Wayward Warbler. He appears every so often and when he does, you better watch out. Whoever sees him will be cursed until such time they change something vital about themselves and their lives. It's serious mojo, for sure. You're in for a bumpier ride than you've already had."

A curse? The bird put a curse on me. Seriously?

"This is ridiculous," I spat. "There's no such thing as curses and even if there were, a bird with a bird brain couldn't dole them out." I checked with the woman, glancing at her documents to check her name. "Back me up, Esme, you don't believe this bird curse crap, do you? This was just a simple accident."

The cop's condescending tone was starting to eat at me. "Sweetheart, you don't know who you just ran into, do you? This is Esme Doe, of the famous Doe Tea House. She reads tea leaves for a living. She knows all about curses, including this one put on our town by a witch named Cinderella Loveridge years ago." She stayed motionless and non-committal while the cop laughed.

I was seconds away from my head spinning right off my neck. These were grown adults talking about curses and witches. And one of them had given me a ticket! "Let's just say, for shits and giggles, this is all true. If you know the witch who cursed the town, why not go to her house and make nice? Ask her to keep her curse-throwing warbler locked up?"

The policeman leaned forward, looking me in the eye. I noticed a certain cloudiness in his brown peepers. "How old do you think I am, ma'am?"

"I don't see how that's relevant, but maybe sixty or sixty-five." Honestly, I was being kind. He looked older than that.

In a strange turn of events, he pulled his wallet out and handed me his license. "I'm thirty-seven. That's why we don't go talk to Cinderella Loveridge."

Looking at his license and doing the math in my head, I gawked at him for a full minute while my brain tried to reconcile what I was seeing. "Are you saying she—?"

"Cursed me? Yes, I am. But my curse is everlasting with no hope of being resolved. You can rest easier knowing yours can be reversed if you figure it out. Have a nice day. I've got to it the head. Bladder's not what it used to be."

He nodded at Esme and she made a beeline for her car. I don't know why, it wasn't going to start.

Done with the shenanigans, I turned on my heel, marching back to my car and praying to the god of carburetors that it would start and give me this dramatic exit. "Thanks for nothing. The chamber of commerce should give you a raise for the awesome community outreach!" I got in, and slammed the door, jamming the key into the ignition. Before I could turn it, I noticed something in my peripheral vision. A huge white feather was tucked under the windshield wiper. How it got there like that, I'd never know. The bird had just sailed close to my car, not stopped and preened its feathers. Weird. I'd get rid of that stupid reminder real fast.

I held my breath and cranked the ignition.

Thank damn, it started. I shifted into reverse, looking up at the cop and the woman and as she slid back into her car, I swear she looked terrified.

It didn't matter how fast I drove to my shop, that damn feather would not blow away. As soon as I parked and got out, I yanked that feather off and threw it in the trash on my way in.

Good riddance.

My sister had done a total of nothing to prep for opening, so of course, I had to rush through everything, leaving some of the first customers waiting to order. She had many strengths, but being a responsible partner in the day-to-day business of Read Between The Grinds was not one of them. "Zoey, could you ring the customers up at least? I'll make their coffees."

She released an audible sigh but jumped off the counter to take care of it for me. She was better at people than me anyway. Everyone loved Zoey Westwood. Including me. We were all we had now.

An hour later the morning rush was over and I had the time and headspace to sip my own cup of coffee. "Hand me a mug, I think I want an Ernest Hemingway today." Bold, straightforward, with no sweetness or light to it.

"You know, I'm never going to remember what all the coffees are, right? You could've just said, I want it black and strong."

"Ha! You did remember what a Hemingway was."

"Not even a little bit. I just saw the stress on your face and made an informed guess."

I poured my coffee and took a big whiff of the life-giving aroma before I attempted to sip. "When is Oscar back?" He was our only full-time worker and I needed him. Badly.

"Two more days on quarantine. Says he's feeling better though." At least that was something. He was an asset. All our weekend part-timers were too. They all worked great under my direction. We'd hired well.

Zoey blew a bubble with her signature grape gum "Tell me again about this curse you're under. How does it manifest? How long does it last? What's it all about?"

Great. Just what I needed: another curse believer.

"I don't know and I don't care because curses aren't real. So, if you'd drop all talk of curses, I'd appreciate it."

"Uh-oh, did the Warbler catch you?" I swiveled slowly, hoping I'd misheard the comment, and spotted a regular customer Bennie, sitting at the end of the counter sipping her super-sweet Nora Roberts. She was from the college campus down the street.

We had lots of their students and faculty in the shop daily. Bennie whistled. "I feel for you. Warbler got my Aunt Kris once. She walked around for months unable to eat thanks to the curse. When she finally realized she was being a total bitch about what my cousin ate every day and stopped measuring her food and monitoring her weight, the curse went away."

I didn't know what to say. The entire town of Between was cuckooing over this bird.

Smiling, I offered her another pour of coffee, which she declined. "I've got to run to class. Best of luck with the curse. I'll check back in this afternoon to see how things are going for you. My aunt will want to hear what you got."

What I got? She said it like I'd won a prize.

After she left, I rounded the corner to pick up her mug. We did to-go cups in RBtG, but I insisted on serving sit-down customers at the tables in an actual mug.

As soon as my fingers grazed the handle, an odd burning feeling shot through me. It was like the coffee was still hot, but there was only a dribble left in the mug, so that couldn't be it. Weird.

I turned walking to the sink with Bennie's mug in my hands. "Something will prevent her from coming back today."

Zoey arched her pierced eyebrow. "What makes you say that?"

"I don't know. I was just guessing she wouldn't come back. That's all."

When I turned my back to wash the mug, the odd burn was gone. I didn't think I was hurt in the accident, but maybe I should've taken it easy and not gone to work immediately afterward.

Nope. Couldn't leave Zoey alone like that. She might have burned down the shop. Or worse, not opened.

I put the mug down and squirted some soap in. There were already things piled in the sink—thanks for nothing, Zoey—so I used a little more just to do all the wash at once.

I turned my back for two seconds, long enough to reach the dish Zoey was eating her pastry on, but when I turned back around, the entire sink was full of suds and they were growing. "What the hell?" I grabbed the soap and realized it was a different brand than we usually bought. "What's with the soap?"

Without even turning around, she called out, "Oh, I got a discount on that. Aren't you proud of me? It's extra industrial strength, so you only need a drop."

"You don't say." The soapy mess kept expanding, out of the sink on the counter, all over the front of my shirt. I reached up to turn the tap off, but it did no good against the mass of monster foam. Shit. How would I get rid of it?

Sticking my hand in the sink and getting even more sudsy bubbles on me, I stirred the bubbles, attempting to break them. When they didn't work, I pulled the dishes out, one by one, finally finding Bennie's mug on the bottom of the Sudzilla.

The door chimed, indicating another customer had walked in. Great. Way to look professional. A couple of moments later Zoey ran up behind me. "Oooooh, your Café O-*lay* just arrived."

That was her little code for a hot guy entering the shop. It was her sole purpose in life to get me laid. I insisted I could and would take that job upon myself, but she was constantly trying to hook me up with some dude. Said I worked too hard and never got out to have fun. My point was if I didn't, we'd be destitute, so…I won every argument, with the caveat that I had to listen to her go on for hours about hooking up with this guy or the other.

"Fallon, turn the fuck around and look at this man." She pulled on my sleeve to turn me drenching my chest in even more soap.

"Damn it, Zoey," I whisper-yelled, turning around to let her have it when Mr. Café O-Lay stepped up to the counter.

My mouth dried and the foam-laden mug I'd been holding slipped out of my hand, landing on the concrete floor with a clattering clash.

I had to admit, for a lesbian, her taste in men was outstanding.

He was stunning. Like a 'don't stare too long at the sun or you'll go blind' kind of attractive. His dark waves fell over his forehead, stopping right at his bright turquoise eyes. He flashed an apologetic smile at me and it was panty-melting.

Perhaps because I worked in the coffee industry, I was incredibly turned on by gorgeous white teeth. These were set off by plump, moist lips and a dimple in his olive skin.

Damn. *Dammmmmmmn.*

"My apologies. I didn't mean to startle you. Do you need help cleaning that up?" He pointed to the mug, then leaned to peek behind me at the pile of bubbles taking over the workspace. "Or with the tidal wave of suds you have back there?"

Zoey shoved me at the register. "Nope. I got both of those things. No sweat. She'll take your order. This is Fallon Westbrook, age twenty-eight, Virgo, relationship status, single." Now my cheeks were giving enough heat to warm whatever coffee he was about to order.She looked at him innocently. "And you are?"

He chuckled as it made that dimple grow bigger. "Um, okay. I'm Quinn Murphy, thirty, Scorpio." His gaze flicked to my chest. I went through a range of emotions over it. For a second I was excited he was checking me out, then offended that he'd started with my breasts, and then I remembered I was covered in sudsy, foamy gargantuan bubbles with minds of their own, so I let it slide. His tongue flicked over his lower lip instead of answering the relationship status part of Zoey's inappropriate questions.

Of course, this made me wonder if it was purposeful or if he forgot. Or hell, maybe he figured it was none of our damned business. Because it was.

"I'm so sorry. Ignore her. She's a bit delusional, but she's right. I'll take your order."

I most certainly would take his order. Especially if it was ordering me to my knees and telling me I was a good girl.

Wait. This was a customer.

I shook my head, trying to dislodge my intrusive naughty thought.

Yeah, that didn't work because he pulled out a pair of glasses so he could read the menu and I nearly had to clutch the register for support.

Glasses were not hot. Why was I about to drool all over him for wearing them? It made him fall squarely into the hot nerd category and I had no clue why I was finding him so…ugh.

As he perused the menu above my head, laughing at the drink names, I took the opportunity to check him out. He'd done it first. Sort of.

He was wearing a navy blazer over one of those sexy low V-neck t-shirts in gray. It hugged his chest down to his similarly snug dark-wash jeans.

I grabbed a towel from the counter and tried to sop up the wetness from my shirt. I mean, he'd already seen me looking like a dirty dishrag so I don't know what I was thinking, but I did it anyway. It did nothing to help the wet stain on my peach shirt.

"Oh, that's good. An espresso is Chekov for his short stories, right? Short stories for smaller cups?"

My heart ramped up. "Yes. So few people get that."

"I love it. I think I'll have a Sylvia Day. I have to ask; is it because it's steamy?"

This guy. He was pushing all the right buttons.

"It is! Hardly anyone uses the special menu names. I don't know why it's so hard for everyone to figure out."

From behind me, Zoey cackled. "Because not everyone is a book nerd like you, sis."

Quinn smiled. "I think they're clever, so I guess that makes me a book nerd too. I don't have much time for reading fiction now, but maybe one day I'll get back to it."

He pulled out his card to pay and once we got that out of the way, I went about making his cappuccino, while he went over to the booth in the corner.

As I was fumbling around with the drink, Zoey joined me, giving me a play-by-play. "All right, he's sitting facing the counter, to get a better view of you while you work."

"Or so he can see the door in case he's meeting someone, say a girlfriend or boyfriend."

"Nah. Gaydar isn't pinging. Oh, he's pulling out a laptop and books. Lots of papers. If he's thirty, he's too old to be a student. So grad student maybe? TA? Ooh, a young hot professor who will keep you after class!"

I sighed. "Thirty is not too old to be a student. And what difference does it make if he is? Why are we guessing his profession? He's a customer and he'll be leaving soon."

"So you can stalk him on social media, duh. Oh, he's taking a phone call." She ran off, grabbing a towel and pretending to wipe down the table next to him like it was her duty. When she returned, I got the full report. "It sounds like he's talking to a professor. He said he'd get back to her later today. Do you think they're having an affair?"

I finished up the foam on his drink. "For chrissakes Zoey, how am I supposed to know that? Just chill. I'm taking him his cappuccino because he's our customer. We are going to leave him alone and let him enjoy it in peace. Got it?"

I didn't stick around long enough to hear her reply. It was important to our business that the customers were happy and got hot coffee when they wanted it. At least that's what was on repeat in my head. Trying to convince myself that I wasn't, in fact, curious about his relationship with some random professor.

"Here you go, Quinn. Let me know if you need anything else."

"Thanks, Fallon. I will. I hope you don't mind if I camp out here today. I couldn't take another long day in the library. I needed to be around people enjoying life so I could soak up the vibes vicariously."

I wished he'd take the glasses off. They were doing things to my insides. *So* not like me. I usually went for the tatted bad boys who treated me like crap. "No problem. Stay as long as you like. What are you working on?"

Damn it. I didn't mean to ask that. None of my business.

"I'm studying anthropology, working on my grad school thesis."

Impressive. "What's your thesis on?"

"I haven't got a title yet, but I'm studying urban legends, with an emphasis on curses and their effects on local culture, specifically their relevance in shaping the communities who actively engage in belief and proliferation of these curses. I'm sure that sounds perfectly boring to you, but I love this shit."

"Not boring at all."

"It's so exciting. I've heard and seen some wild things throughout my research. For example, did you know there's a local legend about a curse in Between?"

"Ya don't say?"

I managed to extricate myself from Quinn when a new customer walked in the door. It was a good thing because I was going to need a minute to process how this otherwise perfect—so far anyway—man was flawed enough to believe in curses.

Not that it mattered because he'd soon be just a memory in my mind. One I may bring out in the shower from time to time.

I was in the process of fixing the customer's F. Scott Fitzgerald when a large guy wearing a football jersey from UNB across the street came running in. "Is it true? Are you the one?"

"I'm not sure what you're talking about."

"The Wayward Warbler got you, right? You have the curse. What's it like? Have you done anything crazy yet?"

"Where did you hear that?"

"A friend of mine said that his ex, Bennie, heard you talking about it this morning."

Quinn was up from his seat in no time, sauntering while tugging on his bottom lip with those perfect teeth. "Is that true? You've been cursed?"

They both looked at me like I was wearing a tiara and handing out hundred-dollar bills. "I don't believe in curses. I saw a big ugly black and white bird. So what? My life is the same as it was before it, only I'm a couple of thousand dollars more in debt because of that asshole bird. Speaking of debt, would you like to order something?"

The guy looked disappointed in my response, but he ordered a Tolstoy anyway. He stood there at the counter eyeing my every move as he drank it. Waiting, watching for the curse to manifest itself on me in some way. I had half a mind to send him packing, but that wouldn't have been good for business. Especially since he ordered a second cup.

Okay, number twenty-one. I'll serve you more coffee even if I don't like you.

Eyeballs still on me, I plastered on a smile and tried to find other things to occupy my mind, like wiping down tables, ordering more napkins, and adjusting all the artwork and books in the room. No matter what I did or where I went, number twenty-one's eyes followed. "Is he making you nervous?"

"Huh?"

I looked up and found Quinn leaning over the counter. His eyes were pinned on me and full of concern. Before I could answer his question, he turned to face number twenty-one. "Look man, you're creeping her out. Why don't you take your coffee to go?"

"Nah, I want to be here when the curse drops."

"I don't think that's a good idea."

The two of them stood a little too close to each other, even matched height-wise, fighting for dominance. I had no trouble picturing the brutish football player beating the crap out of Quinn, but Quinn stood there looking completely unintimidated. He took a step, bumping chests with the curious football goon. "Get out. Don't come back until you find where you left your fucking manners."

Oh my.

Oh, my, my, my, myyyyy.

Was that a flicker of lust heading downtown to Ladyville?

Why, yes it was.

Number twenty-one clenched his fist for a few seconds—likely trying to decide whether or not to slug Quinn—but ultimately decided it wasn't worth it. He slammed his ceramic mug on the counter and left.

Two broken mugs in one hour. Had to be a shop record.

"Sorry about that."

"Sorry about what, defending me and sending a creep packing? No need."

"Nah, I'm sorry he broke another mug. I can pay for it."

"Yeah, I don't think so. It's no big deal. Thanks for sending the creeper away though. Let me just get this. Honestly, I had no idea I needed security on my payroll."

I began picking up the shattered pieces of the mug. There was a section of the bottom still intact, so I picked it up first. As soon as my finger touched the small pool of coffee in the bottom of the mug, I got that same weird burning feeling I did from Bennie's mug earlier.

Standing to toss the mug, my head swirled and everything around me disappeared. It was like the counter of my coffee shop had morphed into a football field.

"What the hell?" I muttered, shuffling back in search of the stool that was somewhere behind me. I hoped.

I backed into a surprisingly solid wall of muscle that smelled amazing and felt warm. Quinn was hiding stuff under that blazer. His arms snaked around my waist, and his breath tickled my ear.

All of that while a football game was happening on the field in front of me. I tried to speak, but I seemed to be frozen in place and struck mute at the same time.

The football crowd screamed as I witnessed one of the UNB players cross the line for a touchdown. Before he could do any kind of victory dance, another player from the other team, wearing a green uniform, plowed into him, knocking him into another downed player. He went flying over the player, landing on his head. His neck twisted unnaturally and his body went limp as it hit the ground with a thud.

"Fallon, I need you to talk to me."

A surge of heat washed through me. I blinked a few times and I was standing back behind the RBtG counter, looking at the stacks of to-go cups and coffee machines, breathing in the telltale coffee shop aroma that I loved. "What happened?"

Suddenly able to move, I took a step but found myself being hauled backward. Into the arms of Quinn. "Hold on. You're not going anywhere until I know you're okay." He pulled the stool over, lowering me onto it before stepping in front of me. "You just zoned out and turned into stone. Tell me what happened."

"I-I-I don't know. I was cleaning up the mug and my vision changed. I was here, then poof, I was watching a football game.

UNB versus a team in green jerseys. It was so real. And so awful. That guy that was just in here, number twenty-one. He was hurt badly. Maybe even paralyzed."

Zoey came out of the office, having finally realized I was in some kind of distress. "This has to be the curse."

"What? No, don't be silly. It was probably just my imagination. If anyone was cursed it has to be him. What I saw was gruesome. I probably just had an intrusive thought because he was rude and bothering me."

Quinn raised his eyebrow. It was a hot move on him. "Excuse me for saying this, but you don't seem to be the type that would wish paralysis on someone, even if he was an asshole."

Okay, he had me there. "I don't know. Whatever it was, it's gone now. I'm fine."

They both looked like they didn't believe me.

Which was fitting because I sure as shit didn't believe myself.

It took a lot of convincing, but I managed to get both Zoey and Quinn to agree to go back to their prospective spots. I didn't want either of them to worry about me. That was my job, thank you very much.

Even after the odd flash of whatever it was, I wasn't sold on the curse. I was far too intelligent to get caught up in all the nonsense. I thought Quinn was as well, but I guessed I was wrong about that. Maybe he was one of those 'book smarts' people with no common sense.

He'd lowered his head to read his screen and those adorable little flops of hair kept getting in his way, forcing him to blow them upward. Some might say he needed a haircut, but I wouldn't be one of those people. Every time he did it, I practically swooned at the thought of his warm breath skating over my ear when he'd tried to save me from my…whatever that was.

"You've got it bad."

"I don't."

"Don't lie to me, bitch. I know you. Your panties are drenched as we speak and it has nothing to do with the water you spilled on yourself. You have the hottie-totties for the Professor over there."

I whirled around and out of the corner of my eye, I caught Quinn shifting on his seat and I immediately wished he was back in my line of sight again.

Okay. Maybe she was onto something.

Didn't matter.

"His name is Quinn and he's not a professor. Do I find him attractive? Sure. Does that mean I'm going to throw myself at him? No."

She crossed her arms, tsking like she was disappointed in me. "Mm-hm."

The bell chimed announcing another customer and I took the opportunity to skirt away from her judgment. "Welcome to Read Between the Grinds. What can I—?" My brain stopped functioning when the woman walking in the door stepped out of the sunlight.

It was her. The woman from the wreck, Esme. She had a white bandage over her left eyebrow. I didn't remember her bleeding from the wreck, but I *was* preoccupied with the steam coming from her engine and the supposedly cursed bird to say for sure. She eyed me up and down and back up again, a scowl crossing her pretty face. "You."

"Um, hi again. I'm still sorry about what happened."

"Don't be sorry. Be forthcoming with your portion of the bill. You've put me out in the worst way. You wouldn't believe the mechanic I was forced to use to fix my car. He's unbearable." She pushed her sunglasses up, revealing dark eyes that looked everywhere but at me. I was about to tell her my insurance company was taking care of everything minus my large deductible and that would have to wait a hot minute on that, but I couldn't because she barreled on with her discourse. "Whatever. I'm meeting someone."

Quinn swept in, eyeing us both cautiously. "I'm here, Esme. Do you know Fallon?"

In the hasty moments it took for her to answer my mind went into overdrive. trying to determine what relationship Quinn had with Esme. Study buddy? Best friend's wife? Cleaning lady coming to pick up his keys?

She pointed to her bandage. "Our cars were well-acquainted this morning, so yes, I guess I know her." She leaned up and pecked his cheek, her fingers twirling in the curly bits. "You need a haircut."

Sister. Yeah, a sister would go for the cheek and give him bad grooming advice. Must be his sister.

"Eh, maybe I like hair this length. Es, this is Fallon who's a creative coffee genius, and Fallon, this is Esme." There was a pause. A pause, I say. A long one. Four seconds minimum. "My girlfriend."

Zoey passed by us, leaning into my ear with a well-timed, "Wah, wah, waahhh."

Quinn directed Esme to his booth by putting his hand on the small of her back, then jerking it away quickly as he glanced over his shoulder at me. "She'll have a Virginia Woolf."

I smiled as big as I could, then turned to get her coffee, hoping the disappointment in his relationship status didn't show on my face.

"You need to learn to school your features, Fal. Anyone could see right through you to that heart beating out of time for Quinn but don't worry, I'll help you out."

"Zoey, what are you doing?"

She failed to answer me. Instead, she waited for me to finish Esme's coffee and when I handed it to her she went over to the booth, promptly sliding in next to Quinn like she'd been invited. I prayed to the god of intrusions to make the bench open up and swallow her whole.

It didn't.

Thankfully another customer darted in so I could focus on her. She drummed her fingers on the counter as she ordered a small which was a ristretto, having the highest amount of coffee beans and caffeine we had on the menu. I called it a George Orwell, but she couldn't be bothered to use the proper moniker.

As soon as it cooled enough for her to drink, she downed the entire cup in one gulp and asked for a second. Which she downed in one gulp. "Thanks so much. That was delish. Which way to the restroom?" I pointed to the far corner and she set her empty mug on the counter, then dashed to take care of her business.

Okay, the last thing that woman needed was more caffeine. She was as jittery as anyone I'd ever seen. I started to feel bad for giving it to her as I picked up the mug to wash it.

Just like before, a rush of warm heat soared through my body, my head swam and my vision blurred into another section of my shop. Namely the ladies' room.

It was happening again. I was seeing things. This time, the woman was taking apart my toilet, piece by piece. There were gadgets and tubes and all the guts of the toilet strewn around her. It made zero sense. She stuck her hand inside the gross part up to her elbow, then frantically moved it around like she was fishing for something.

When I was certain I was going to throw up over her sticking her hand where the human waste was supposed to go, she pulled her hand out and bolted out of the restroom, flying by Quinn and Esme who looked like they were arguing. She sped through my sitting area, then outside to her car. She wrenched her door open and found her cell phone sitting on the driver's side seat. Her look of sudden relief turned into riotous laughter, then got in the car, and peeled away.

Had she thought she'd flushed her phone?

My vision cleared and I found myself, once again, in the arms of Quinn. "Whoa there, Suds. We've got to stop meeting like this." I turned to look up at his face to see if it looked as soft as his words sounded. The second our eyes connected, he smiled. When he began stroking my cheek with his thumb, shivers went right through me. "Seriously, are you okay?"

"I think. What happened?"

"You tell me. You zoned out again and I couldn't get you to respond. When I saw you teetering like you were going to fall, I ran over to make sure you stayed upright. A bump on the noggin might ruin your gorgeous face. Not on my watch."

Did he just call me gorgeous? And do so with a smoldering look that warmed my girly parts? Yep. Not only that, he'd said a total of zero words about Esme's bump on the noggin.

Still.

"And your girlfriend?" I slapped my hand over my mouth. Why did I say that? Why? The vision must have rattled my common sense.

His eyebrows knitted together. Fuck me, even his frown line was hot. "I'm more concerned about you."

I pulled away from him, knowing it was the right thing to do. "I'm fine. Just got a little dizzy."

"What did you see this time?" I shook my head trying to play it off, but he didn't buy it. "Spill the beans, no pun intended. I know you saw something."

Sighing, I gave in. Way too easily. I had a deep desire to do anything this man told me to do. "Just that customer wrecking my bathroom and running away, but I'm fine. Don't tell me it's the curse, okay? It was just my vivid imagination mixed with guilt for giving her more caffeine than she should've had. Just… I need to go back to work. Esme's waiting for you."

He glanced back at his booth. Indeed she was waiting and frowning and scowling and looking more pissed off than when we bumped cars. Quinn shrugged as the corner of his mouth kicked up. "I'll be right over here. Shout if you need me. I don't give two shits what Esme thinks about it."

Needing to take a breather, I leaned against the counter. Within moments, Esme was shouting. "Maybe she needs to see a doctor, not a handsome grad student."

Oops.

Zoey popped in like the ghost she was. "Where have you been?" I whisper-yelled. I had another vision and Esme is probably going to murder me in my sleep now. Could've used some backup that wasn't in the form of a yummy dude wearing glasses."

"Oh, you mean, Clark Bent-Me-Over?"

"Geez. Where do you come up with these names? Yes, he came over when he saw I was feeling off. Again, where were you?"

"Going through her bag, of course. She was focused on watching him dote on you. Did you know her family is famous around here? She's part of the Doe Tea House that read tea leaves and fortunes and all that mysterious stuff. She's the face of the brand."

"Makes sense. And please don't do that again. She hates me enough already."

"Yeah, well, Ms. Tea Pot, tall and curvy, has one train ticket for out of town. One way. It doesn't feel like she's too invested in her relationship since the ticket is for tomorrow and I heard Quinn making plans with her for the weekend and she failed to mention she'd be out of town."

Interesting. Very, very, very interesting.

The bathroom door swung open and the jittery woman burst out, flying past Quinn and Esme who were arguing——no doubt about me—then hit the door. Just like I'd seen in my vision.

Shit.

I sprang from behind the counter, breezing past the booth and hitting the bathroom in record time. I had to see if it was true.

Somewhere deep inside me, I knew what I'd find in there.

My toilet was completely upturned, just like in my vision, and the sound of a flush in the men's restroom next door caught my attention. Before I could say Charmin, water began gushing from the broken toilet.

No, gushing wasn't the right word. It was more like erupting. It hit the ceiling, raining water down all over the walls, and yep, all over me. I was drenched in toilet water.

Shit, was it clean? I had no idea.

All I knew was I was covered in it.

"What the fuck?" Quinn spat as he pushed inside the door. "What did you do, Suds?"

"It wasn't me!" I stupidly put my hands over the spray of water coming from the toilet like that would magically stop the flow. "I don't know what to do!"

By this point my hair was drenched, my makeup running, I had not a dry speck of clothes on me, and the water was still cascading all over the bathroom. Quinn splashed—yes, it was pooling on the floor now—over to me, picked me up, throwing me over his shoulder like a sack of beans. "You can start by getting the hell out of here."

He walked with me outside and deposited me next to the booth where Esme was now standing. He pointed at me. "Stay."

I opened my mouth to argue with him. It was my bathroom, my problem, but he put his finger to my lips—right there in front of his freaking girlfriend—and said it again for emphasis. "Stay."

"I'm not a dog," I blurted.

"No, you are *not*," he said with a liquid tone to his voice that matched the water gushing in my bathroom.

And in my panties.

I needed to get a grip on my emotions with him.

He marched back into the toilet tsunami, closing the door behind him. That left me with Esme. She took one look at my wet clothes and stepped back so I wouldn't drip on her. "Well, while he cleans up your mess, the least you could do is get me a free coffee. These are Jimmy Choo's." I looked down and found a steady stream of water flowing over said Choo's.

Great. Afuckingmazing.

Not sure what else to do, I got her another coffee, handing it over with yet another apology. "Sorry about that. I don't know why that woman dismantled my toilet."

"Hm." She looked down her nose at me, then sipped her coffee like there wasn't another thing happening in the world. "I hope your business insurance is better than your car insurance."

Before she could insult me further, Quinn came back out, giving me a raised eyebrow, then shifting his gaze a little to the right where he'd left me. I hopped over that few feet, making that delicious smile cross his face. His voice was pure molten heat. "It's good you take direction well."

What? Did he just make a second sexual innuendo in five minutes? Surely not. I was getting delusional to avoid the problem of the toilet. That had to be it. "I got the water turned off for you, but you're going to need a plumber."

I sat in the booth, mainly because my legs were close to buckling under the weight of his words. "I'll have to close down until it gets fixed. I can't serve food and drinks without a working toilet. Not to mention, I'll have to mop up this mess. I'll be closed for days and lose so much money."

Esme set her mug on the table, then looked down to re-examine her shoes. "Not to mention the expense of the plumber."

I wanted to put my head in my hands and cry. I wouldn't. Not in front of people. In front of Quinn or Esme specifically, and the stream of customers that were bolting for the door, but I wanted to. As I silently calculated how much debt I was now in, Esme took one last drink of her coffee. "I know you don't believe it, but this is the curse messing with you. I'd advise you to think your way out of it soon or things like this will keep happening."

Not what I wanted to hear.

I forced myself up, grabbing her mug to go do something productive. As soon as I touched it, that familiar feeling settled over me. This time I was sitting, so I didn't get as light-headed but the fuzziness overtook my sight, and before me swirled a vision of a dirty garage, with a greasy floor and beat-up cars covering almost every inch. In the middle of the workspace sat Esme's shiny red ride.

It took a few seconds for my sight to adjust, but when it did, I gasped. The windows of the car were rolled down and I saw directly into it. Esme's skirt, top, and bra were strewn over the seat beside her.

And she wasn't alone.

I tried to close my eyes so I could unsee what I was seeing.

Didn't work. The vision was still as clear in my head.

Esme was with a man with long, dirty blonde hair and full pretty lips. He was—

Oh god, they were—

If this was a true vision and not my delusional state of mind, then it had to be a memory.

Except...

She had that white bandage over her left eyebrow.

This, whatever it was, was happening in the future.

How the hell was I seeing the future?

Not the curse, not the curse, notthecurse.

It had to be the curse. I was seeing Esme's future and she was cheating on Quinn. With a guy in a dirty garage. Possibly the very mechanic she complained about before. Well, she was *not* complaining now. She was moaning.

The vision faded just as she cried her release.

I blinked. Again. And again.

Quinn was crouched in front of me, stroking my jaws with his thumbs. I was still soaking from the debacle in the toilet, but the feel of his fingers digging into my wet locks sent a rush of adrenaline downtown. My cheeks flushed despite my best efforts to keep calm.

His voice was barely a whisper, low enough that Esme couldn't hear him, but I did. *I. Did.* "I prefer when you stand up to have your visions. I didn't get to catch you this time."

"C-c-catch me?"

"Mm-hm. How else am I going to get my arms around you?" He held out his hand and helped me to stand. I was wobbly, but it wasn't because of the vision. It was because of him.

Once I was upright I took a glance at Esme. She was glaring at me again, but the anger in her stare wasn't as palpable. It was a level three or four as compared to her normal eleventy-thousand. "What did you see?"

"Uh." How could I tell her that I saw her boning a mechanic? I couldn't. Not in front of Quinn. "Just another customer having a bad day." If a bad day meant sweaty, filthy, grunting, orgasmic sex. "Why are you asking?"

"Just trying to see what I'm in for. We both got cursed if you recall. Whatever. I'm heading out." She jerked her thumb toward the door. Quinn remained still at my side. "I guess I'll see you around, Q."

That did not sound like the typical boyfriend/girlfriend goodbye scenario. There was no emotion in her voice, no passion in her eyes. It was cold and felt more like a farewell than an 'I'll see you later.'

It had been a while since I'd done that myself, but the whole exchange sounded off. Quinn gave her a quick wave and she left. Just like that.

Zoey came out from the back again. "Called the plumber. He can't get here until eight p.m."

"That late? That's suspect."

"Well, I had to find one that would work out a payment plan for us, so I had to get creative and use the next-door neighbor of my ex's cousin. He's good and won't charge us an arm or a leg. He just does this on the side, hence the late hour. I can call the guy up the street that comes in for coffee sometimes, but it'll cost four times as much."

Although sometimes Zoey annoyed me, she was helpful in a pinch. "Okay, great." I strolled over to the door and switched the sign from *Open Book* to *Closed the Book*, glancing at Quinn. "I guess I have to send all customers packing for a while. Thanks for all your help."

He walked over to me, shoulders back, turquoise eyes lit like fire. "You're mistaken if you think I'm a regular customer. I'm not going anywhere. Not until I get you out of these clothes."

True, I wanted out of my clothes. True, I'd be more than accepting of Quinn taking them off for me, but his sudden obvious advances made me blush. "What do you mean?" I screeched.

He pointed at me, running his finger from my head to my toes. "You're soaked again, Suds. You need dry clothes and possibly a gallon of disinfectant. Fortunately for you, my condo is a few blocks away. I have a working shower and soap. Let's go."

He glanced up at Zoey, asking her a silent question with his eyebrow. One she answered with a nod toward the door. "I'll lock up."

"Excuse me, ma'am," a voice called from the men's restroom. A man walked out holding a coffee cup. It was full of water, so everything probably had exploded in there too. "Could I trouble you for a refill before you close? I have a long drive ahead of me. My caffeine spilled in the bathroom."

Zoey jumped into action, pouring him an extra-large in a paper to-go cup, then handed it over to me. I shoved it in his hand, apologizing. "I'm so sorry this happened. I hope you'll come again once we get everything back in working order. Coffee will be on the house, of course."

"That'll be up to the woman I'm going to see. If I'm honest, I hope to never come back because it'll mean she accepts my proposal. I'm driving to her place in San Diego now to ask her to marry me."

Zoey let out an aww as he took a sip from the cup. "Oh, could I get some creamer in this too, if it's not too much trouble?"

I took the cup from him and as soon as it happened, a vision materialized in my head. This time I took a step toward Quinn because I knew the wobbly bit was going to happen. As I felt his arms reach around me, I tried to memorize the feel of them. No time to enjoy it because the vision started.

The man in front of me was down on his knees holding out a small box with a huge diamond in it. The woman he was proposing to, threw herself on her knees too and launched at him, kissing and hugging and crying at the same time, screaming, "Yes, yes, yes, I'll marry you."

Within the next moment, the vision was gone and I was looking back at the man who eyed me cautiously. I handed the drink back for Zoey to put the creamer in. She filled it up, then told me to lock the front and she went out through the alley door, leaving me alone with Quinn and the last customer I'd have for a while.

I thanked him again. "Best of luck. I think she'll say yes. And the ring is beautiful."

He gave me a quizzical look but was on his way out the door for the rest of his life without verbalizing his confusion.

Well, if the curse was to be believed, she would say yes.

If it *was* the curse giving me the weird hallucinations.

"I'm such a headcase," I muttered, mad at myself for the momentary slip of judgment. Curses weren't real. "I think I just imagined his proposal and the woman saying yes. I don't even know him."

Quinn was not letting go of me. "I don't think you're a headcase. I think you're cursed and you're seeing the future in cups of coffee."

That was… a good assumption based on everything I'd experienced, but I didn't believe in curses, so I dismissed it as soon as it came out of his kissable lips.

"That's ludicrous. I don't believe in this shit. No one can read fortunes in coffee grounds or tea leaves or crystal balls." Belatedly, I realized what I'd said about tea leaves. "No offense to your girlfriend."

Still keeping me in a vice grip, he leaned down. "Not my girlfriend anymore. We parted ways. No harm, no foul."

I swirled around, forcing him to drop his hands. "What? Just now? In my coffee shop?"

He shrugged. "Before the bathroom incident. It's no big deal because it was mutual. We'd been heading in this direction for a long time, maybe since the beginning. I just had reasons to end it today. She did too."

In my mind, I was not-so-subtly hoping one of his reasons was me, but I made an effort to look aloof. Even if he had an interest in me, getting together with someone who'd broken up with his girlfriend five minutes ago didn't seem the wisest idea.

However, the way he was looking at me made my girly bits quiver in anticipation of welcoming him right on in there despite the recent breakup.

He ushered me toward the door. "You look like you don't believe me, but I can prove it to you. Come on, let's go to my place. Get you out of this mess."

I paused before we stepped outside, taking more than a sweeping glance at my shop. My baby. It was going to take more than a plumber and a mop to fix the damage to the bathroom, much less the standing water in the entire place. I didn't need to get out of there, I needed to stay and start cleaning up. "Thanks, but it's going to take a while to clean up. No sense showering until I'm done."

Placing his firm hands on my shoulders, he turned me in the direction of the door, shoving just a little to get my feet moving. I groaned and he laughed about it. "That's the wrong attitude, Suds. You've had a rough day and you need some distance from this place. Everything will still be here if you take a few hours away. I, for one, am hungry. Let me get us some lunch and give you time to breathe. I promise it's the best thing for you right now."

I sighed and gave up despite my misgivings. I locked the door as I tried to run all the positives through my head. It's not every day a hot guy offers to get you lunch and use his shower. I could do this. I could walk away from my shop for this reason alone.

Right?

Quinn opened the passenger door of his SUV, but before I'd gotten so much as a toe inside, I paused. Jumping around him, I called. "I just have to make sure the electricity is turned off too. And double-check the office, put away the cash in the safe."

Trailing behind me, he stood in the doorway, leaning against it with his arms crossed, watching me go through all the things on my list. After I unlocked and relocked the safe the second time, he made a buzzing sound. "Bzzzz. Time's up. Everything is locked, put away, organized, and safe. Now get your sweet ass over here so I can get you out of this place."

He thought I had a sweet ass, huh?

"But I need to—"

"Nope. Whatever it is can wait. Come lock this door, get in my car, and leave this shop behind for a few hours. I promise I will make it worth your while."

Realizing he wasn't going to let it go, I reluctantly did what he asked, locking the door and slipping into his SUV. It was difficult to leave the shop in such a state, but once we'd pulled out of the parking lot, something hit me. "Wait, what do you mean you'll make it worth my while?"

The corner of his lip kicked up and that dimple made a spectacular appearance as he took his eyes off the road and pinned them on my lips. "Use your imagination. I know I am."

It was more of an impact than the wreck was. He'd gone from zero to sixty in just a few ticks of the clock. And I had no response for him. None. I just spent the short ride doing what he'd said and imagining all the ways he might make coming with him worth my while.

Turns out I had a vivid imagination.

We pulled into the space in front of his condo. It was half of a building in a very nice area behind the university. "Do you have a job while you're in grad school?"

"I ghostwrite and edit non-fiction books. It's not as fun as reading fiction, but I've been doing this since high school and made a pretty good chunk of change on it. I turned into a good investment, which got me this place and some bank. I do okay enough to get my degree, then we'll see where that takes me. Now that you know I'm not a serial killer, Come on in."

Could've still been a serial killer.

I wasn't sure I cared.

His condo was neat and well-furnished with books on pretty much every surface including the coffee table, dining table, and kitchen island and yeah, I peeped into his bedroom where I caught a stack of fiction books on the nightstand. It had a scholar vibe, but with quirky abstract art and random, black-painted knick-knacks, it was warm and inviting too. "Nice place."

"Thanks. Make yourself at home. If you want to hop out of those clothes and get into the shower, I'm cool with it."

I laughed. "I'm sure you are."

He spread his hands. "That was an innocent comment. I'm not a letch." After a few seconds pause, he added, "Although…"

"Which way to the shower?"

He led me into his bedroom. Points for his bed being made. "I'll tell you what. I want you to be comfortable, so while you're showering, I'll run to the store on the corner and pick us up some food. It'll be better than the cans of soup or ramen I have in my pantry."

The idea did make me a little more at ease. I was having a hard time denying what he was doing to me physically. Maybe a few minutes alone would help me out. "Okay, fine. Just lock the door behind you. I'll make it quick."

"Great. Towels are in the cabinet and feel free to use any and everything in there. I'll be back in fifteen."

As soon as I heard the door click and lock, I stripped out of my wet clothes, leaving them on the tiles, and stepped into the shower. It heated up quickly and I let the steamy water run all over me, hoping any residual cooties from the exploding pipes would be washed away.

Once my muscles had loosened, at least a little, I grabbed the bottle of soap, lathering some in my hands. The heady and manly aroma wafted to my nose and I inhaled. It smelled like Quinn, which made sense, but what didn't make sense was the way it shot through me. The scent was woodsy, fresh, and intoxicating. I couldn't get enough of it.

Just like my body couldn't get enough of Quinn.

I pictured his wicked smile, the dimple, the way he looked in those glasses. I was helpless to thoughts of him. Slipping soapy hands over my breasts, kneading them in the way I liked, imagining they were his hands. Before long, I was arching into my touch and moaning with my breaths coming quicker.

Keeping one hand where it was, I slid my other down, over my stomach, between my legs as the growing heat of the spray pelted my skin with pinpricks of pleasure.

I bet he would know just how to touch me.

And I bet he'd say something like "I can't wait to get my hands between your legs."

Shit.

Did I say that out loud?

Didn't matter. My want for him was ramping up as the pace of my fingers on my clit increased. I angled, letting the warm water rush down my body and pool in the creases of my thighs as I thought about Quinn.

It was bordering on insanity to pleasure myself in his shower while he was gone getting me food, but he'd been right: I'd had a day. I just needed to…let go.

Imagining the deep rumble of his voice in my ear saying, "That's it, come for me Suds," I leaned my head against the shower as my release tumbled through my body, leaving me gasping as I rode the wave of pleasure. I couldn't remember a time I came so hard and so fast.

My legs trembled as I forced myself to stand upright and finish the shower, making quick work of the shampoo and conditioner. When I was satisfied—ha, in more ways than one—the germs were off, I stepped out of the shower and grabbed a towel from the cabinet. After I'd toweled off and the mirror less steamed, I looked around for my pile of clothes.

I couldn't find them.

Shit.

I checked everywhere in the bathroom—the hamper, the cabinet, back in the shower for some dumbass reason, They weren't there.

Which begged the question: where had they gone?

Taking a deep breath, I carefully opened the door to the bedroom, looking around. Still no clothes. Well, that wasn't exactly true. There were clothes on the bed. They did not belong to me.

I tip-toed over, finding a UNB Rugby team shirt that had been cropped with uneven scissors and a pair of black silk boxers.

Yeah. Quinn had left these for me.

Which opened yet another chasm of questions in my head. When did he lay these out? When did he get back? Where did my clothes go? Are these his clothes? And, most importantly, was he within hearing distance when I…

I was flushed enough from the shower, but that was nothing compared to the feeling I got on my cheeks and chest after those thoughts.

Having no options, I completed my drying and stepped into the silk boxers. They were big on me, no doubt, but they felt nice against my skin. Knowing they were his gave me a level of intimacy I wasn't sure I was comfortable with. Well, I was comfortable with it, I just wasn't sure I wanted to be. Especially after I'd just come in the shower.

"Hey, there's a hair dryer in the back of the cabinet if you want. Come on out when you get dressed. The food's waiting," he called from the living room.

No time to get insecure now. I pulled the rugby shirt over my head. It was also big, but it hung low enough to nearly skim the waistband on the boxers. Part of me wanted to dry my hair, but he'd already seen me with a wet head and I was aware enough of the strange feelings regarding Quinn that I recognized it for what it was: a stall tactic. I didn't want to dry my hair.

I was an adult, damn it. I did nothing wrong and everything I thought about Quinn was good. Nothing off about being attracted to him. What had he said? No harm, no foul. I was going to march out there and eat the lunch he'd brought me.

And pray to the god of orgasms he hadn't heard me.

Running my fingers through my hair, I pushed through the bedroom door. Quinn was sipping from a mug with a bevy of food set out on the table in front of him. "Hey, Suds. Nice shower?"

He's just asking about the shower. Nothing else.

"Mm-hm. I smell like you now, but that's not a bad thing."

"Thanks, I think."

I slid into the chair next to him. The table was round and the surface that wasn't filled with food was filled with his laptop, notebooks, and papers. "You couldn't wait to get started with your work, huh?"

"Something like that." He said, shrugging. "Here. I know it's not as good as your coffee, but I figured you could use some caffeine."

I took a big sip from the cup, letting it soak into my veins like the warmth of the shower had. "Thank you. So, tell me what you're working on now. I know urban legends and that's it." I set my cup down next to his, peering over the pasta he'd gotten us.

"I'm focusing on local urban legends and their effects on the community, specifically the Wayward Warbler curse." He grinned. "You could help me with that, you know."

"I'm not cursed. I just had some bad luck." I picked up my coffee—rather what I thought was my coffee—but with one drink I realized I grabbed his instead. We might have had some stuff in common, but it wasn't coffee orders. With one drink I wanted to spit it out, but before I could comment or rib him about the unnecessary sweetness in his, my vision went haywire.

Not again.

Not with Quinn.

As my head swam to make sense of the scene in front of me, I gripped his arm, pulling him to me as the scene morphed from his dining room to outside somewhere. There was an overgrown field of dainty sky-blue flowers mixed with bright orange blooms. Marigolds, maybe. A hazy dusk sky was just starting to dot with stars and Quinn was leaning against his SUV. The driver's window was broken, but he didn't look concerned about that at all. He had his hands behind his head looking down as he panted.

I wanted to run away screaming but I couldn't. All I could do was inhale and exhale as I saw myself on my knees in front of him running my tongue over his hard cock and moaning as he pushed inside my mouth. "You like the taste of me, don't you?" he rasped.

Oh man. This was not good.

From the look of me in the vision, I did, indeed, like the taste of him. I liked the look of him too. He had a ferocious-looking lion tattoo right underneath that curved V-line of his hips. The placement, the artistry, everything about it was as sexy as hell. No wonder I got on my knees for him.

In the vision, he ramped up the pace, grabbing a handful of my hair, and grunting his satisfied agreement as I took him in the back of my throat over and over, spitting out gravelly, "Oh yeah, you're a good fucking girl to take my shaft like this. I'm so close."

Oh, my.

Just when he was about to come in my mouth, the vision faded and I was back in his condo, looking at him across the table, my cheeks hot. He whistled. "That one was different. What did you see?"

I jumped up, grabbing the chair back for support. "Different how?"

Biting his lip first, he shrugged. "Um, it sounded like you were—how do I put this—getting off."

"No. I wasn't… no. It wasn't like that."

It was exactly like that.

He didn't look like he believed me. I wouldn't have either. "Okay, whatever you say. I think we need to figure out how your curse works, not just for my paper, but for you too. But first," he paused dramatically, taking his time to whip a notebook from his messenger bag, flipping a few pages, and angling it toward me while I tried to get my pulse under control. "This is my journal where I make my lists every day. You can see this is today's date. Look at what I wrote this morning."

The handwritten list—nice handwriting, by the way—was at the top of the page. I read it, mumbling out loud as I did so. "Get gas, text Prof Duncan, rewrite the thesis statement, break up with Esme, laundry."

I looked up and blinked. "You put break up with your girlfriend on your To-Do List?"

He nodded and I wasn't sure if I was impressed, turned on, or offended. "I told you I'd prove that we were already on the way out before I met you. Honestly, our relationship was more about the convenience of having another body in the room or the bed. We got along fine, but there was never anything long-lasting between us. That undefinable spark people have when they're really into each other? We never had it. Maybe that makes me a dick for staying with her as long as I did, then giving our breakup the same status as doing my whites, but if it does, she's one too. She didn't even blink when I told her it was over."

"But you were arguing. I saw you in my vision and I heard you raising your voices."

"Yeah, well she was pissed I brought it up first. She likes control and wanted to have the severing of our relationship on her balance, I guess. Our argument didn't last more than a minute. We both knew we'd had fun for a while, but now it was over. Which reminds me…"

Fishing a pen out of his bag, he pulled the journal over and scrawled something to the bottom of the list, looking up at me with that eyebrow cocked.

Kiss Fallon

id I stare at the page for several seconds while my brain processed? Yep. Did my brain process properly? Not at all. My brilliant reaction to his obvious flirtation was to remark, "You have great penmanship."

You have great penmanship!?

I'd just envisioned his cock in my mouth and my response was to comment on his penmanship.

Maybe I *was* cursed.

He laughed as he got up from his chair, stepping toward me with one long stride. "Fine motor skills. Wait until you see what else these fingers can do." My eyes went wide as he grasped the back of my neck, bringing me to him. "I'm going to kiss you now. Unless you tell me to stop." He zeroed in on my mouth like he couldn't look away from it. "Are you going to tell me to stop, Suds?"

The low liquid of his voice was like honey dripping through my veins. "No."

"Excellent."

The explosion between us was quick and brutal. He planted his lips against mine and we just combusted into a tangle of heat and touch and taste, all the good things I could imagine. His lips were soft, but confident, moving against mine like he was desperate to drag all the secrets from my soul. Ones I'd be willing to give him freely.

When he deepened the kiss, nudging his tongue inside my mouth, I sighed, opening for him and finding myself gripping his waist to bring him closer. Before long our tongues and teeth were nipping and stroking to the sounds of our moans while he took further control, guiding me to the couch and lowering me onto my back.

His lips never left mine.

I didn't know how he'd gone from a 'nice, good-looking guy trying to help me out' to a fire-breathing hottie who was hellbent on destroying me with his kiss. Not that I was complaining. I enjoyed the juxtaposition of him.

He crawled over me and the weight of his body on top of mine made my stomach dip as a fire ignited between us. I gripped his hair in one hand as he finally tore his mouth from mine, kissing and licking his way over my jaw, down the column of my throat.

"Maybe I should've been more specific on my list. When I said kiss you, I meant…" His words trailed off as he stuck his hand inside the waistband of my boxers—his boxers. The promises of what his fingers could do jumped to the front of my mind as he found my center, running his fingers over my clit, down the middle of me, then back up again.

I arched into his touch when he pressed a finger inside me. "So wet for me, aren't you?" All I could do was nod and grip his shoulders for support, writhing under the feel of his toying. "Yeah, that's it. I'm going to make this little pussy purr."

Frozen, I gasped. "What? Oh my god, my underwear!"

He kept going, stroking, pushing inside as he feathered kisses along my neck, "This is *my* underwear, but I'm not going to be too picky about correct pronoun usage right now."

I slapped his bicep, which was remarkably hard. "No, you saw my panties. I was wearing those silly bridesmaid gift panties with the cat on them that says, 'Make my cat purr.'"

"Guilty. I put your stuff in the laundry, so yep, I saw them. Gotta say they were a huge turn-on. Made me want to do this."

He pushed two fingers inside me and began using his thumb to rub against my clit. The sensation was unreal and when he added more fiery kisses, all I could do was throw my head back and moan. "That's it. There's the purr I want."

His voice was too much. Not only the sound of it but what he was saying too. I was seconds away from coming apart, moaning his name and making it clear who I was coming for. "Oh god, Quinn. Don't stop."

"I wouldn't dare stop when you're so eager for me. I knew your pussy would be perfect and I couldn't wait to get my hands between your legs."

At the sound of that choice nugget, my orgasm ripped through me. He didn't let up until I had gone slack underneath him. Pressing a sweet kiss to my temple, he finally pulled his fingers out of me, promptly sticking them in his mouth. I watched in sheer awe as he sucked my juices from them, then he ran his wet fingers down my thigh and back up again. Cocking an eyebrow. "Was that better than imagining me in the shower?"

"You heard that?"

"I did. That's going to live rent-free in my head for a long time, but I'm sure we can find other things to add to it." He pulled his shirt off by grabbing it behind his back and lifting it.

His body was insane. Immaculate. Perfect.

Taut and smooth olive skin, which defined abs and perfectly cut pecs. His arms were more of the same. I couldn't stop myself—why would I—from reaching up and running my hands over his torso, pulling his jeans down to see if that lion was on his hip.

It was.

There's no way I could've known about it. We'd never discussed it, I'd never seen it before the vision. I had no clue it was there.

Unable to reconcile what I'd seen in my head and the stark reality of this beauty of a man staring at me like he wanted to devour me, I focused my attention elsewhere. To his broad shoulders and muscular arms. "So you played rugby as mentioned on this shirt I'm wearing."

He smirked. "You can tell?"

"You know I can." I sat up, going a little wonky from the intensity of the orgasm. "This is not the body of a bookworm who reads indoors all the time."

"You like?"

"Yes."

"I get some great workouts with the rugby team. I've been the assistant coach since I graduated, but I don't want to talk about sweaty assholes right now. I want to talk about making you come again."

He scooted back, giving me space and also making room to take his jeans off. My mouth watered at the sight of him undoing his top button and getting my first real look at his tattoo, but I got a whiff of something in the air that broke me out of the spell. "What's that smell?"

He sniffed his armpit, then looked around. "Um, is it lunch? We can get back to that as soon as I'm finished with you." Such a delicious promise, more so than the food, but that's not what it was.

With his hand on his zipper, he cocked his head. "Okay, I smell it now. Is that…?" He jumped up and ran into the kitchen with his fly open. I tracked behind him until we got to the laundry room.

Smoke billowed out from behind the dryer, fogging the air with heat and an acrid smell. "Shit!" Quinn screamed as he gripped the dryer, yanking it from the wall with one big jerk. Just watching the muscles of his back rippling during the action, got me revved up again.

It wasn't the time or place, but his body made me loopy with desire. Even in the midst of another calamity.

Reaching behind the dryer, he pulled the silver pipe out of the wall. Fire erupted from the remaining hole, licking the wall in flames. Quinn was quick-thinking, ripping a fire extinguisher from the shelf inside the door and putting out the fire in a couple of minutes, while I stood there gaping at him and having a series of fireman fantasies that made me wonder if I needed the extinguisher between my legs next.

When he was sure it was all out, he pulled me back into the living room and sat me on the couch. Of course, I started with apologies. "I'm so sorry. You kept saying I was cursed and I didn't believe you. I'm starting to believe it now."

"I do think you're cursed, but that fire wasn't your fault just because it was your clothes. I should've been keeping a better watch on my lint trap."

"Maybe, but if you'd never met me, this wouldn't have happened today."

"No, I guess it wouldn't, but this is the way I see it: you saved me because normally I put my clothes in the dryer right before I go to bed. Doing laundry in the middle of the day may have just saved my life." He ran his hands through his hair, forcing the cute strands to flop around. "So, I don't believe this was part of your curse, and I'm not pissed about the fire. Although I have to admit, I'm fucking gutted your cute panties are gone."

Though neither of us was too thrilled about having been interrupted, we both agreed we needed to take a moment. Quinn went to shower the extinguisher gunk off him and I took a second to check in with Zoey. She assured me the plumber would be there on time and that all was fine. I had the intense urge to go to check and be sure, but I stifled that when Quinn came out of the shower wearing a towel slung low over his hips. It was too much.

Or too little.

"Like what you see?" he drawled. I didn't answer, but it didn't faze him. "That's okay, you can play coy, but I see you. Your emotions are all over your face and right now you're warring between coming over here to rip this towel off and doing what you think is the right and sensible thing by refusing your urges and focusing on your shop or your curse. Or both."

He pegged me pretty well.

Wait, not pegged. Pegged sounded too much like what I wanted him to do to me. He figured me out.

Smiling, he turned on his heel, dropping the towel and giving me a stellar view of his phenomenal ass as he pulled out some gray sweats, throwing them on without underwear.

Not fair.

He slid into another tight V-neck shirt, this one black, and toed on some slides before joining me at the dining table. I'd reheated lunch and we were both famished, so we tucked in right away. After a few minutes of silent munching, Quinn pulled his laptop open. "Here is the low-down I've been able to gather from the curse if you want to hear it."

I nodded with my mouth full. Of course, I did.

"Legend has it that Cinderella Loveridge had some relationship issues back in the nineteen-twenties. I know that would make her over a hundred years old, but I've done my due diligence and I can find records of her birth in eighteen, ninety-nine, but nothing about her death."

"Already you're not making sense. The oldest living person was what, a hundred, fifteen years old or something like that. This would make her even older. It's not humanly possible."

"True, but if you believe in the curse, you have to give in to the fact she isn't human in the strictest sense. She's a witch. If she can curse Officer Simmons or the poor Postmaster and has a bird who delivers curses, then I'd bet she can extend her own life if she chooses."

I didn't want to know what had happened to the Postmaster, especially if it was worse than the aging Officer Simmons experienced.

If he was to be trusted.

"*If* I believe in the curse." I tried to make my voice as matter-of-fact as I could, but I was starting to wobble on the fence about this curse. Especially after seeing myself with Quinn in one of my visions. Although, that could've just been my wishful thinking and nothing more. "What else?"

"From everyone I interviewed so far, the consensus is that the Wayward Warbler chooses his victims by watching everyone and everything in the town. He picks people who are on the precipice of making a wrong choice or decision. The cursed have the power to get rid of it if they can figure out what it's trying to tell them and make the necessary choice or change. The problem is that it's not so easy when you consider how many decisions or paths our lives take in a day."

I took a sip of water, mulling the thoughts in my head. "Okay, but wouldn't the curse be interested in something life-altering? Seems to me like it would be simple to figure out."

"You'd think, but I've got a list of people here with the weirdest curse resolutions." He pulled his laptop over and clicked a few times, opening a file. "KG eliminated her curse when she returned overdue library books, TY got rid of his curse by eating with chopsticks instead of forks when he went to the Chinese place, SW changed deodorant, so no, not all life-altering changes."

It was difficult to process something so ridiculous. "If you're trying to make me believe in this, you just took a step backward."

"I can't tell you what to believe. I'm just saying that sometimes getting rid of the curse isn't obvious. I'm going to try to help you, but if you don't even believe in it, I don't know how I can. Unless…"

It was his turn to take a big drink, leaving me hanging.

"This is probably a bad idea, but I've been considering visiting Cinderella Loveridge and asking her for an interview myself. You could come with me if you want."

"Really? You're not scared of getting cursed yourself? Like Officer Simmons?"

"Nah, because I'm not going to berate or make her or get rid of the curses. I just want to know about them from her perspective. I can tell you're a seeing-is-believing kind of girl, so maybe if you talk to her you'll understand what's happening."

I stood up, gathering the plates and taking them to the kitchen as I thought about it. To his credit, Quinn gave me the space I needed. Once I'd rinsed the dishes and come back to the dining room, I'd made my decision. "Or, talking to her may convince me this is all nonsense."

"True. I'll take that risk. We've got a few hours to kill before the plumber comes and while I'd like to spend it with you on the bed in there, I think we both need to see Cinderella."

Quinn had said she lived outside of town, but that may have been an understatement. We were at least a half hour outside of the Between city limits and the terrain was getting—for lack of a better word—spooky. The trees and foliage on the way had been nice and normal for the first of May, but when we turned off the main road and onto a beaten-up asphalt track that was probably once a real road, it was like we'd entered another dimension.

Everything around us was dead. Brittle yellow grass blew in the wind as the skeletons of trees stood silently among it. There was a loneliness to the terrain that I felt deep in my soul. I couldn't remember feeling that desolate since my parents were killed. "I'm not saying I believe, but I'm getting witchy vibes for sure."

"Yep. We're going in the right direction. I'm told there's a cemetery beyond Cinderella's house. I can't imagine it getting much creepier than this dead zone."

Goosebumps erupted all over my body when we turned a corner and an ancient house and barn appeared on the horizon. The barn looked like a strong wind would knock it over, but the house, looked sturdy, just old. It was a Victorian design, but the paint had long since faded, making it look like a black-and-white photo in an old newspaper clipping instead of a vibrant residence indicative of its time. "I guess painting isn't high on your priority list if you're a hundred and twentyish years old."

Quinn slowed his SUV, pulling into the dirt drive, but turning around and facing the road. He looked over as he turned the ignition off. "In case we need to make a quick getaway."

Smart.

We climbed out of the car, nerves skittering through me. Quinn didn't look as jumpy as I felt. I hoped that was a good thing. We made it two steps up the porch stairs when a terrible screech drew my attention. I whipped my head around to find that damn bird sitting on a low branch on the nearest tree. A bitter taste coated my tongue as dread flooded my veins. It was watching me with cold, crystal-blue, *human* eyes.

I yelped, practically throwing myself at Quinn. "The Wayward Warbler is watching me."

He pulled me close, putting his arm around my waist. "A few people have told me the Warbler tends to revisit those he curses. I think he knows who you are." He turned to check. "Don't worry. I don't believe he wants to hurt you."

"You mean beyond the supposed curse? Great. Outfuckingstanding."

Quinn laughed, then marched right up to the door and rang the bell. Within a literal second, it swung open and we were face-to-face with Cinderella Loveridge.

Her face was tight and drawn, covered in wrinkles and age spots. She looked every bit of her years. When she opened her mouth to speak, there were no teeth left inside it. It gave the illusion of innocence and youth, but the creaking of her voice said other things. "What do you want? You have ten seconds to convince me not to put a spell on you."

I gripped Quinn's arm even tighter. He smiled, throwing that disarming dimple at her. One second down, but it was a good choice. That dimple probably got anything it wanted. "Sorry to bother you, Mrs. Loveridge. I'm Quinn. This is Fallon. We'd like to ask you some questions about the Wayward Warbler. All we want to do is talk. We've heard a lot of things in town and I think it's time to tell your side of the story."

She eyed Quinn up and down. "It's *Ms.* Loveridge."

"Of course. Ms. Loveridge. Can we take a few minutes of your time?"

She stepped aside, allowing us entry and guiding us to the right into the sitting room. As I was taking in the fact that the furniture must surely have been the original items from nineteen hundred, I also pondered the fact that she'd corrected Quinn when he used Mrs.

If she weren't an ancient potential curse-giving witch, I would've pegged that move as flirting.

Shudder.

We gingerly sat on the crimson settee she pointed to and she took her place across from us on a floral chair. Somewhere in the old house, a clock ticked, giving us a soundtrack to the awkward silence in the room.

Quinn pulled out his notebook and pen, setting his bag on the coffee table. "Let's get started, Ms. Loveridge. Tell me what you want us to know about the Warbler and the curses."

She smacked her gums. "Not much to tell."

"Anything will do. Where did you get the Warbler? When was the first curse? Why do you curse the people of Between? Is there a way to get rid of the curses?"

I sat on the edge of the settee, anxious for the answer to that last one. She ignored Quinn completely, turning her head toward me and making my blood feel cold. "Wouldn't you like to know?"

So, she knew I was personally cursed. "Yes, I would."

"You'll get no help from me, girl." She shifted in her seat, addressing Quinn. "As for you, young man, you have no idea what forces you're dealing with. The whole blamed town has it wrong, but I'm not inclined to enlighten them. No one came to my aid when I needed it most, so why would I come to theirs? We're done here."

Undeterred, Quinn continued. "I get that, but what I don't understand is why you let us in if you weren't going to share any information with us?"

"That's a very good question. I haven't let anyone in this house in years. I think…I think you reminded me of someone, boy. But he's gone and I'm an old fool for allowing myself a little sunshine on this darkest day. You two can get now. Don't come back or I'll make you regret it, just like I did those others who tried to control me and my Warbler."

She stood and we took our cue. That was a big bust. Two minutes and we got zero information.

After Cinderella shuffled us to the porch, I was met with the glaring eyes of the Warbler. It would've been bad enough for the bird to be staring again, but the humanness in his gaze was terrifying. "Why does the bird have creepy human eyes?"

It shot out of my mouth before I could stop it. The look on Cinderella's face when it did told me I'd fucked up.

"What did you say?" she screeched. "Not as creepy as the consequences you'll face if you don't end your curse." The green veins in her neck popped out as she advanced on me. Spittle was flying everywhere. "How dare you have the audacity to insult my

Warbler. He is the greatest gift this town could ever wish for, but you come here you're your silly nonsense and simpleton boyfriend and try to trick me into telling you things.

"You think you can end your curse, but you can't because nobody will ever catch the Warbler. The only way out is through. Get off of my property now, girl. You've riled me up. Get."

Quinn grabbed my arm and we scrambled down the stairs, making a beeline for the car. For some unknown reason, I turned behind me and caught Cinderella raising her arms to the sky, muttering as she did so. I wasn't sure how witches administered curses, but it sure as hell seemed like raising your hands to the sky and mumbling would be it.

I dove into the car as Quinn spun around and got in the driver's seat. The Warbler had left his branch and was flying right toward the vehicle at a speedy rate. "We need to get out of here now, Quinn."

He revved the engine up and dust spewed behind us as he peeled out of her driveway. I held my breath as he swerved onto the road and put as much distance between us and the witch as he could. I sat there clutching the door handle until he said, "You can breathe now. We're miles away from her."

I laughed. I mean, what else could I do? "Maybe I believe now."

"Good. You're halfway to clearing up your curse. We just have to work through it and figure out what's making your curse tick."

Glancing in the rearview and finding that damn bird was sailing in our direction was yet another disturbing encounter looming on my horizon.

"Do we though?"

Quinn cocked an eyebrow.

"Cinderella said something at the end when she got crazy-mad. She said nobody would ever catch the Warbler. What if it's as simple as that? He's already following me, so what if we stopped and used me as bait? You can open your hatch and I'll sit in the front. When he flies in to get me, I can jump out the door and he'll be caught. If that doesn't break the curse specifically, we could kill the bird and put the town out of its misery."

"You're feisty. That's going to be fun to explore later, but I'll put a pin in that. I don't like the idea of you being bait, but maybe you're onto something. Some old-timers in town mentioned that people used to try and trap the Warbler in the past, but they weren't sure why. Maybe this is it." He bit his lower lip. "Okay, we can try it, but I reserve the right to abort if it looks dangerous."

"Pshh. I'll be fine."

I didn't know that I would, but I was eager to get the whole business behind me. My shop needed me.

As I checked in the rearview again, Quinn turned a corner. "Oh shit! What the fuck?"

The SUV swerved violently, as a battered old car with wooden panels on the side blew past the turn for the main road and headed straight for us.

The driver's head was tilted back against the seat and wasn't even close to watching the road as his vehicle angled in our direction. Quinn gripped the wheel and swung the car onto the shoulder of the road to miss the collision. We bumped along the dry grass for a little way, and then our SUV hit a deep rut in the ground, sending us spinning for a second and then landing back on the other side of the road with a thud.

We were halfway on the shoulder, so the SUV rocked as soon as it hit. Quinn floored it, maneuvering the car back onto the road completely. As soon as we hit the asphalt, our tires screeched and we spun and the car went twirling in the opposite direction, finally skidding to a stop on the other side of the road near a tree.

With my stomach in my throat, I turned around, trying to get the license plate, but another head popping up distracted me from my quest.

"Oh god, that guy was getting a blow job. He almost killed us for fellatio." I shouted.

"What? You're kidding."

"Nope. I saw a woman's head pop up at the last minute."

Quinn laughed. "No wonder he wasn't watching the road."

I slapped his chest. "Yeah, it's not funny."

He grabbed my hands, pulling me toward him and pressing a quick kiss to my temple. "It's a little funny. Let's check out the car before we try to move."

We got out and determined pretty quickly there was no damage. Quinn's car hadn't even hit the tree. Everything was in order, so I moved to climb back in and get out of there, but Quinn wrapped his arms around my waist, pulling me back so I was flush with his chest. I assumed things were about to heat up—because let's be honest, I wanted them to, despite the witchy encounter—but instead of getting handsy, he dipped his head and whispered. "Do you still want to be the bait?"

Moving my chin with his finger, he pointed my head in the direction of the tree we'd almost hit. The Wayward Warbler was literally six feet away at most, sitting on a branch and eyeing me like I was its next meal.

Slowly, I disengaged from him and slid into the front seat of the car, closing the door, but keeping my hand on the handle. He crept behind, opening the hatch and giving the Warbler plenty of room to get inside. "I'm going to just…" he hitched his thumb behind him, pointing to an area with tall dead grass behind the tree.

The moment he was out of my view, and I guess the Warbler's, the bird struck. It darted from the tree, circling the car like a predatory shark, giving me the stink-eye on each pass. After the third time, it moved, sailing into the hatch and landing on the headrest of the back seat. Again, his haunting peepers were glued to me. He squawked as Quinn jumped into view, slamming the hatch shut behind the bird.

Thank the god of rugby for his swift moves.

Yelping, I jumped out of the car, slamming the lock down for good measure. Like the bird could unlock it with its beak.

My chest was heaving as Quinn made his way to me. "You good?"

"Yep." We'd done it. We'd trapped the Warbler. Too bad neither of us knew what to do next. "What does your research say about capturing it?"

"Only that they tried. We must be the first ones to be successful." He cocked his head. "I feel like that deserves a reward of some kind." He hauled me against his chest and before I could say cursed, his lips were on mine. The languid way he moved against my mouth combined with the hard ridges of his body pressed to mine was enough to cause a volcano of lust to travel through me.

His hands traveled down my back, grabbing my ass and lifting me. I wrapped my legs around his waist and moaned as he arched against me with his hard cock. I wanted him. I didn't care we were in the middle of nowhere after almost being hit by a guy getting blown and cursed by a witch. Nope, this man was above all that noise in my mind.

I pulled away to tell him so, but I didn't get the chance. A loud crack sounded from the car. He swung me around and we both gasped as we found the bird using its beak, pecking at the driver's side glass. "It's trying to get out."

Another few well-placed pecks and the window shattered, glass cascading to the ground. The Warbler flew out and instead of getting out of there, it made a huge loop in the air and dove.

For me.

It was like looking up and seeing a bullet coming in your direction. I ducked, but he swooped in and got a handful of hair in its claws, yanking and flying away with a clump. "Ouch, you asshole."

It had gone from watching me suspiciously to attack mode.

He sailed in for a second pass, this time I was smart enough to cover my head, so he clawed at my arm, drawing a stream of blood out. "Get in the car," Quinn demanded.

Of course, why didn't I think of that?

I wrestled with the door, finally getting inside, but when Quinn didn't immediately appear next to me, I got concerned. "What are you doing?"

The hatch lifted again and he fumbled with a bag in the back. The Warbler was coming in hot again, but Quinn was ready for him. He raised the rugby ball and aimed, sending it flying at the exact right angle to smack into the bird.

Bulls-fucking-eye.

The bird fell to the ground with a thud. Right next to the rugby ball. Sadly, the bird got up and shook himself off, but apparently, he'd decided we were too much trouble to mess with. He took off in the direction of the witch's house.

My muscles relaxed as relief flowed through me. While Quinn retrieved his ball, I glanced to the other side of the road. It was the first time since the wreck I'd had time to pay much attention to it. There amidst the dead grass and trees was a field of flowers, light blue and marigolds. I didn't know a lot about gardening, but I knew enough to know these two flowers should not be growing together, especially in the middle of a dead field. Yet there they were. These familiar flowers.

I jumped out of the car and ran over to Quinn, realizing what was about to go down.

Specifically me.

Nice rugby skills there. I think you've earned that reward."

"Eh, I just scared it off, nothing major."

I put my hand on the door handle. "Oh, if that's the case, we can just cancel the things I had in mind to do to you. I have to admit, I'm disappointed about it."

That dimple came out in full force. "Don't be so hasty. What did you have in mind?"

"You asked me earlier what was different about my last vision. I guess I should tell you that it was about you."

"Is that so? What was I doing in this vision?"

"It wasn't so much what you were doing as what I was doing?"

"And that was?"

I ran my hand over his crotch. Yeah, the sweatpants were still on, but I enjoyed the feeling of him hardening in my hand as I stroked him. "In my vision, we were here next to this field of strange flowers. Your window was broken and you were enjoying the things I was doing to you while I was on my knees."

He arched into my grip, moaning a little. "On your knees? Please tell me you weren't praying."

"I wasn't, but you were sure as hell thanking god."

The sexy laugh was going to kill me. "If that's true, you better get down on those knees for me right now. I want to feel everything you saw. Show me, Suds."

He looked down, using his foot to scrape the broken shards of glass away. The gesture was sweet and it made me want him even more, so I dropped to my knees, looking up at him and smiling as I slowly—and I mean slowly—pulled the waistband of his sweats down, kissing the smooth skin of his stomach, then running my tongue over that hot V in his hips, then finally making my way to the lion. "I saw your tattoo in my vision too. I gotta say, it's hot." I pressed a kiss there, soft, light, barely grazing his skin.

Goosebumps erupted on his skin. "Do that again."

I did what he asked, enjoying the way he squirmed, but I wasn't there to kiss his tattoo. I wanted something else.

Dragging his pants to his knees, I grabbed his cock in my hand, bringing just the tip inside my mouth, then ran my tongue over the sensitive flesh at the top. He groaned, so I made another pass, taking him in just a little, then drawing out again, this time flicking my tongue over the head. His hips bucked. "You're going to be a fucking tease, aren't you?"

"Am I?" Starting at the base, I kissed all the way up, softly grazing the hot fleshy cock with my tongue. He tasted so good. It wasn't a particular taste I could define like men sometimes said women tasted like honeydew or something, but it was more of a general flavor of salty-sweetness. I wanted to take my time, but honestly, I was struggling to hold back. Especially with those heated turquoise eyes watching every stroke of my tongue and that dimple playing with my emotions.

Quinn slid his legs further apart, angling toward me with that delicious cock, urging me to give him more. Since he'd just saved me a couple of times over, it was the least I could do to give him what he wanted. So, I ran my tongue over the underside of his cock, from the base to the tip and back again, "Mmm," I murmured.

His response was to grab my chin and push his cock inside my mouth. We both groaned as he went deep, then pulled out again. I almost went feral at the sensation, so I grabbed his base and started pumping with my fist as I took the rest of him in my mouth, setting a rhythm, sucking as I jerked him too.

He placed his hands behind his head. "I want to watch you take my dick."

Never taking my gaze off him, I moaned my agreement as I continued to pump him with my mouth and hand. My heart was hammering my chest as we both picked up the pace. He was thrusting and I was taking all of him in my mouth, savoring every second until I had to pull back and lick him like a lollipop, letting that salty-sweet flavor coat my tongue.

"You like the taste of me, don't you?"

Hells yes, I did.

As things heated even more, he took a handful of my hair in his grip. Ironic that I was pissed about the Warbler doing the same thing earlier, but I fucking loved the stinging tug as he pumped into my mouth.

I gripped his thighs for a minute, then reached around and got a hold of his ass, just to give me something to steady myself. He cupped my chin to help with my jaw as I worked him to the back of my throat. "Oh yeah, you're a good fucking girl to take my shaft like this. I'm so close."

I was dizzy with desire. Since he'd said he was close, I wanted to give him all the pleasure as the explosive orgasm he gave me earlier with his fingers alone. So I took a hand and began to fondle his balls as I sucked.

He hissed his pleasure. "That's it. You better get ready because I'm going to come so fucking hard for you." With his warning lighting my blood on fire, he came, throwing his head back and gasping as he emptied into my mouth. "You're going to take it all, aren't you? Yeah, all that's just for you. Drink me up."

He was already at level eleven sexy for me, but that dirty talk just edged him up even more. I couldn't decide what I liked best about him, the dirty talker or the nice, studious guy.

I held on to him tightly as he finished and I swallowed all of it down. I wasn't normally a big swallowing fan, but something at that moment told me it was because I wasn't sucking the right men.

His release, the sheer pleasure of tasting him did funny things to my insides. To my brain too, if I was honest. The vision in my mind earlier had come true without me even trying to make it happen. If it was the curse, then how could I be pissed about it if it brought about such amazing things as this? Unless there was something more to it than I hadn't seen yet.

I helped Quinn pull up his sweats, then stood up, flexing my knees to get the feeling back. Before I could say a word, he pulled me to him, giving me another steamy kiss that made all my insides flutter. How did he do that so easily? It was like his kiss was made of magic. Everything around me seemed to fade into nothingness when his lips were on mine. I'd never been that invested in kissing before.

We were both breathless when we parted. I couldn't stop myself from telling him what he did to me. "I don't know who taught you to kiss, but I'd like to send them a thank you card."

Laughing, he reached up to toy with the ends of my hair. "Funny, I was just thinking of the guys you'd blown before me and getting so damn jealous."

"The list isn't that long and it's been a while. My business takes precedence, unfortunately."

"I guess it's good I live so close, hm?" he teased. "It's getting dark. Let's go wait for the plumber and talk about your curse. Then maybe we can figure out something else to do."

Quinn held the mug in his hands for a few minutes, then offered me his cup before opening up a new document on his laptop. "Let's chronicle our trials. We've established the curse manifests in the coffee somehow. I've held this, but not drank any of it. Can you see anything when I give it to you?"

We were back waiting on the plumber and he'd been a little more than excited when I told him I was starting to believe in the curse. I wasn't sure when that happened. Sometime between the blowjob and Quinn taking out his phone as we pulled into the shop. The asshole football player, number twenty-one, was all over the news. His neck had been broken just like I'd seen in my vision.

After that solid confirmation, there was just too much to ignore about the curse. I mean, yeah, I always had a creative and vivid imagination, but I had true proof that what I'd been seeing came to be. It was disconcerting, but also a little exciting to think about. Now that I believed it, I was set on solving it, on figuring it out so I could get rid of it. On top of that, I liked how Quinn wanted to help me. He was a good guy and smart. If anyone could help me solve it, it was him. Then maybe we could keep it from happening to anyone else in the town.

Taking the mug, I stared down into the depths of the dark roast, focusing on the heat, and the aroma, then glancing up to Quinn. When nothing happened, I squinted, straining to get something out of it, but all I got was the fact that he needed to drink it soon before it went cold. "Nothing."

He took it back, sipping it a few times as he grinned. When he handed it back, he cocked that eyebrow for me. When I had the mug back in my hands, my vision immediately went swimmy, blurring and swirling until I was no longer in the booth of my shop, but in a large, well-appointed office. Glancing around, I found several diplomas on the wall with the name Dr. Julian Meadows. Guessing it was him sitting in the cushy chair behind the desk. He'd tented his fingers and was looking at Quinn with a grim expression. "This is a serious accusation with serious consequences. Are you certain you want to go down this road?"

Quinn was dressed in a suit, which looked stellar on him, but also out of place from his normal look. Well, normal in the one day I'd known him. HE appeared to be a jeans and sweats sort of dude.

He ran his hands through his hair. "I understand, but I can't stand by and let this happen. I'd be culpable. Lives are more important than league standings."

Dr. Meadows nodded. "They are, but you understand this will become public. It could hurt your reputation. I know that seems counterintuitive, but I've seen this happen before. This team is important to the university and the town. You'll be ripping it apart."

"You think I don't know that? I don't care. It has to be done."

"I want you to give this twenty-four hours. If you still want to move ahead, come back at seven tomorrow morning."

The office faded and I was back in the booth with Quinn giving me a questioning look, fingers perched on the keyboard. "Well?"

"First, I guess we know that the person has to drink at least some of the coffee before I see a vision. As for the rest, I don't understand this fully, but you were in Dr. Meadows' office at UNB. You were making some kind of serious accusation to him and he was questioning you about it."

"The university president? What was the accusation?"

"Unsure. I think it had something to do with the rugby team. It was important to you. I could tell by the way you were dressed up and the worried look on your brow. Your eyes were dark and serious."

"When will this happen?"

"Not sure. Out the window it was daylight and the trees were blooming. I'd guess sometime soonish. Before Fall anyway."

He put all this down in his notes, stopping now and then to think first. "I don't know what I'd be accusing anyone of. I guess I need to be on the lookout."

"Yeah, maybe. What else do we need to figure out?"

"We need more data. More people to drink coffee. We need to find out if it happens every time. Can you turn it off and on? Is what you're seeing important only to them or to you too? Can you change the vision since you know what the future is?"

I rubbed my temple. "That's a lot of questions."

"True. How about I give you a kiss for each one of them?"

He leaned over, taking me by the nape of the neck and pulling me close. He pressed his lips to mine, so quickly, so softly that I barely felt it. He followed it up with another graze of my lips, and a third, and a fourth. One for every question he'd already asked. It gave me shivers, and definitely left me wanting more. Damn, he knew how to kiss. These soft little pecks were just as panty-melting as the ones where he devoured my mouth. "Keep talking."

"Does Esme have the same curse? Do you have any clues on how to stop it? Do you want to stop it?" Kiss. Kiss. Kiss. I was short of breath as heat coiled in my stomach.

"What about—"

A banging on the door broke the spell Quinn had put me under. "Shit. Plumber's here," I grumbled as I slid away from Quinn and went to open the door. All he did was laugh. Did he know how under his spell I was? Probably.

"All right, ma'am. I've got everything back in order and the water is turned back on. The issue wasn't just the toilet as the surge of water caused some serious damage to the old pipes. I had to do more than I expected. I suggest putting signs in your bathrooms about dismantling the toilets in the future."

I sighed. "You'd think that would be a given."

"True, but you'd also think not eating detergent pods would be a given too, but that's where we are in the world." He pulled out a clipboard and started writing all the expenses down. My stomach knotted more with every line. "Here's the total for the costs, minus my regular billing fees. Small businesses have to stick together. I'm happy to take what you have today and work the rest of it out later."

He was being kind. Kinder than he needed to be given the price on the bill. I went into the office and grabbed a hundred dollars from the safe. It was not even a tenth of what I owed him, but all I could spare. "This is what I can do now, but I promise I'm good for the rest. As soon as I can open back up and make more money, you'll hear from me."

The plumber nodded and was packing up his things to go. Quinn slapped him on the back. "How about a cup of coffee for your trouble?" He shot me a conspiratorial look. Of course, I was going to offer anyway, but now I had other motives outside of being polite to think about.

After I served the plumber his Stephen King we chatted about his business and family, he took one last swig and headed home. We wasted no time grabbing his mug, channeling all my thoughts to him, trying to produce a vision. Within seconds I was knee-deep in water again. This time it was fly-fishing. Rather, the plumber was fly-fishing and after three casts of his rod, he pulled a huge fish out of the stream. It was gigantic and he was so happy about it. There were kids behind him, jumping up and down on the bank. Then my vision cleared and I was back in my shop.

"Okay, that was happy. He's a fisherman and he's going to make a once-in-a-lifetime catch soon."

Quinn clicked keys as he talked. "What were you thinking right before your vision?"

"Um, I was thinking about how happy I was that I found a plumber willing to work with us on billing and how nice he was. Nothing else specific."

"Interesting. What were you thinking about when you had the vision of me with Dr. Meadows?"

I searched my mind. "Oh, I was thinking about how lucky I was to have you helping me figure this out, how smart and good you seem to be."

"Aw, you're making me blush."

"Stop, it's true. Thank you, by the way."

"It's my pleasure." He smiled and kept typing. "What about the football player? What were you thinking before his vision?"

"Just that he was making me uncomfortable and being a jerk."

"Hm." Quinn reached out, grabbing my hand and lacing our fingers together. "The pattern seems to be that you see things based on your mood. You were feeling upbeat about the plumber, so you saw him having a huge success. You were annoyed by the football player, so you envisioned him getting hurt."

"Wait. I didn't want him to get hurt. I wouldn't wish that on anyone."

"I know. I'm not saying you caused it. You saw it. It was already going to happen anyway, no matter what. If you weren't uncomfortable with him, you might have seen him making a touchdown or something. Your vision simply took your mood and ran with it." He brought the back of my hand to his mouth, kissing it softly.

"As for me, tonight you thought of me as an ally, so you saw me being an ally to another person in the future."

"Oh wow, I didn't even notice that."

"Yep. So now I know how badly you want me."

"Um, excuse me, Sir. What do you mean?"

"You envisioned yourself giving me the best blowjob of my life, so you must have been thinking about how sexy I am. By the way, feel free to call me Sir anytime you like. Preferably when you're naked."

I jerked my hand from him, feigning shock, but in reality, I loved how he flipped from sweet to dirty so fast. "I'll keep that under advisement. I don't think I'll have an opportunity for nakedness until I clean up this water and mess."

"Or we could always clean up while we're naked. Just saying."

I stood up, surveying the shop and trying to determine how much time it was going to take and what supplies I would need. It got overwhelming quickly. I hadn't even peeked in the restrooms yet. I took a deep breath to calm my frayed edges. "I'm going to have to rent a shop vac or two."

Quinn was up with his arms around me in record time, pulling me so my back was flush to his chest, encasing me with warmth and that delicious scent that was all him. "You will, but I doubt there's anywhere open at nearly midnight to do so. I think you should go home, put on some sexy jammies, and go to sleep. Everything will be here tomorrow, including me."

The idea of sleep sounded phe-freaking-nomenal. "I can't leave it like this. And you've already done so much to help me. You don't have to feel obligated for cleaning duty. Zoey and I can handle it. I can get started on some of it tonight."

"Don't." With an unusually stern tone, I turned around to face him, finding his beautiful eyes soft and caring. He cupped my face, running his thumbs across my skin in that way of his that was almost so light I didn't feel it, which sent waves of desire downtown. "I know it's your first nature to take care of the shop, but you can't do that if you're exhausted. Do you trust me?"

Did I? We'd only known each other a day, but he'd saved me, cared for me, given me orgasms, helped me, and basically been the closest thing to a real companion I'd had in a while. "Yeah, I trust you."

"Okay good. I'm going to follow you home in my car and while it goes against every instinct I have to not take you inside and spend the night figuring out all the dirty little things I could do to make you squirm, I'm going to leave you at home. You need rest. Get some. I'll meet you here at eight in the morning, ready and willing to help."

There was so much sincerity and tenderness in his gaze that I swooned. "Okay." It was all I had in me. My strength was waning as we talked and I just wanted to put a lid on the very long day I'd had.

With one more tender kiss, he helped me lock up and did exactly what he said, following me home in his car, and honking a few beeps as he drove away.

I took a quick shower, slid into my pajamas, the non-sexy variety, and plugged my phone in. No sooner than my head hit the pillow. I got a text from Quinn.

Just checking to see if you're all tucked in.

I am. What about you?

Almost. I couldn't go to sleep without telling you what a fun day I had. I know that sounds shitty on paper, but it's true.

I know what you mean. Me too. I'm glad you're coming tomorrow.

You bet your sweet ass I'll be coming tomorrow. So will you. ;-P

OMG. You're so bad.

Nah. You love it when I talk dirty. Get some sleep, Suds. Good night.

Night.

When I pulled up to the shop the next morning at six-thirty, I was shocked to find half a dozen trucks and cars parked in my lot. There was a cluster of college-aged guys assembled around the door. My first thought was 'Oh great, I'm going to have to tell them I'm not opening today' but I spotted Quinn leaning against the wall, laughing at the dude who was trying to juggle empty coffee cups and failing.

I pulled in and jumped out of my car. "What is going on here? You know I can't serve these guys. I'm sorry, but I'm not about to lose my license."

Quinn kicked off the wall in that sexy way. "Relax, Suds. I wouldn't make you compromise those cute principles of yours. We're here to help." He turned to the guys, gesturing. "Fallon, these are some of the most dependable guys on my team: Luke, Wyatt, Cass, Alec, Dante, North, Hayden, and Playboy, it's a nickname, don't ask. Guys, this is Fallon, the capable damsel who is definitely not in distress, but we're going to help her anyway."

The guys all said hello or waved and I stood there dumbfounded. "Um, hey."

Quinn whistled and the guy that was sitting in the back of a truck hopped out and opened the gate. "Alec and Playboy, you guys help Cass get the shop vacs inside. The rest of you get the supplies from the back of my car. We'll meet you inside."

He waited patiently while I fumbled with my keys. I was in a state of shock, or at least mild surprise. I'd gone in an hour and a half earlier than we'd agreed just so I could get started before Quinn could come and try to do the bulk of the work. He'd beaten me to it in a lot of ways. "You're here super early. And you brought your team?"

"Not all of them. Just the ones I trust to work hard and not goof off. And yeah, I knew you'd try to slip one in on me, so I made sure to get here around six. We've got all you need to clean everything and spruce up the place too. I bet we can knock it out by lunch so you can open this afternoon."

"I don't know what to say."

"Thanks is customary in these situations, but it's not necessary."

"No. I mean, thanks. But why?"

"Hm." He tapped his chin like he was thinking hard. "Why would I help the devastatingly sexy woman whom I want to get closer to out with something she needs, especially when I had the ability and resources at my disposal? I don't know. Got me."

"Quinn. I can't accept this help. It's so sweet of you, but it's my—"

"Responsibility? Yeah, I know. But just because it's your responsibility, it doesn't mean you have to do it alone. Let us help."

It was hard for me to admit I needed help, much less accept it, but he'd already gotten all the equipment and labor there, I'd be a fool to turn it down. Especially if it meant opening later in the day. "Okay yeah, but they get all the coffee or pastries they want for free. For life. I won't do this any other way."

The door burst open and the rowdy bunch strolled in, weighed down with all kinds of cleaning equipment. And books. Lots of books. Quinn pointed to the main seating area near the bathrooms and told them to set up before he leaned down to whisper in my ear. "If they get free coffee, does that mean I get free sex? For life?"

"I've known you less than twenty-four hours. Let's see how today goes and I'll get back to you."

He pressed a kiss on my temple. "I'll take it."

Three hours later they'd run all the shop vacs, dried the floors everywhere, mopped and sanitized both bathrooms, and helped replace the soggy books I'd used for décor that had been damaged in the flood. It was remarkable. "Where did you get these books? I almost hated to use them because there are some classics here."

The red-haired guy, Alec I think—it was hard to keep up with their names because they moved around a lot and called each other by their last names most of the time—shrugged. "My mom's a librarian. She goes through books constantly. There were piles of them in our garage. Dad's going to be stoked he can park the car inside now."

I gasped. "Your mom knows you took them, right?"

"Oh yeah, she was all about helping a fellow reader. Said to let her know if you want more." I couldn't imagine more books, but I filed that away for future reference.

"Tell her I appreciate it." He handed his empty mug to me and I took it without even thinking. The vision spread as the others had. Quinn was right there helping me as my brain wobbled into Alec's garage. At least I thought it was his. He was there, playing a beautiful set of drums while a young woman with a guitar sang into a mic. Sounded great, especially when he added harmony. Their song finished and she paused for a second, then set her guitar down and ran over to kiss him wildly before telling him how thankful she was.

As I came out of the vision, the players were gawking at me like I'd grown a second head.

"What just happened?" I recognized that one as Playboy, because who's going to get that one confused?

Quinn spun me around, looking at me with a questioning expression. "Was what you saw negative?"

"I'd have to say no from his perspective. He looked like he was enjoying it."

"So, tell him."

"I don't know. If word gets out that I'm cursed to see the future, then people are going to be hounding me."

"Yes, true. Stay with me here—think about what you need to do to tell a future."

"I have to touch their cups after they drink coffee."

"Okay, right. And how do they get this coffee, if they were, let's say, in this shop?"

The light bulb clicked.

He was right.

If people knew I could see futures, they'd flock in here. Much like Esme's family's tea leaf reading business, only true.

Could I use the curse to make money for all the damages the curse caused me in the first place? The wreck, the shop, I could pay Quinn's new washer and dryer too.

I mulled it over in my mind while the group of rugby players and Quinn waited for the response. After a few moments, I found it to be morally acceptable, at least to me.

"I saw your future Alec. You were playing drums in a garage. There was a pretty girl with long dark hair and lots of black eyeliner playing guitar and singing with you. You sounded fantastic, by the way. Great voice. When the song was done she was so thankful to you so she kissed you. And it was not a chaste kiss." Alec went slack-jawed. "Does any of that make sense to you?"

He scratched his head, grinning like a madman. "I play drums and I fight with my parents all the time about the noise. I keep bugging my parents to let me move to the garage and now that we brought the books to you, there would be room."

Quinn leaned against the counter. "What about the girl?"

Dante, I think, slapped Alec on the back. "Oh, that sounds like Jett. He's had a thing for her since Middle School. You didn't tell me you were hooking up with Jett, man."

"I'm not," he muttered.

"Not yet," I offered.

"Aw shit. I gotta go take a shower. She was going to come over this afternoon. What was I wearing? Did I look hot? Did she? Of course, she did. Did the kissing go further?"

"Woah there Cassanova, slow down," Quinn said. "She only sees a few minutes at a time. And I'm not comfortable knowing about the sex lives of my players, so maybe we stop here."

Alec nodded, and then he ran out the door. Two seconds later the rest of the team were shoving coffee mugs at me.

Quinn winked. "One at a time and be sure to tell everyone you know about this. To get a reading of the future, they've got to buy a large coffee and be patient with Fallon. Got it?"

"Yes, coach."

I had no idea how much could change in a day. After I'd read the futures of the rugby guys, one of them, North approached me about a job. He was doing online classes and about to graduate off the rugby team so his practice days were over. He was looking to line his pockets and get out on his own before he went into his full-time career.

He was the biggest of the players and Quinn made him promise if he wasn't there at the shop to be my security if anything went wrong with the future predictions. It turns out I didn't need him, but it made me feel better he was there. Especially when Quinn had to leave for a meeting with his advisor.

The morning had gone well. There weren't too many customers above the normal amount and I handled the predictions fine. Most of them had been positive and mundane, so that was good.

The afternoon was more daunting. Never had I had so many customers want coffee at three p.m. I was thankful for it though. By the time I finished my day, we'd made three times what a normal amount brought in. The only issue had been when Zoey appeared and I had to let North down and tell him she was too old for him and into girls.

He got a good prediction out of it though because his future was full of a leggy blonde with an intense attraction to his muscles.

As I closed the shop, looking forward to getting home and putting my aching feet up, Quinn appeared, holding a pizza box and a bottle of wine. "Come home with me. I want to, well, you know what I want. No sense trying to disguise it as anything else. But we can talk as we eat." He never failed to make me smile, even with the aching muscles I was suffering from.

"I don't know if I'd be good company. I'm tired and I need to get up early to get some accounting done."

He shot me a pout, complete with the dimple. "I'm not going to force you, but if I consume all this pizza and wine myself, the next time you get your hands on my abs, you'll be disappointed."

Laughing, I locked up the door. "Okay, but if I fall asleep on you, don't blame me."

"I won't. I just fondle your tits until you wake up."

He was too much.

But I couldn't get enough of him, so I don't know what that said about me. I got in his car and we made the short trip to his condo.

The smoke smell was mostly gone and he'd tidied up too. It was nice when he tucked me under his arm on the couch and handed me a slice of pizza. Normally I wouldn't lounge and eat, especially when plastered next to a great-smelling man, but I was comfy and he was willing to risk me dripping pizza sauce on him or his tan couch, so I went with it.

When we'd finished eating and had gotten to our second or maybe it was the third glass of wine, he lifted my legs and lay them across his lap. Downing his drink and setting it on the table, he began massaging my feet.

"Oh god, does that feel good? My dogs are tired."

"I figured. Let me help with that. Lay back, close those pretty green peepers."

I did as he asked, relishing in the way he worked the muscles in my feet. Before long he'd stripped me of my socks and used his thumbs to drive in deeper. I moaned. "Yep. That's the spot."

"I'm just getting started, Suds. Just you wait."

"Mm-hm."

After I was nearly a puddle on his floor from the relaxing effects of his hands, he spoke again. "Esme came to see me today. She's not seeing the future like you. She's seeing people's pasts. She looked haunted by what she'd learned these past few days."

My eyes popped open. "Isn't that what she does for a living?"

"Her family, yes. She never could see anything in the leaves like her mother and grandmother. She just faked it enough to make it believable because she's the face of the business, but now she's really seeing people's pasts and it's freaking her out. She wants us to hurry and solve the curse."

"Okay, but she could help with that."

"That's what I told her, but she said she had too much shit in her life than sit around with her ex and his new girlfriend guessing about the curse, but I don't want to talk about her now. Not when I'm about to make you moan like that again."

Sitting upright, I gawked at him, unsure how to respond. I went with ignoring the impending orgasm and sputtering. "Sh-she thinks I'm your…g-word?"

He laughed. "You can say it." He took my face in one hand and forcibly moved my mouth. "Girl. Friend."

"Quinn. Seriously. Why did she just assume that?"

"She made me drink tea so she could read my tealeaves to show me what it was like. She saw our little rendezvous on the road beyond Cinderella's house. She assumed we were officially together because she knows me well enough to know I don't go around sticking my dick in women's mouths unless I'm really into them. News flash: I'm into you. And don't you try to bother denying being into me?"

"Man, you're so confident."

"It's all over your face when you look at me, Suds. By the way, I love that your emotions are right there on the surface. Makes it easy for me to know what you're thinking."

He'd been massaging my feet throughout this entire conversation and he chose the moment when I was trying to frown at him to hit that one sore spot on the ball of my left foot. I attempted to school my features, and my actions, but my mouth dropped open and I moaned despite the effort.

Dropping my foot, his gaze traveled from my feet up my body as he leaned over me. "Thanks for making my point." He pressed his lips against mine and my body went from relaxed to wired between heartbeats as he kissed me.

When he finally broke our kiss, I was panting and wanting more, but he seemed to read something else in my face too. "I'm sorry if I freaked you out talking about Esme and the g-word. I'm just a guy who goes after what he wants and I want you, Fallon. I'm not going to apologize for doing everything I can to make sure every single bit of you is mine. If that's too much, tell me to back off and I will. Just know I'm not going away until you make me."

No man had ever talked to me like this. He made every pitiful boyfriend I'd had in the past seem like a child. I wanted to take his words and physically wrap myself in them. It was crazy how deep I was getting in a few days. Maybe this is what the curse was trying to tell me. I needed a partner, someone who would treat me well. Is that how I met him? The curse brought him to me?

If that's the case, it wouldn't be a curse, would it?

"Hey, where'd you go? Did you have another vision without coffee?"

"No. Sorry, I was just mulling over what you said. If I can be honest, I've never met anyone like you. I've enjoyed being with you and, yeah, I'm into you, but the practical part of me is waving red flags right now. Okay, maybe not red, but pinkish flags. I want to leap into this with you, but I don't know if I'm ready to throw that g-word out just yet."

That immaculate smile crossed his face and then he was back to kissing me, my lips, my jaw, my throat. "Fair enough. How about another g-word then?"

It didn't occur to me what he'd said until after he'd picked me up and carried me into his bedroom. Once I was gently placed on the bed, he stripped his clothes off fast, then I was treated to him taking my jeans off at a snail's pace. As he peeled them down, he spent time kissing my thighs, my calves, all the way down and back up again until he was right between my thighs, frowning.

Frowning?

"Now Suds, what did I say about your panties? I liked your cute kitty ones." He ran his knuckle over the purple silky material of my panties. I sucked in a breath as my entire body sparked. "I don't hate these, but we have to get you some new cheeky ones soon." Yeah, okay. I was willing to do anything he wanted just because of the way he was stroking me. "This is good, yeah?"

I bit my bottom lip and tried to answer, but it came out as a "V-n-huh" sound.

He laughed and I was starting to love the sound of that. His voice was deep and rich and when he laughed it seemed to come from his toes. Before I could comment on it though, he put his fingers inside the waistband of my panties and drew them down my legs, hissing between his teeth as he looked at me. "Damn. I'm going to have fun with this pretty pussy."

Diving down, he took one long stroke with his tongue. I nearly shuddered apart right then and there. He was just getting started though. Like a man possessed, he put his hands under my legs, pulling me to him as he went on his knees before the bed. My pulse rocketed as he put his head between my legs and began to lick, his tongue flicking over my clit and back down again.

I fisted the sheets and writhed against his face as he went harder, licking and sucking and moaning against me until I was lifting my ass off the bed. "Quinn, you have no idea how good this is."

"Mm, I have some idea, but it's not good enough yet."

Was he joking? Not good enough?

I discovered he was not joking when he pushed two fingers inside me, taking his sweet time to drag them out again. "The pipes bursting had nothing on you, Suds. You're gushing for me."

"Okay, but that's your fault." I heaved, panting to get more oxygen as he used his fingers. He'd begun to pump in and out of me and I was having a hard time staying focused enough for conversation.

"You're welcome. Want more?"

"There's more?" I screeched, uncertain I could take anything else. I was riding that high spot, enjoying the feeling of his fingers, the scent of his sheets, and the sound of his voice, I couldn't imagine anything else.

"Yeah, let me show you another g-word."

I wasn't ready for it. Not at all, but when he curled his fingers to reach that spot, I swear I blacked out from pleasure. "Oh god."

He flicked his fingers, toying with me for a few seconds, then he dipped his head again and took my aching clit into his mouth, sucking and moaning as his fingers pumped inside me, grazing the g-spot. I gripped his soft hair in one hand and his pillow in the other as I came apart. The wave of euphoria that swept through me was like no other before.

I'd known about the g-spot, but no guy had ever tried to point it out so vividly to me.

As I slowly came down from the intense orgasm, I got that feeling of being watched so I managed to crack open one eye.

Quinn and his insane body were standing at the edge of the bed looking at me. He had his cock in his hand, stroking himself and smiling. It was a beautiful sight. "I was just enjoying watching you come down. You're gorgeous like this, but I'm going to rail you with this cock right now."

I would have expected nothing less from my sweet, dirty guy. "I'd enjoy that very much."

"Oh, we both will," he purred as he crawled over me.

The bed dipped with his weight and I swear even that was a turn-on. It was like everything with him was heightened to the point right before pain. I pulled him down to me, praying to the god of romance that I was as good a kisser as he was. He moaned into my mouth, swiping his tongue inside before nipping my bottom lip with his teeth. "Are you ready for me, Suds?"

"Yes, please."

He ran his hard cock over my slick entrance. Shivers hit me like a lightning flash, and then he rolled his pelvis, pushing the tip in and waiting for me to adjust. I didn't need adjusting. I needed fucking.

Rising to meet him, I grabbed his ass and pushed his hardness inside me. He made a sound somewhere between a moan and a laugh. "Oh, what an eager little pussy cat you are."

The rest of our words were eaten up with grunts and moans and the sounds of our bodies slapping together as he did what he'd promised and railed the rail out of me.

Not only was he a good kisser and great at going down, but he was an expert at setting a perfect rhythm, going fast and hard, then pulling out slowly, rocking his hips to the side so he could touch every part of me. It didn't take long for me to get worked up again, especially after he reached between us and rubbed his thumb on my clit. "I want you to come with me now."

With that, I threw my head back and let myself go, lost in his fingers and cock and body, swimming in his dirty words, eating up the way he looked at me. "Fuck yes, Fallon. Fuuuck."

He dove for my mouth as his release came, kissing me and laying his body over mine to the point where we were consumed with each other. When we'd both been spent beyond measure, he slowly pulled out and then collapsed on the bed next to me.

I didn't wait for him to tell me. I snuggled up next to him and reveled in the post-sex haze and the feel of his arms as he tucked me against his chest. "We don't have to settle the g-word now, but if you think you're leaving this bed tonight, you're mistaken."

Realizing I hadn't planned to go was my first indicator that maybe the g-word thing had already been settled.

For five days I told futures and made money. More than enough to cover my deductible and pay the plumber fully. I was shopping online for washers and dryers for Quinn, but it was difficult because he refused to tell me the size he needed and every time I was at his place and tried to measure, he'd get frisky and distract me with his kissing abilities or more. I was determined to find a way to get it done though.

Everything was going well at Between the Grinds. North was fitting in great and working like a mule alongside Oscar who'd come back from the plague or whatever he'd had. Zoey was doing her usual flitting in and out and Quinn was spending most of his days interviewing my customers about their predictions. He'd even set up a system where they came back in and reported to him after my prediction had happened, earning me more coffee revenue in the process. His paper was going to be killer because he was getting some great perspectives from the customers. To say he was pumped would be an understatement.

So, why did I feel like something was off?

The business was booming, great community connections were being made, and I was at the start of a wonderful relationship with an awesome guy yet…

"Hey Boss, read my future," Oscar said as he shoved a mug in my hand. I was glad to have him back, but I was feeling wobbly from all the predictions. I had no choice though because the vision appeared seconds later.

Oscar was in his bed asleep, tossing around so much that the covers were twisted between his tattooed legs. His phone rang. The time and date I caught when it lit up was that night at three, fourteen. He flopped his tattooed arm over to slap at it until it silenced. A few seconds later the phone went off again and he managed to get upright enough to pick it up, running his hands through his dark curly mane as he did so. "Hullo?" There were ten seconds of silence, then, "Well, shit. Okay." He hung up and threw himself back down on the bed.

"What did you see? Me hooking up with one some or all of the members of Twice?" He was a K-pop fanatic and they were his favorite group. Went on about them relentlessly. He was still a big draw for the female customers in his age bracket. They loved to talk to him about that stuff and loved it even more when it seemed like he was flirting with them.

"Not exactly. Unless one of them calls you tonight when you're sleeping."

"Are you kidding me right now? You're seeing all these other folks doing awesome things or hooking up with interesting people and you see me sleeping? I want my money back."

"You didn't pay me."

"Well, it's a good damn thing I didn't. I feel robbed."

"Get back to work, will you? You have beans to roast."

"Yeah, yeah. Fine. That call better be someone interesting tonight is all I have to say."

I turned my back leaning against the counter. "Something's up. What is it?" Quinn was there with a smile and a warm hug.

"I don't know. I feel off. Drained. I think I just need to sit down. I'm heading to the office."

"Do what you need to do, but I suggest you take a real break and get out of here. We can go to the park or my place or wherever you want to go. Leave the world and the future-predicting behind for an afternoon."

I glanced around the shop. It was tempting, but I had things to do in the office and who knew when another slew of customers would come in for a prediction? "Eh, will you take a rain check?"

"Sure." He pressed a kiss to the top of my head, watching me walk away with a concerned look in his expression.

I woke the next morning with a raging headache.

And a racing pulse when I realized I didn't remember driving home or getting in bed. I was still in my clothes from the night before, but that's all I knew.

Glancing at the time, I jumped out of bed. It was past eight o'clock and I was late for the shop. I took the quickest shower possible and changed into my RBTG tee and jeans, threw my hair in a messy bun, and headed out the door. The entire drive over I was trying to piece together what my night had consisted of, but I simply couldn't. It was like I'd been trashed, but I hadn't had a thing to drink.

When I got to the stop light, I finally thought to check my phone. Several missed calls and texts from Quinn and Zoey early in the morning along the time I should've been there, but none after, which was odd. I guess they weren't too concerned. Which made me feel icky if I was honest.

It was so unlike me to sleep in without telling anyone.

Parking the car, I slid out and went inside the shop. Several customers were there drinking coffee, and Quinn was in his usual spot typing on his laptop. Zoey and Oscar were behind the counter chatting.

"Um, guys."

Zoey waved. "Hey, did you enjoy your sleep-in'?"

"I guess. I didn't mean to sleep in."

Oscar shook his head. "The fuck you didn't. You called me at three last night telling me you'd decided to sleep in and I had to open up for you. Very funny, by the way, making your own prediction come true."

"Wait, what? I called you?" I scrolled through my calls and he was right. I'd made an eleven-second call to Oscar. One that I had no recollection of. "Okay, this is weird. I'm sorry. I don't recall that, but I'm here now, so let's just get to work."

Oscar squeezed my arm as I went behind the counter. He'd been joking with me because that was just his personality, but there was clear concern on his face. "I don't mind coming in early. Maybe just tell me before the middle of the night next time."

Quinn came over, grabbing my shoulders and massaging them. "You're starting to scare me. You look pale and your eyes are glassy. I say we ditch predictions for today. You've got the money and I've got the data. Let's go home and spoon in bed."

"Eh, I'm tired, but I'll be all right. I'm happy to be your little spoon tonight though."

He relented, but I could tell he didn't like it.

Three more days of me forgetting things, Quinn trying to get me to slow down, and then me making excuses. I hadn't meant to push him away like that, but I guess from his perspective, I was.

"Look, Suds, I'm not upset. I'm concerned about your health. If this curse is giving you headaches and memory loss, it's time to solve it."

"Maybe you're right. I don't know how though. I've been trying to figure out what the curse is saying to me every time I see a future, but I don't see patterns or clues, or any kind of hint. It's just all jumbled-up events and people. I even tried to read my own future every time I sipped coffee, but it never worked. If I could just see it I…" my voice trailed off. I wasn't even sure what I'd been planning to say. The rest of my sentence was gone.

It was going to be pretty damn hard to resolve the curse if I couldn't remember anything. I bit my bottom lip to stop the trembling I felt in my body. I didn't know what was happening to me, but the fear I felt when I could no longer fill in some gaps in my day was palpable.

Quinn hugged me to his chest, letting me melt into him and tremble as he stroked my hair and told me everything would be okay. I did not feel okay at all. "What do I do, Quinn? I'm scared."

"You don't have to do anything, Suds. Go to the office and lie down. I'll be back within the hour." He turned to Zoey and said a few things to her, but I was so zoned out that I couldn't discern what they were saying. Numbly, I shuffled into the office and lay on the couch, covering myself up with a fluffy blanket that Quinn had brought me sometime over the course of the week.

I closed my eyes, simmering and churning on everything I'd learned since the curse struck me. I'd wondered if the curse was showing me I needed a new kind of man to date, or if I was supposed to consider options for the future of the shop, or if I was supposed to connect and take an interest in more people. Hell, I even wondered if I was supposed to move back home to California since I'd seen a couple of people moving to a new location in the future I read..

None of it seemed to click and I went to sleep clutching myself and wondering if I'd even remember my name when I woke up.

Quinn brushed the hair from my face and then kissed my cheek. "I've got something for us to try. You awake?"

"I am now." I sat up, stretching and looking around the room to ground myself. In my office at the coffee shop. Hot guy in glasses in front of me. Yep, everything was normal. Ish. I still had a foggy feeling in my brain though. "What do you want to try, because if it's a new position, I'm going to have to pass until I'm fully recovered from…whatever this is."

"I have so many positions in mind, but that's not what I'm talking about. Come with me."

I shuffled behind him as we pushed out of the office and into the main room of the shop. He led me over to the high-top bar that seats four and put his hands on my waist to help me onto the stool. He slid in next to me just as the door chimed to indicate customers.

I could not believe who walked in.

She was wearing an oversized hoodie and sweats, with sneakers and big hoop earrings. Her hair was in a messy bun and for once, she was not scowling. It was so opposite from her normal look I almost didn't recognize her. "Esme? What are you doing here?"

"I was kidnapped by your boyfriend."

Quinn shook his head. "You were not. You want this over as badly as we do. Sit down and let's figure it out."

She sighed, then climbed onto the seat opposite me. A gorgeous man with shoulder-length blond hair sat beside her. He had a scruffy five-o'clock shadow and full lips that made me think he might be as good a kisser as Quinn. Esme whispered something in his ear and the dark grimace he was wearing morphed into a big smile. He was pretty.

I mean, not enough to sway me from Quinn, but still. Nice looking would be an understatement.

Quinn made the introductions. "This is Fallon. Fallon, this is Esme's…friend, mechanic, boy toy, I don't know, Rex." The only response I got was a dip of his head.

The four of us stared at each other until Zoey breezed by with a well-timed, "Awkward."

"Go away, Zoe." When she'd disappeared into the office, I turned to the only person in the group who wasn't giving me stink-eye. "What are we doing?"

He pulled a deck of cards from his pocket. "Simple. Esme is suffering like you are. The curse is on both of you, so it stands to reason and I've backed this up with research and old interviews, that the two of you need to work it out." He shuffled the cards. "Now, I'm not sure about you, Esme, but what Fallon sees is a direct reflection of her mood or thoughts at the time."

Esme did not indicate if that was the case for her or not. Neither did Rex. They both sat very still as Quinn shuffled again. "Since neither of you can read your own grinds, so to speak, I thought we should take a look at what happens when you try to read each other's."

That was actually a good idea. A twitch of hope sprouted from my chest. I didn't want to know about her future, but if it could help us, I would sure try. "Okay, let's do it."

Rex folded his arms over his chest, stretching the tight white t-shirt to its limits. "Hold it. How do we know you won't lie to Esme about what you see?"

"Because I want this over," I replied, biting my lip because that sprig of hope had just vanished. "I hadn't even thought about her lying until you said something, so now I'm not so sure about this."

Esme adopted the same position as Rex. "Me either. This is dumb, Quinn."

"No, it isn't. This is why I've come prepared." He reached into his bag, pulling a bottle of rum, then four shot glasses. After he poured a splash in each one, he continued. "For you two to relax enough to get accurate predictions I propose we play a drinking game first. Rex and I will participate too, so it doesn't seem too creepy."

Esme sighed, but Rex pulled a glass over downed the first shot without the game even starting, and then turned to Esme. "The quicker we do this, the quicker we get out of here and do what we have to do."

She finally relented. Not that she said anything verbally. It was more of a nod and sigh that told Quinn she was in. He shuffled the cards one last time before giving us the rules. "I thought we might do Never Have I Ever, but then I realized Esme and I might be drinking on some of the same things—sorry about that—so we're going with a game my rugby guys taught me.

"We turn over a card and whatever number it is, we take turns giving an example of that number. For instance, if I turned over a seven, I might say 'Seven Days in a Week,' the next person might say 'Magnificent Seven movie,' the next might say 'Seven Habits of Highly Effective People,' then 'seven dwarves, and so on. You have three seconds to name a seven-something and if you don't, then you drink your shot and we go on to the next card."

I smiled. "This sounds like fun." Esme didn't concur verbally, but she reached for a glass anyway.

Quinn gave us one last rule. "If you get a Jack, name famous Jacks, Queens are famous queens, Kings, name kings, and an Ace means you get to name any category you like. Let's start. You go first, Fallon."

He turned over four of clubs. Okay. Four seemed easy. "Four seasons."

Esme went next, glancing at Rex with a beaming smile, "Four-leaf clover."

Rex smirked in response, adding, "Four horsemen of the apocalypse."

Yeah, that was an inside joke or secret thing between them for sure.

Quinn added, "Four elements."

"I am Number Four by Trevor Negus."

"Four calling birds.

"Fantastic Four."

"Four ninja turtles!" Leave it up to Quinn for that one.

"Four…ack…I can't think of another."

"Time's up. You drink, Fallon," Quinn said, as he slid a glass to me. I took the swig, downing the burning liquid as fast as I could. I wasn't a shot kind of girl, but it wasn't too bad. Besides, I was determined to get this over with.

We went on to the next card. King of Diamonds.

"King Charles."

"King Louis the thirteenth."

"King Kong."

"Elvis, the king of rock and roll."

"Burger King."

"The King. Movie with Timothee Chalamet."

"Oh, good one. The King's Speech."

"King Tut." Rex may have been quiet, but he had a funny streak.

"Stephen King, of course."

"King…what was that guy's name? King…"

"Bzzzz, you lose. Drink, Esme," Quinn mocked. She laughed and took her shot.

The game went on for over an hour. Rex and Quinn were very good at it. Or maybe we girls were letting them win to get drunk fast. I couldn't say. I know I was anxious and I could see Esme's concern etched in her pretty face as the game went on.

After I don't know how many rounds I was feeling loose. I leaned up and placed a kiss on Quinn's cheek. "I think we can go now."

It was funny that both he and Rex hopped off their stools, each of them helping us get what we needed. Quinn went to fetch Esme her coffee and Rex followed behind, coming back with one of our few teacups and some tea. "I hope you like it black. It'll get the best results for her if you sip slowly and make sure to swirl around the last bits."

I picked up the cup, taking in the musky aroma. It wasn't as nice as the coffee smell I was used to, but it wasn't too bad.

Esme tucked into her coffee right away, taking a huge gulp, then looking over her cup at me. "Do you think this will work?"

"I have no idea. I've been doing a lot of fortune readings and I've developed a sort of skill, I guess, to drive the vision where I want just by thinking certain things before I start. I'm hoping I can focus on the curse and your part in it to get an answer."

"Yeah, I was shocked the first time I saw something from the past, but I've found that if I ask a few leading questions, things appear easier. For example, tell me about your family."

I took another sip of tea. The bitter taste coated my tongue. "You've seen my only family, my older sister, Zoey. My parents were killed in an airplane accident a few years ago. Grandparents had already passed. It's just us now."

"That must be hard. I lost my father to cancer when I was eleven. Sometimes it feels so raw, but other times, I have trouble remembering his face."

"That's sad. I hope you have photos or something to remind you."

"She has a lot of reminders," Rex grumbled, throwing his arm around the back of her chair. He was protective of her and there was a vulnerability about her when she looked at him.

The conversation went back to the wreck and the cursed police officer, then we told Esme and Rex what happened with the Wayward Warbler and Cinderella at her house. Left the part about the blow job out, but Esme already had seen it, so I'd bet Rex knew too.

When we neared the end of our cups, Esme held out her hand. "Since I see the past, I think I need to go first. Take my hand. It helps me read better."

I took one last swig, then swirled the tea like Rex had said. Some of the leaves clung to the sides of the cup, others were floating in the bottom. To me, it looked like clumps of tea leaves, but when I glanced up at Esme, her expression changed. Her gaze turned glassy and she seemed to stare beyond the bottom of my cup. She squeezed my hand and I didn't know if it was for her benefit or mine. I clamped tighter just in case she needed it.

Moments later, it was over.

She took a deep breath and looked up from my cup. "Your parents loved you very much."

I smiled. "Tell me something I didn't know. I miss them." Quinn was quick, slinging his arm over me and offering his warmth.

"Well, I saw a conversation between you and your mother. You look just like her. Have the same smile and determined look in your eyes."

"Yeah, Zoe looks and acts like Dad. I'm Mom's clone."

"I could see that. I think it must have been maybe ten or so years ago. You were younger, your hair shorter, and you were wearing a t-shirt from Benedict High School.

"Your mom was going over some accounting ledgers and had about fifty tabs open on her on her laptop. There was a veritable mess strewn out on the bed around her. You'd asked her to come get ice cream with you, Zoey, and your dad. She said she couldn't go."

The memory of that conversation already played in my head more than I could say. It was like a defining moment in my life. "That was the day I realized that Mom was the driving force of their business. Dad was the face, Mom was the brain. She kept everything running at their shop and our home simultaneously. I remember thinking it was a shame she had to do it by herself, but she told me she enjoyed what she did because it was her strength and it freed Dad up to, well, be Dad."

Esme smiled. "Yeah, I saw him and Zoey in the hallway, running after a scruffy dog and laughing. I got the sense your Mom was trying to tell you something with that conversation. Do you know what it was?"

"She told me I was just like her; that I was the responsible one in the family and one day I'd be the one to take care of everything myself, just like she did. She said I needed to put my focusing skills to good use, take a look at things from every angle, use my brain to solve problems, and seek solutions when there were none.

I guess she was passing the torch without knowing she was going to die sooner than anyone expected. She kept repeating how alike we were. I think she was proud of that. She was helping me see my strengths and showing me how to use them like she did."

Quinn shifted on his stool. "Are you sure that's what she was trying to say?"

"Yeah, it's what I've always known. It's up to me to keep their business going. Yeah, I moved to a new town for a new start, but I brought all of Mom's principles and lessons with me. I'm doing everything the way she would have. I know it'll be a success this way. Zoey can be all…Zoey and I'll keep us afloat. I'm capable of taking care of things, just like my mother did when she was alive."

Esme gave me a sad smile. It was as surprising as it was unusual. "I'm sure you can, but that's not the message I was getting from seeing that memory."

"What do you mean?" My voice was louder and screechier than I'd intended. I had no idea what she was saying and was starting to regret even letting her in my head.

"Fallon, I think you're seeing it from the perspective of a person who has lost their parents, not from the perspective of a young girl who didn't know what was coming.

"I'm sure your mom was happy in her life and I could see she loved your family, but I took what she was saying as a warning. She didn't want you to be like her and have to miss out on family ice cream runs. She wanted more for you. She wanted you to use your brain and abilities to seek more than she had. To enjoy life and ice cream and chase dogs down the hallway. She was warning you about balance, Fallon."

"No, that can't be right. She was proud of my practical brain, my organizational skills, and my dedication to finishing anything I started. She wanted me to be like her."

Esme reached across the table for my hand. I didn't know what to do because goodness knew I didn't want to hold her hand again. She was sitting there saying the last ten years of my life had been a lie. A misinterpretation on my part. I pulled away, but she reached forward and grabbed it anyway. "I didn't mean to upset you. This is why I hate this damn curse." She glanced over at Rex. "I want it to go away, so I can be free."

My mind was reeling. Could I have gotten it all wrong? I remembered feeling a lot more grown-up after the talk. I'd just graduated high school and was gearing up for college, so it made sense that I was thinking about the future and how I wanted my life to be.

I was so impressed with my mother's ability to do it all that I could've missed the mark on what she'd said that night. Maybe Esme was right: she might have been telling me not to get in my own way.

If that was the case, I'd done everything all wrong.

And *she'd* been the one to see it.

I'd need to think about it more. A lot more. But first, I had to steer us out of this curse. My voice tightened. "The only way to be free is to solve this curse. Give me your damned cup."

Quinn picked me up from the stool and carried me over to the counter, shouting over my shoulder, "Hold up a sec, guys."

Esme and Rex looked slightly confused, but they bowed their heads and started whispering as Quinn placed my ass on the counter next to the register. "What?" I snapped at him.

"Woah there, pony. No need to bite my head off. That's actually what I wanted to tell you. You're too angry about what she said to read her future now. You'll end up getting some argument between her and Rex and not the clue you need."

I clenched my jaw. He wasn't wrong.

"I don't know what to do. I'm angry about what she said. How could I have gotten it so wrong? Do you think I'm not remembering it correctly?"

"No, I think you went into survival mode after your parents died. To cope with the loss, you compartmentalized and organized your life into neat boxes and took the weight on these little shoulders of yours."

He put his finger under my chin, raising it so he could kiss me. It was brief, and light, but the trademark promise of what might come after it was there. "It's admirable. You took on the responsibility and never looked back. I am here for you now. Zoey too, obviously. You're not alone in this anymore.

"Maybe the curse is telling you to consider a life beyond this shop. You can have both, you know? A profitable business and a smoking hot boyfriend who wants you to get off as much as possible when you spend time with him."

Laughing I leaned my head against his hard chest, feeling the familiar thump of his heart. "I do like that last part."

"Mm-hm. You have no idea what I'm going to do to you later, but first, we need to see what we can do to bring Esme's half of the curse to light. Now that you have something to think about, it's only fair to give her the same."

He was right. I wanted to help her too. Yep, I was pissed, but I could put it behind me so we could get out of this.

I hopped down and went over to get my prediction on. Grabbing her mug, I concentrated on Esme and what I wanted for her. What I wanted for myself. Happiness, yes, but more than that. Now that I was looking at my situation from another perspective, I wanted her to be able to do the same thing.

My vision went wonky as the coffee shop swirled into another place. It was dark, almost too dark to see, but there were pinpricks of light coming through the walls.

Esme was curled up in the corner, from the best I could tell. She was staring off into space when the door creaked open, flooding it with light.

She was in a beat-up, dirty, rusty old rail box car.
What?
That did not seem like an Esme-type place at all.

Once the door was open, Rex appeared. He hopped into the car with ease. As soon as he saw her, his face lit up. "I knew I'd find you here."

"Yeah, well I knew if I went here, you'd come. You always do."

"And I always will."

"I know."

He strolled over to her, throwing himself beside her, then pulling her into his lap and wrapping her with as much of his body as he could. For the first time since I'd had the visions, I felt like an intruder. This was something private, more intimate than seeing people having sex. I could feel it emanating from both of them. "Have you made a decision?" he asked as he toyed with the ends of her hair.

"Yes."

"And?"

"The past is the past. The cold won't hurt me anymore."

He took her hand, lifting it to his mouth and kissing the back lightly. "No one will hurt you ever again. I would pull the fucking sun from the sky if it would warm you, T. You and I. Always."

"Yeah, well..."

The vision faded and I was back in the shop with both Esme and Rex glaring at me, waiting for answers. I wasn't sure what to say. While the vision had been a nice and quiet moment between them, it didn't seem big or life-changing like mine had, outside of the mention of a decision. I couldn't help with that part though because I didn't hear what she'd decided.

"In the future, I don't know when exactly, but you both looked the same as you do now, so I'd guess soonish, I saw you curled up in an abandoned rail car. Esme, does that make sense to you?"

Her gasp told me everything I needed to know. Yes, she recognized it, and no, it was not a place she normally would go.

"You were alone at first, sitting in the corner in the darkness. I couldn't tell if you were sad or what, but as soon as Rex opened the door, you both looked pleased to see each other."

Rex chuckled under his breath. "Of fucking course, she was pleased to see me."

She put her hand to his jaw, then pushed him away from her, playfully. He retaliated by grabbing her by the throat and pulling her to him so he could bite her bottom lip, then kiss her.

Okay.

Carrying on...

"Rex said something about finding you, so I don't know if you were hiding from him or someone else or what, but he said some sweet things to you. I don't want to repeat them now because I think you should hear them from his mouth in the future, not mine." I glanced at Rex and he nodded his approval. "He asked if you'd made a decision. I think you'd decided something but I don't know what your options were or what the final choice was because my vision faded before you could tell him."

The two of them looked at each other. They knew exactly what I was talking about, even if I had no clue. "I'm sorry. I didn't give you as much to go on as you did for me."

She fiddled with the many bracelets on her arm before responding. "No, you did. In a way, it's exactly the opposite of what I told you. My vision said that you should re-examine the path you were taking. Your vision told me I should stay the course." Sighing, she stood up. "If only either of those things were easy."

Rex pushed away from the table. "What do you think I am? Or Quinn for that matter? I've been telling you that you're not alone. Neither of you are. So, maybe you should stop sighing and wringing your hands, both of you, and do what you need to do to end this fucking curse and get on with your fucking lives."

Quinn chuckled. "Couldn't have said it better myself."

Agreed. "So, now that we know these things, do you think the curse is done?"

"My research says the curse will be done when you get another feather from the Wayward Warbler. Some people said the feather shows up in places the bird itself never could have gone. Like indoors. One person found one inside her refrigerator. Don't ask me how a bird without opposable thumbs opened a door and a fridge, but she swore it. There are plenty of accounts to back this up."

Rex was already on his way out the door, but Esme lingered next to the table awkwardly. "Okay, so I guess we're done. Keep in touch." She gave me a quick hug, patting Quinn's arm, then rushed over to Rex and they left.

Immediately, I started checking everywhere for the feather, which was nowhere to be found. Naturally.

Quinn came up behind me and snaked his hand inside my waistband, skimming his fingers over my pussy. I yelped. "What are you doing? I have customers!"

"Just checking to make sure your feather isn't in your panties."

"Oh, my god, you are beastly."

He took the shell of my ear in his teeth. "Mm-hm. As much as I'd love to get dirty with you, I think the best thing for you to do now is focus on what Esme told you and go about your normal routine. The feather will come when the feather comes. Maybe tonight, after I make you come."

"Quinn. Seriously."

"Yes, seriously." He removed his hand, then spun me around, putting his arms around me. "Hey, I'm glad you're getting to the end of this. I don't like seeing you tired and struggling to remember things. I want all of you and you won't be able to give me that with the curse hanging over you."

"Oh, I see. The curse is all about you and *your* needs."

"Not at all. The curse is about you. I just plan on reaping the benefits when it's gone. Now," he said, swatting my ass playfully. "Get to work. I'm going be over here in my booth sneaking peeks of your hot ass for the rest of the day and make a list of all the naughty things we can do tonight. The curse may not be completely over, but it's on the way out and I want to celebrate."

The list had been extensive. It took us three days to get to the bottom of it. Not that I minded.

Things went back to semi-normal at the shop. I mean, I was still pushing out predictions and waiting for the curse to end, spending every spare second thinking about how to change or what to do about the vision I'd been given by Esme. I knew I had to change, but I had no idea how. It's not like I could rewire my brain to start shirking my responsibilities.

I tried.

I went to lunch with Quinn two days ago, leaving the shop for Oscar and North. Zoey was around too. I'd called halfway through to remind them to roast the beans, a task they did every day. They'd done fine. *Fine.* Yet, I couldn't stop thinking about them, ruining the lunch date.

Quinn was accepting, but I could see I was starting to lose him when things like this happened.

I didn't want that.

At all.

"Hey, wanna see a movie tonight? I feel like I need to get off this laptop for a while."

I glanced down at the accounting ledger I had between my legs. I was reconciling on the daily and all the revenue was taking up more time. Not that I was complaining. "Can we do it tomorrow night? These numbers are not going to add themselves."

"Um, they will if you go electronic. Like every other business started in the past five years," North quipped as he swept the broom between Quinn's legs. He was good about cleaning before I asked him.

"I have it electronic, but I feel more comfortable with hard copy. It's how I learned from my mom."

"I get that, but if you want, I could set it all up for you. You know my degree is in Accounting."

"Wait, what? Quinn, you told me he majored in Business."

Quinn shrugged. "Accounting is business, is it not?"

"Not exactly, coach. But, the offer stands. I'll get it all set up for you before your movie ends. I'll even do your payroll and other things for you, free of charge."

"No way. If you do this, I'll pay you."

"We can discuss it later. Show me what you have and I'll get started. Oscar and Zoey can fill the drink orders while I work."

Thirty minutes later, I was strolling out the door with Quinn. He slung his arm over my shoulders. "I think you're worse than a first-time mom leaving her baby with a sitter. It'll be fine. North knows what he's doing."

"I know. I trust him. I just feel fidgety when I'm doing frivolous things for myself, you know? A boss needs to boss."

I slid into his SUV as he shut his door. "True, but if you recall, this is what you need to do." He cupped my face with his warm hands. "Look, I'm invested in this relationship and I'm not going anywhere but think about how many things your mom missed out on. How many times your Dad may have been lonely without her."

Turning it around and looking it that way, a twang of sadness pinged my heart. "Okay. You're right. I'm good. You better buy me the large popcorn."

Afterward, Quinn informed me, "I texted North. He's all done with your books and software. Oscar is closing up shop. They said to have a good night. There may or may not have been a few eggplant emojis involved, but the Read Between the Grinds is now being put to bed. Daddy and Mommy can feel free to have their playtime."

We'd left the theater and Quinn drove right past the shop as I leaned against the window watching it whiz by. A strange sense of satisfaction overcame me when I turned my head to Quinn and he was grinning widely, the dimple on display. "Playtime with you sounds nice."

"Phhhsh. Nice isn't what it will be. I bought you some new panties and I'm going to need you to try them on one-by-one and let me see which I like best. I promise to take you to the shop first thing in the morning in plenty of time to open up and get your little Sudsy fingerprints on everything."

"Eh, maybe tomorrow we sleep in."

When I woke, the first thing I noticed was the hard chest pressed against my back and the warmth of Quinn's arms and legs wrapped around me. I took a deep breath, letting the scent of his sheets and the morning sounds of the birds outside wake me fully.

We'd had our playtime and talked into the wee hours of the morning. I couldn't remember a time I'd stayed up so late. I'd always been worried about being tired in the morning, but last night I'd ignored that urge and enjoyed the conversation with my boyfriend.

Yeah, I said the B-word.

Quinn had opened up to me about the future I saw in his coffee cup that day. Dante had told him that the head coach, Quinn's mentor and friend, had been dosing some of the players with steroids. None that I knew, but still it was disheartening to hear and even harder for Quinn to accept. He had a decision to make, but both he and I knew he'd do the right thing and turn him in. I'd seen it.

We talked about my family, my dreams for the shop becoming a chain, we talked about what he'd do after he turned in his paper, and his career options. We even got around to an extensive conversation about books.

It was nice.

And to think my first reaction after we'd had sex was to rush to sleep.

"Daddy needs five more minutes."

"Of sleep?"

"Oh wait. I have options? I'm going with five more minutes to rock your world, Suds. Then we can get to the shop. Promise."

He was already reaching between my legs and as much as I didn't want to stop him, I grabbed his hand, then rolled over to face him. "What if we had more than five minutes?"

He stretched like he was warming up. "In that case, I'll be starting with my fingers, then adding a little tongue action between those silky thighs, then I'll probably get you on your knees and make you clutch the headboard while I take you from behind. Then we can shower and I'll order you to suck my cock like a good girl. From there—"

"Okay, okay. I get it. Fun time to be had. So let's do it."

"Do what? I need to know which of those things you want specifically."

"All of them. Then more. But first, I have to call Oscar and tell him I'm taking the day off."

I grabbed my phone from the nightstand as Quinn made a big show of clapping and whistling for me. Once I was done with the call, he picked me up and dragged me over on top of him. We were both naked and the feel of his skin on mine made my heart patter faster.

When he kissed me, I wrapped my arms around his neck, reaching under the pillow so I could get as close as I could. My fingers grazed something, so I pulled it out and started laughing.

"What? Am I tickling you with my morning scruff?"

"No. Look."

I held up my hand. A glistening black feather had appeared under the pillow. It was too big to be one of the feathers from inside the pillow. Nah, it was the Wayward Warbler's feather.

The curse was over.

Quinn kissed and I melted for him just like I did every time. "I say we celebrate."

I could think of no better idea.

I didn't make it back into the shop for two days.

It was still standing.

ESME'S Black Tea

Four miles.

I was four miles from the town border when the Wayward Warbler decided to mess with my plans. I should've known. It was the kind of luck I'd had my whole life.

Moving my bracelets so I could see my touchstone—the shamrock tattoo with Lukey written inside it—on my wrist, I tried to make some semblance of peace wash over me. Sometimes that was all it took to calm my nerves.

As I surveyed the steam rising from the hood of my car I knew remembering what led to that tattoo wouldn't help me today.

Four damned miles.

Officer Simmons took one look at the wreck of a woman who ran into me but strolled up to my car first. Of course, he would. I was the famous Esme Doe of Doe Tea House, known throughout the town as a prolific reader of tea leaves. Bullshit, of course. I didn't get the Romani gene for fortune telling considering how I was adopted. Not that my family would admit that in public.

He tapped on my window, glancing inside. I jumped out at lightning speed hoping he hadn't taken notice of the suitcases in the back seat. If he mentioned them to Uncle, even in passing, I would be in trouble. I should've put them in the trunk, but I was in a hurry when I left.

Escaped.

I took a second to prep, putting my Doe family mask on so I'd be on-brand when I responded to the wreck. It was old-habit now. Sometimes I even forgot to take it off when I was alone.

Okay, Esme. You've got this. Remember people are always watching.

I pointed at the girl in the beat-up silver car and shouted something vaguely Romani in the direction of Officer Simmons. He was a true believer in my family and the curse, so it was all I needed to get him ramped.

I would blame the girl publicly because it's what Uncle would've insisted on, but I knew better. I saw the Warbler. I didn't know he'd cause the wreck seconds later, but one glance at that bird and I knew my plans were dead.

Much like my black heart.

My act worked. They both thought I was two beats from going crazy, but to her credit, she swallowed down her fear and marched over to me anyway.

Officer Simmons pushed me back from her, thinking I might do something violent and Romani-like. He addressed her. "Okay, ma'am the best I can tell she believes that you caused the accident when you swerved into her lane at an advanced speed. My Romani is a little rusty though, so maybe you should tell me what happened."

The girl went through all the details, trying her best to keep from admitting guilt, blaming the Wayward Warbler instead. I listened to her intently, schooling my features to seem disinterested. "Mm-hm."

She got more animated as she spoke. "You saw it, right?"

I threw some more Romani at her then spat and ended up calling her a cunt. Maybe she was. I had no idea.

As she and Officer Simmons went into a discussion about the curse and the Warbler and all that came with it, I checked my nails, keeping my exterior aloof. Inside, I was shaking like a leaf. I'd have to call Uncle and tell him about this. He was going to be upset and when he was upset he was unpredictable.

Not only that, I'd have to stay in Between until I figured out the curse. I knew better than to try and leave after this. I didn't want to do that to myself or this innocent woman who was currently losing her shit over the curse and her disbelief of it.

She'd learn.

Just like Officer Simmons did when he stupidly approached Cinderella Loveridge in an attempt to get her to stop her bird. Ha! My grandmother warned him. My mother warned him. I warned him.

He did not listen.

He'll never mess with a witch again. I guess that was a good thing, although I didn't think he saw it that way. "My curse is everlasting with no hope of being resolved. You can rest easier knowing yours can be reversed if you figure it out. Have a nice day. I've got to hit the head. Bladder's not what it used to be."

He nodded at me, so I spun on my Jimmy Choo's—shoes were my thing—and went back to my car as the girl made a dramatic exit. Good for her. She had spunk. Maybe she's smart enough to get us out of the curse. Jesus, Mary, and Joseph knew I couldn't. I had no Romani blood, no witch blood, there was nothing special about me at all. Outside of my shoes. Of course, I was never to utter a word about my lack of Romani blood to anyone outside the family. I hadn't even told my boyfriend of months, Quinn.

He was a good guy. Great guy. An amazing kisser, fucked like an Olympian champion, was nice to my grandmother, and was a fantastic listener. It was just too bad that I could never talk to him about *real* things.

He deserved better than me.

I'd been on my way to meet him and tell him so, to say goodbye, when my car's hood had been crumpled like a piece of tissue paper.

Waiting for Fallon—I got her name when he handed her a ticket—and Officer Simmons to leave first, I sat in my car. The more seconds that ticked by, the more inside my head I got. I closed my eyes and tried to keep the demons from seeping in, but it did no good.

I always felt it before it happened, like there was a little squirrel in my head tapping on my brain saying, "They're coming, they're coming, here we go."

The rushing wind sound came first. It overtook my mind and signaled the beginning, then my heartbeat became erratic, filling with blood, then whooshing out when it got too full. I don't know if that was technically what happened, but it's what it felt like to me.

Then next came the cold sweating, the clenching fists, the tightness in my chest.

Then I was there. Right *there*.

In a box car, bumping over tracks, smashed against other kids, crying, praying, grasping onto a firm hand, and rocking back and forth.

I'm only eight years old.

Only eight.

Only eight.

In the present, I was aware that I was rocking back and forth in my car. I knew it was a memory. I knew that the time in that awful railcar was over. Yet, the coppery taste of adrenaline was on my tongue and my heart was thumping wildly.

This is what always happened when I let the memories in. They overwhelmed me and erased my logical thinking.

"I've got you. You're okay. Look at me, Twenty-three." I looked up into Twenty-two's eyes. He was four years older than me, but he may as well have been an adult. He was the only reason I hadn't died of fright from the moment I got taken. "What do we say?"

"We'll be okay if we stick together."

"Right. Do you feel my hand? Do you feel it?"

"Yes."

"I put super-glue in there and we're stuck. You and me. We will be okay. Say it."

"We'll be okay."

"Good."

He squeezed my hand and the memory rushed out of me like the wind.

My hands were clenched as if I'd been holding onto that hand from twenty years ago as tight as I could, and I was freezing even though it was May in Nevada.

I was not in that rail car any longer. Right? Right.

Taking a deep breath, I took one more look at my tattoo, trying to gain the strength from it to do what I had to do. It didn't take long for my head to return to normal.

I was a Doe now. Does don't let the past bother them. Picking up my cell, I hit Uncle's number.

What do you mean your car isn't running? What did you do?"

He'd heard me the first time. This was his way of taking control, forcing me to repeat the words we both knew would piss him off.

"It was her fault. She got the ticket. I'm just going to need a tow and maybe another ride until my car is repaired."

"Is that so? Well, perhaps I don't feel so generous today. Perhaps I think you should strut in those pretty heels and find your own mechanic."

I swallowed. This was the part where he wanted me to beg. To show my humility. It should've been easy. I'd done it a million times.

That day, I just couldn't do it.

I'd been so close.

"If that's what you wish, Uncle. Sorry to waste your time."

"Wait. Don't be hasty. I said *perhaps*."

Just the sound of his voice made my skin prickle. He was the head of our family and what he said was final. More often than not, what he said was vile. "You test me, Esme, as usual, but I'm not a cruel man. Text me your location and I'll send a tow truck. You can get them to bring you to the Tea House. I'll be waiting for you here."

There was no goodbye, no inquiry about my safety. Just dead silence on the other end.

Having no choice, I texted him the info and waited in my car until I could no longer stand the heat.

The squeak of the tow truck slowing drew my attention from my spiraling thoughts. It was about damn time. I'd been waiting for over an hour.

A man jumped out of the passenger side, immediately going to the back of my car, and started the process of hooking it up by the rear bumper.

The other one, the driver, just stood there with his body half in and half out of the truck. He was wearing those ugly gray mechanic overalls but had the top of his slung over his hips, revealing a tight white wife-beater that hugged his lithe body. He pushed his aviators up, sliding them into his shoulder-length dirty blond locks, and stared at me for what seemed like a lifetime. He was so still that he resembled a statue.

I didn't know if he was trying to intimidate me or found me attractive or maybe he was a little star-struck given my reputation as the face of Doe Tea House.

Finally, he jumped out of the cab and sauntered toward me. The way he led with his hips, the tilt of his head, and the confidence of his stride told me he wasn't star-struck. When he got close, he glanced at my car and then whistled. "What a tragedy."

"How long do you think it'll take to fix it? I need my car as soon as possible."

He took a pack of cigarettes from his pocket, slapped them against his hand to get one out, then fished a lighter from the other pocket and lit it. The whole time, his dark hazel eyes were peeled on me. Taking a drag, he tilted his head back and blew the smoke upward. "I wasn't talking about the car."

"Did you just call *me* a tragedy?"

"Yeah. Look at you with all those delicious curves, juicy lips, that expensive perfume. Here you are on the street sweating in your designer clothes when you should be lying on someone's bed, having grapes fed to you while you prepare for your next orgasm. You're a walking tragedy if I ever saw one."

I huffed. "Let me guess: your bed."

"If that was an invitation, I accept."

I did not have time for this kind of bullshit. "It was not an invitation. You can put it back in your pants. I'm not interested. Just hook up my car, take me where I'm going and I'll see you when you deliver my repaired car. Wait, better yet. Let the other guy bring it. We can part ways and never see each other again now."

"That would be yet another tragedy, Tragedy."

"Jeez. Let it go. I'm not into guys like you and I have a boyfriend." At least for another few minutes.

He took another drag. "Does he like to watch? I'm down for that, but I'm not knocking boots with a dude. Not my thing."

Insufferable. Jerk. Dirtbag.

"Look, kar, which is Romani for dick, by the way, I'm not in the mood for your lip. Just get the job done and shut your overactive mouth."

He smirked again, taking one more drag on his cigarette, then thumping it out of his fingers. "Yes, ma'am," he barked, then he turned to help the other guy, mumbling, "Maybe my mouth is just what you need to make you less bitchy."

I fumed for another ten minutes while they hooked up my car. When the asshole mechanic was satisfied it was ready to tow, he came around to me. "Got you a present." A big black feather was in his hand. "Found it under your windshield. I guess this means you're going to be an even bigger tragedy."

Snatching the feather from his grease-stained fingers, I huffed. I didn't need the reminder that my future was in real jeopardy with the curse. I was already annoyed, but his innocent disregard for the seriousness of my situation crawled inside my skin and rooted there.

Not that he would give two shits about that. In fact, I was certain he was trying to push every button he could find. Case in point, he opened the cab of the truck and bowed. "Your chariot awaits, Tragedy."

Looking up into the dirty cab I sighed. "Don't call me that. And right now I'm going to stop at Read Between the Grinds coffee shop for a few minutes—I don't think it'll take long—then you can take me to the Tea House."

I climbed up into the cab of the truck, using whatever I could get a grip on to help me up and in, knowing that the mechanic was watching my ass as I did so. My white skirt was loose and short. I'm sure he got a great view that he'd probably jerk off to later.

Whatever. I wouldn't be giving him a second thought after he dropped me off at the Tea House. I was going to let Uncle take care of the specifics of the repairs.

When I was settled in the middle of the cab, the other mechanic climbed in on my right. He was middle-aged. Could've been his father. It was hard to tell. "Hey, I'm Charlie. He's Rex. I'm sure he didn't introduce himself. He forgets manners sometimes."

Rex hauled himself into the cab. "I don't forget them because I don't have any."

That tracked.

He started up the truck and maneuvered easily into traffic. It was rush hour now, so that was a skill. I didn't want to compliment him on anything so I kept my mouth shut.

Charlie, on the other hand, felt the need to fill the silence all the way to the coffee shop. I learned that the RR Auto Repair once stood for Richard Richardson, Rex's father, but he'd passed away due to cancer and left the shop to Rex. I learned Charlie was divorced with two kids, went bowling every night of the week, and didn't drink tea or coffee. I also got his favorite food, color, movie, song, and month.

Why I needed to know that was beyond me, but I certainly wouldn't forget Charlie when April came around next year.

I was fearful he was about to launch into his favorite sexual position when Rex pulled to the curb outside of Read Between the Grinds. I sat there awkwardly waiting for Rex to do or say something, but he didn't. He just looked straight ahead, fixing his eyes somewhere on the horizon.

Clearing my throat, I said, "Excuse me. I can't get out."

He turned his head slowly. "Have we met before?"

"Still trying to pick me up? I told you no several times. Not interested in the likes of you."

"It's not a line. It's a legitimate question. Answer it."

"No. I've never seen you before today. Can I get out? I'm meeting someone and I'm late now."

He took his sweet time gazing at my face, looking at me like I'd lied to him. I hadn't. I'd remember a guy like him if I saw him before. Yeah, he was dirty and rude, but he was what most people would call pretty. His nose was a little bit bigger than it should've been and a teensy crooked, his lips were full and the dark stubble along his square jaw looked like he groomed it to be just a little longer than a normal day's growth. He was like a good-looking man, plus.

He was still a jerk though.

I was within seconds of asking Charlie to let me out on his side when Rex suddenly moved, reaching across me and Charlie, pulling a plastic storage container from under Charlie's seat. "Good idea," Charlie mumbled. "I didn't want to intrude, but it looks nasty."

I wasn't sure what they were talking about until Rex flipped the top open. It was a first aid kit full of bandages, antiseptic, and the like. He wrestled a white handkerchief from his pocket. It looked clean, but he was a mechanic so I had my doubts. Before I could protest, he'd pushed my hair away from my face and started wiping blood from my forehead.

"What? Is it bad?" I reached my hand up to check, but he swiped it away.

"I don't think it needs stitches, but you might want to check it out. At least you won't bleed all over your pretty pink shirt now." Pulling the rearview mirror down, I checked out the wound. The blood hadn't dripped down my face too far, but it was a pretty big scrape where a bump was starting to form.

I don't know how I missed the fact that I was bleeding.

Rex readjusted the mirror, then pulled out a big white bandage, opened it, and wiped antibiotic cream on it. "You'll want to keep it clean and reapply the bandage often."

"Thanks, I guess."

Again with a smirk before opening the door and getting out of the truck. I scooted along the seat to get out myself and Rex stuck out his hand to help me. I didn't want to take it, but I also didn't want to jump the distance in my heels. It was rough like you'd expect from a guy who works with his hands, but his grip was unexpectedly tender as he guided me out of the truck.

I wobbled as my foot landed and he grabbed my waist to steady me, leaning in to whisper in my ear. "Look at that. I *do* have manners after all."

"Yeah, thanks." I dislodged myself from his grasp. "I'll just be a few minutes I think. If you'll wait here—"

"I'm not your fucking Uber driver, Tragedy." He climbed back into the cab, slamming the door and looking down at me with that smirk. "If you have somewhere else to go, I suggest you ask your boyfriend to take you."

He drove off, leaving me standing on the curb and gaping, knowing I wouldn't have a boyfriend when I was finished here.

The bell chimed announcing as I entered the shop. It was nice and homey inside, with books everywhere. I could see why Quinn had been texting me for an hour raving about how cool it was. It had his kind of vibe. The woman behind the counter looked up, swishing her long blonde hair out of her eyes before smiling a smile that was way too big for the kind of day I was having. "Welcome to Read Between the Grinds. What can I—?"

Of course, this was my luck. The woman who'd plowed into me this morning was behind the counter. "You," I snarled. Was it a bit mean girl? Yeah, but the mechanic had pissed me off and I wasn't in the mood to be nice.

"Um, hi again." She bit her lip before finishing her sentence. God help her, she was trying to be friendly to me. "I'm still sorry about what happened."

"Don't be sorry. Be forthcoming with your portion of the bill. You've put me out in the worst way. You wouldn't believe the mechanic I was forced to use to fix my car. He's unbearable." I pushed her sunglasses up, scanning the place for Quinn. Whatever. I'm meeting someone."

He appeared from the main dining or sipping area, whatever it was called in a coffee shop. He looked good today, which was nothing new, but there was something in his expression. Something foreboding. 'I'm here, Esme. Do you know Fallon?"

Fallon looked like she was doing calculus in her head. Several different expressions passed her face.

I pointed to the bandage Rex had just given me. "Our cars were well-acquainted this morning, so yes, I guess I know her." I leaned up and pecked Quinn's cheek, my fingers grazing the long bits that hung over his eyes. It was a shame to cover up those teal beauties up. "You need a haircut."

He gave me an easy smile. "Eh, maybe I like hair this length. Es, this is Fallon who's a creative coffee genius, and Fallon, this is Esme." He paused. Way, way too long for my liking. "My girlfriend."

Although, I guess I didn't have any right to be upset about it. I was here to break up with him. Still, he didn't have to look so damn bewildered by the statement. We'd been together a while.

A dark-haired woman passed by us, whispering something under her breath as she did so. Fallon looked mortified at whatever it was. I didn't care. I just needed a few minutes alone with Quinn.

He put his hand on the small of my back, something he did all the time because he had that gentlemanly way about him. Honestly, it was the first thing in my day that had felt somewhat close to normal, so when he pulled away from me, I was left with a prickly cold feeling. "She'll have a Virginia Woolf," he called over his shoulder.

It would be like him to pick a shop with cutesy bookish names on the menu. No idea what that was, but he knew my coffee order, so I trusted him.

Quinn led me to a booth in the corner and I slid into the seat across from him. He'd obviously been there a while because he'd set all of his papers and things out like he was settling in for the winter. Maybe he was. Maybe this place would be good for him.

He reached across the table, pushing my hair back from my face and lightly grazing the bandage with his thumb. "You were hurt?"

"It's nothing. I'm fine."

"If you say so. Keep an eye on that. You might need stitches."

"The mechanic doesn't think so."

"Right. And he's qualified to make that call? Last time I checked under your hood you didn't have a carburetor."

Why did he have to make me laugh? It was going to make this so much harder.

Before I could get a word out, he started talking. "Hey, before I forget, Professor Duncan wanted me to ask you to come to his book signing this weekend. I told him I wasn't sure you'd want to go, but he insisted you come. I could make an excuse if you wanted." He shrugged, giving me an open opportunity to say no and looking like he wouldn't care if I did.

I should've stopped him there and just ended it between us as I'd planned, but since the curse wasn't going to let me just sneak away as I'd planned, I was going to be around. "Yeah, I guess. Sure. I'd hate to disappoint him."

The woman who wasn't Fallon came over with my coffee, sitting it down for me, then slid into the seat next to Quinn like she was invited. She'd make a good match for the mechanic. They could go around and be rude to each other all day long. Quinn swung his arm around the back of the booth, already comfortable with her. "Esme, this is Fallon's sister Zoey."

She gave me her hand and I shook it. "Nice to meet you."

"Yeah, you too. So, how long have you guys been together?"

Quinn kept silent. At first, I thought he was just going to let me answer, but he wasn't even looking at me. He was staring at Fallon behind the counter. "A while."

"Good. And how did you meet?"

Vaguely, the chime of the bell sounded, indicating another customer. I hoped it would get Zoey up from the table—our table— but it didn't. She stayed where she was. "We met at a party. One of his friends had been in one of my classes at UNB. He introduced us. We hit it off. Um, don't you have something better to do than get to know your customers? I don't mean to be rude, but I need to speak with him privately."

That seemed to get his attention back on me. "What's up?"

Zoey stood. "Of course. I'm sorry. Fallon just takes an interest in all our customers. Just being friendly. I'll give you some space."

"Thank goodness."

She went about cleaning the tables around us where no one had been sitting. I was about to call her out for snooping when Quinn suddenly jumped up from our table. I gaped as he ran over to Fallon and clutched her into his arms. She seemed to be having some kind of seizure, and it was painfully obvious he wasn't going to let her fall or move or even breathe without his protection.

I couldn't remember a time when he'd ever done something like that for me. Yeah, he was always nice and a gentleman, opening doors and serving me food and drinks, but that look of sheer concern in his eyes over her? Never got that. Not even when he commented on my forehead just now. It wasn't concern. It was…observation.

Fallon didn't look like she was doing so well. She was pale and trembling. I could see that from where I sat.

Something must have happened to remind Quinn I was waiting because he suddenly looked up and our gazes locked. It took several heated seconds for him to wrestle his way away from Fallon. He gave her the smile that he *knew* would highlight his sexy dimple, then he ambled over to me. Finally.

Little spots of light formed in my periphery. Some might call them jealous sparks. I raised my voice, making sure Fallon could hear me when I spoke. "Maybe she needs to see a doctor, not a handsome grad student."

She had the decency to blush at my remark.

Quinn didn't take it so well.

"What are you doing? That was a bitch move and you aren't a bitch."

"Maybe I am and you just never realized it."

Fighting with him was not the way to break up. I knew that, but I couldn't control myself. I was angry and scared and all that malice was seeping out of my pores. It was like the curse was already turning me inside out.

The new customer that had come in whizzed by, on the way to the toilet. I waited for her to move past us before I spoke again. "Do you know how it makes me feel to see you fawning over the woman who wrecked my car? Who caused me to be cursed? You're making a fool out of me, Quinn. I hate that."

"Fallon had no control over the curse. The wreck either since the Warbler caused it. Think about what you're saying, Esme.

You're better than this." He reached out to take my hand and I let him. I don't know why. "Listen, you know I care about you, but maybe we've reached the end of this thing. I hate that this comes on a bad day for you, but I'd already planned to talk to you about this before I met Fallon." He glanced over at her and I swear, his eyes lit. He was into her. After what, two hours? "You and I both know we've been going through the motions for a while."

I went nearly mental at the tear that was threatening to fall. I'd come here to break it off with him and now that he was doing it first, it ate at my soul. "Is that what you want? To ditch me right here in her coffee shop. That would make it very convenient. You wouldn't even have to go anywhere to fuck her. You two could get at it in the storage room between the cups and coffee beans."

"Es—"

The woman burst out of the restroom, flying across the tiles and out the door. Everything in me wanted to follow right behind her, but I wasn't going to leave until I had the upper hand.

Does always had the upper hand.

"Don't Es me, Quinn. You picked the worst day of my life to do this. You *know* I was cursed today. You *know* what Uncle will do to me. You know everything."

No, he didn't. Couldn't. He knew a lot, just not all. I'd never told him. Never told anyone.

"Look me in the eye and tell me you still want me like you did. Give me a list of all the things you love about me. I want to know how many times lately you've been sitting there hoping and praying for me to call so we could meet up. How many times, Es? Tell me."

One of the things I liked most about Quinn was his logic. He had a way of looking at the world and narrowing it down to its basest parts to make sense of it. He'd done that with one paragraph.

I sat in my seat, sighing. "None."

Fallon raced by us, not even sparing us a second glance. Quinn on the other hand, tracked her every move as she ran into the restroom before looking back to me. "Exactly. We had fun, but there's someone better for each of us. I don't know who. Maybe Fallon, maybe someone five years from now. It's not that I want her so much that I have to dump you. It's that I care so much about you that I have to let you go and find the right person, Es. He is out there. It's just not me."

"God, I fucking hate when you make sense."

"I know, it *is* annoying to be right all the time."

"The kicker is I was going to break it off with you today too. I just got caught up with the curse and the rude mechanic and then seeing your expression when you look at her, I lost it."

"You keep mentioning the rude mechanic."

"I don't."

"You do."

A loud whoosh came from the restroom. It was like a dam broke inside there. I wasn't sure what Fallon was up to, but it didn't sound pleasant. Quinn got up, shouting, "What the fuck?" as he barreled in the door.

I looked around. Zoey had gone inside an employee-only door. There were a few customers still in the shop. None of them seemed worried about what was happening. A man went into the men's next door even, bringing his coffee with him. Ew.

I waited a few minutes, wondering if that was it between me and Quinn. If so, there was no reason for me to stay. I had hoped for one final kiss, but I doubted I'd get that now that Fallon was on his radar.

Funny how that thought didn't even strike a chord of emotion in me at all.

When they burst out of the bathroom, Quinn was carrying her over his shoulder. He dropped her on the floor next to the table, telling her to "Stay."

Her face said she was about to give him the smackdown, but he put his finger on her lips to keep her from it, repeating himself. "Stay."

Was it bad of me to be amused by this interaction? It was funny to see her be both angry and definitely piqued by Quinn's actions. "I'm not a dog."

"No, you are not," he drawled. Oh, I knew that voice. That was his bedroom voice. This girl was going to have the ride of her life if she knew what was good for her.

I wished she would.

The curse was already messing with her if the disaster in her restroom was any indication. The least she could do for herself is put a hunky, good guy with sexual prowess in her bed for the night.

When I looked at my feet I realized the curse was already messing with me too. I knew I shouldn't have worn my favorite heels for my grand escape. "Well, while he cleans up your mess, the least you could do is get me a free coffee. These are Jimmy Choo's."

She went off to get more coffee for me, bringing it back and looking more friendly than I was ready to accept. "Sorry about that. I don't know why that woman dismantled my toilet."

"Hm." I looked down my nose, then took a long slurp of coffee, giving my time to get my Doe mask in place. We were not friends. I needed her to help me get rid of my curse, then it was *la revedere* to her, to Quinn, to Between. "I hope your business insurance is better than your car insurance."

Quinn arrived from the bathroom, cocking his eyebrow at her. then using that eyebrow to get her to move a few inches to the right. Man, she was in for it. When he spoke, he was all-sex appeal. "It's good you take direction well." Remembering I was standing feet away, he adjusted himself and put a more professional tone to his words. "I got the water turned off for you, but you're going to need a plumber."

That seemed to break her spirit. To her credit, she didn't start bawling, but she definitely took that as a hit in the gut. She started droning on about closing the shop, needing money, health codes, and a bunch of woe is me.

I put my mug down, then glanced at my favorite shoes again, lamenting their ruin. I'll never get them back in mint shape with all that water damage. "Not to mention the expense of the plumber."

I ignored the heated glare Quinn was now giving me. He was right. I was being a bitch. I was a Doe, after all. "I know you don't believe it, but this is the curse messing with you. I'd advise you to think your way out of it soon or things like this will keep happening."

She picked up my mug, already on her way to clean it up when her eyes crossed. She got violently still as she stared into what was left of my coffee in that mug.

I knew that look.

This is what my Mama and Grandmother Baba looked like when they got true visions from the tea leaves. It's what I tried to emulate as best as I could since I was faking it all the time.

Her gaze was glassy, fixed on one point and she trembled.

Quinn went right into action, crouching down to meet her eye-to-eye. He ran his thumbs along her jaw before gripping her wet hair, whispering something only she could hear. Seeing him like that with her made my stomach clench. Not because I wanted it to be me. I didn't.

But I wanted that feeling of being taken care of. Of knowing I had one person who was there for me no matter what. I had that once. In a different way, but it was no less important. Moving my bracelets so I could see my Lukey tattoo, I sighed.

Lukey.

Fallon blinked over and over, trying to clear the vision I knew she'd just seen. "Just another customer having a bad day. Why are you asking?"

"Just trying to see what I'm in for. We both got cursed if you recall." I hooked my thumb over my shoulder. Whatever. I'm heading out." I looked up at Quinn, wondering if that last kiss was coming. When he didn't move an inch toward me, I had my answer. "I guess I'll see you around, Quinn."

I steeled my shoulders as I headed out into the sunlight. I should've maybe felt bad about our breakup, but I didn't. I was relieved about it. I had far more pressing things to deal with anyway. Namely, the curse.

And the fact that my ride had left.

I Ubered to the Tea House, uttering every Romani curse I'd ever heard at Rex on the way. They weren't going to stick, but it made me feel better to get them out. And hey, it fit the brand. I was certain my poor driver was going to come in and buy every charm that my family sold in the gift shop to make sure I wasn't cursing her.

Skirting in the door, past my cousins Charity and Selene, my tanti Rhoda, my mom, and grandma who were both engaged in a tea reading at tables in the back of the room, I turned for the stairs to Uncle's office. My female relatives congregated together all the time. They welcomed me, always, but I never felt like a part of them. Not really. Besides, I couldn't avoid the inevitable.

The Tea House was a converted Victorian which, frankly, looked odd in a desert town, but it fit the vibe, so the Doe family bought it years ago. Back when my grandpa, God rest his soul, was in charge of the family. Not that I knew him. He'd died before I came to Between. I'd just heard so many stories about the legendary Eli Doe it was hard not to feel like I knew him somehow.

Now that Sampson was the patriarch, the family and the business were run differently. Eli had been a traditionalist, so yes, the women had been made to wear skirts and gold jewelry. The entire family looked and acted every bit Romani. Uncle had kept those principles intact, but he was big on updating and bringing the Romani life into the modern world, so we were reading tea leaves on YouTube, live streaming, selling merch, performing shows, and doing God knew what other stuff to make money.

Which is just one of the myriad of reasons I wanted out. I didn't trust anything about him. He was always looking for the angle. Always.

With every step climbed, my stomach clenched more. It was like the descent into Hell, only I was going up.

I knocked on his office door, waiting for permission to go inside. He, of course, made me wait several minutes before calling for me to enter.

"Ah, Esme. I was expecting you earlier. I suppose you had trouble getting here without your expensive car the family money bought for you."

"My apologies Uncle. There was a misunderstanding with the mechanic. I had to take an Uber. Would it be possible for me to get a loaner car until he fixes mine?"

I stood tall and straight with my hands folded, just like he expected of me. He stood from behind his desk, walking around to lean on the edge facing me. "You must think I'm an idiot, Esme."

"What? No sir."

In truth, he was very smart. And connected to people and things I'd not like to be associated with.

"Why did you think you could get away with leaving out the most important information this morning? You told me all about your poor little car and how you needed my help, but you failed to mention the Wayward Warbler had cursed you?" He slammed his fist on the desk. I flinched.

How had he even found out about it? Had that damn mechanic told him?

"I didn't leave it out on purpose. I was just more concerned about other things." I pointed to the bandage on my head. "I was injured."

"You seem to be fine, but now I'm in a dilemma. You know that something stirs in the air of this town when the Warbler strikes. Our clientele always increases, and our revenue skyrockets. If word got out that you were the one cursed, how would that look? Our customers might fear a cursed Romani reading their leaves."

"But you know I don't have the gift anyway. I could still fake it like I always do."

He crossed his legs and arms at the same time, drumming his fingers, the shiny gold rings on his fingers clicking together as he did so. "That's irrelevant. It's all about perception. I'll have to think about how to handle this unfortunate event."

I nodded and he suddenly jumped off the desk, walked over to a file cabinet, and removed the key from his pocket. Once he had the cabinet open, he pulled out a manilla envelope. When he turned around, the look in his eyes had gone from cold and aloof, to sly and devious. "While I ponder the situation, you can do something for me."

"Yes, Uncle."

"I want you to remove your panties."

"What? Why?"

"Am I not the patriarch of this family, girl? You'll do it because I said so."

"I'm not comfortable with that."

Beyond uncomfortable. It was an insane ask, even for him.

I once had a best friend in Jr. High School, Nomi. She told me Uncle gave her the willies because he seemed to want to touch me in inappropriate ways. It was true that he got handsy when he was drunk, but he had never forced himself on me. If he had, I'd have left sooner.

Staring at him now as he asked me to remove my underwear I was beginning to wonder if Nomi was right. "I'm sorry, Uncle, but I'm not going to give my panties to you. Nor will I give you anything else."

The thought of his hands touching me was making my stomach turn.

He growled. "Don't be dumb Esme. You think I want your whorish little pussy? I don't. Just give me the underwear. Now."

I turned to get away, but he ate the distance between us up and grabbed my arm to stop me.

The stench of alcohol wafted around as he leaned in to speak in my ear. Already drunk that early in the day. Seemed about right. "You will show me your respect by giving me what I'm asking for or I will take them forcibly from you. One way you'll get a car to drive while yours is repaired, the other way will get you punished. Your choice."

Punishment could mean any number of things. I didn't even want to consider the list. I truly had no choice. Shaking, I went to stand behind one of the chairs he had for visitors, then carefully, I stepped out of my panties, using the chair to block most of my body so he wouldn't see.

When I finally had them off, I balled them up and threw them at him. He caught them in one hand. "White lace. Nice choice." He put the panties inside the manilla envelope, sealed it, and then filed it back away in the cabinet. Then he silently returned to the chair behind the desk. The matter was closed for him.

My stomach was burning and I was starting to feel pressure between my ears. I needed to get out of there. "Am I free to go?"

He pulled a drawer open and fished out a set of keys, tossing them to me. I guess in exchange for the panties. "You can use Grandpa's car until your car is fixed. Keep your phone on. I want to be able to reach you at all times. As soon as the curse manifests, I want to know what it does. I'll let you know what I decide to do about it then."

I glanced down at the keys on the horseshoe keyring. According to my Grandma, the horseshoe was the symbol of good luck. We had them hanging on our home and business too. This one was Grandpa's and had stayed with his truck ever since he bought it years and years ago. It was a family joke. Every one of us had learned to drive in the Jalopy, as we called it. We were told if you could drive that, you could drive anything, so once we passed the Jalopy test, we were given cars.

Driving it at twenty-eight years old would be an insult. Which is exactly what Uncle was attempting to do. Perhaps with my underwear too.

I was not going to let this humiliation get to me.

"Thank you, Uncle. I appreciate your kindness."

I walked out of the office with my head held high, making sure I'd dried the tears before I made it to the kitchen.

"Esme, come to your Mama. Let me hug you."

I buried myself in my mother's arms. She was a good woman and I'd miss her when I left, but knowing she was not my biological mother always stuck in my mind. Maybe it was the circumstances that led to my adoption, I couldn't say. There was just a chasm between us. At times, large, but sometimes, like that moment, it was small. I loved her, and I could feel the worry in her embrace. "Sampson told me the Warbler got you. My poor baby. Let us help you figure this curse out. Pull up a chair."

All around me, the women tutted and patted my arm. It did give a measure of comfort, but I knew there would be nothing they could do to help me. "It's okay. I haven't even seen the effects of the curse yet. I'm sure it'll be fine."

My tanti Rhoda, my mom's sister, Charity, and Selene's mother was especially keen to find out about the curse business. She was a busybody and a nosy know-it-all, so she was either pumping for information or spilling information, whichever the occasion called for. "Tell me about the one who bears the other side of the curse. Do you know?"

Sighing, I accepted the cup of tea my Baba slid to me. Out of all of them, my grandmother was my closest friend and ally. She would likely have been the only one to understand why I was leaving. Though, I doubted she'd understand why her son just made me give him my panties.

I shuddered and tried to push it out of my head. "The one I was in the wreck with owns a coffee show if you can believe that irony."

Rhoda tsk-tsked. "Oh, it's not irony. The Warbler knows things. He has his ways. I'm not surprised she's in a similar profession as you. What do you know about her?"

"She's a little jittery and uptight, definitely a control freak, but seems decent. She'll probably be in bed with Quinn before the night ends though." The collective gasp around the table was audible. "It's okay, we parted as friends. It was mutual. I don't want to talk about him."

Because I didn't, I kept talking so they couldn't interrupt me. "From what I could tell, the curse seemed to make her see visions. It reminded me of the tea leaf readings, but her trance was deeper. That's it. That's the extent of my knowledge."

"Okay, well you must tell us when the curse manifests."

"That's what Uncle said too."

"Hmph. We want to know so we can help you, not control you."

Baba swatted her arm. "You best be careful how loud you say things like that. You know Sampson has ears everywhere. If he heard you talking down about him, you'd be in for it. You need to respect him."

Rhoda bowed her head, knowing she was right. I knew for a fact that Baba was the one who respected him the least in our family. She always abided by his leadership, but underneath her obedience, laid a will that told me she'd prefer to run the family and the business both.

Alas, we lived in a patriarchal situation.

Yet another reason, I wanted out.

"Uncle just said he was waiting for the curse to manifest before he decided what to do with me. He doesn't want the taint of it on the Tea House, naturally. I may have to go into hiding for a while."

"Nonsense. You'll do no such thing. You're my baby and I will take care of Sampson if he needs to be told off. I don't care what he says. He can't hide you."

Baba sighed. "Is something in the water today? Shush, all of you." She leaned forward, using her hands to gather us together in a tight huddle. "At least wait until he's out of the house!"

We erupted into laughter and for a moment I forgot about the curse and the panties and everything else weighing on me.

Later, finished with my tea, I reached out to get my cup and Selene's. The moment I touched hers, I felt something.

It wasn't so much a physical feeling as an overwhelming rush of adrenaline and chill chasing through me. It came on so quickly, I thought I might fall off the stool. I grabbed her hand to steady myself.

"Are you okay, Esme?" Her voice was hollow. I tried to answer her, but I couldn't speak or move. All I could do was sit there clutching her hand and wishing the awful feeling would stop.

Since my gaze was locked on her teacup, I focused on the leaves. It was second nature to me by now. This time, however, I didn't need to make up a vague prediction of the future or some nonsense designed to get more money out of our customers. A vision appeared in the cup, strange as it sounded. It was like the tea leaves changed and morphed into a room. Uncle's office. Selene was there.

"Take off your panties, Selene."

"Are you joking? No way. And newsflash: my father will have your head for asking me something so wildly inappropriate. You're my uncle, Uncle." She spat out the last part and I took a little pride in the fact she was telling him no.

"I'm the patriarch of this family and he would not bat a single eyelash over this order. Take them off. I promise no harm will come to you. I just need your underwear."

Knowing she had no choice—just like me earlier—she slipped off her panties and handed them to him. And, like before, he put them in a manila envelope.

"What are you doing with those? It can't be anything good."

"I'm going to forget you questioning my authority."

"I'm questioning what you're doing with my underwear."

He slapped her and I swear I felt the sting of the slap on my own face. "It's not your place to question anything I do. You're dismissed."

My vision faded and I looked up at Selene, blinking. "What just happened, Esme?"

"I-I-don't know. I think I had a reading. A real, actual, honest-to-god reading. Mama, when you and Baba read leaves do you see the events in your head like they're happening?"

"No. We interpret what we see in them. Tasseomancy isn't like movies, Esme. The leaves are leaves. We look at how they're arranged and the location in the cups to determine the prediction or the recollections. We translate meanings from that. You know this."

Shit.

"Well, it must have been the curse then."

Rhoda grabbed my hand. "What did you see?"

"I don't want to say. I just saw the past. Can we leave it at that?"

She frowned. "If we're going to help you, we need to know everything."

"No, you don't. I will figure this out. Or Fallon at the coffee shop will. I don't need your help."

"Leave it alone, Rhoda. She'll tell us if she wants."

Thanks, Baba.

Suddenly, I wanted out of the kitchen, out of the Tea House, out of… my skin.

I needed to shower, to change shoes to—

I laid my head down on the table, silently cursing myself. I'd forgotten my bags in my car. Not only were my favorite clothes and shoes inside them, but my most prized possession was inside too.

I grabbed the keys off the table. "I have to go. I'll be back later. Um, please don't tell Uncle about this yet. I need to think. See you later."

Rushing out of the kitchen before anyone could stop me, my heels clicked on the hardwood floor. I pushed out the back door and was halfway to the garage in the back of the Doe family compound when I was suddenly whirled around by a hand.

Selene.

"Will you tell *me* what you saw? You were looking into my leaves when you had the vision."

I had a decision to make. I could give her some random memory that I participated in with her in the past to satisfy her curiosity, or I could give her the truth, essentially outing what Uncle had done to me.

When it was just me, I could chalk it up as punishment for the wreck and insubordination, or hell, Uncle just having a morning, but when I acknowledged it was more than one of us involved in the…whatever it was, it felt dirtier. More important.

I didn't want to give credence to it.

But I didn't want to ignore it either.

"I saw you in Uncle's office. He made you take off your panties and give them over to him."

Her hand flew to her mouth. "I didn't know what to do. I had no choice. He's done that multiple times now and I still don't know why."

"It isn't just you, Selene. He took mine too. Just now. He's probably gotten Charity's too."

"What could he be doing with them? That's so gross and strange."

"It is. I'm not sure what's going on, but if I were able to read his tea leaves, maybe I could figure it out. Trouble is, he rarely drinks tea."

"No, he rarely drinks tea in front of Tati and Baba, given their abilities. He knows you fake it, so if you can put off the news of the curse, maybe you can sneak a reading from him beforehand. Catch him off-guard."

That was a perfect idea. I just had to figure out how to make it happen. I hugged Selene. "Don't worry. I'm going to find out. But it would help if you ran interference for me. I've got to go somewhere now. I'll be back later and we can figure out how to make this work."

She nodded, then scurried back into the Tea House.

The rest of the long walk to the garage I mulled everything over in my head. Spending even more time with Uncle was not what I wanted to do, but I'd do it to get to the bottom of this strange mystery. Hell, if I could catch him doing something immoral or illegal with our panties, maybe he'd end up ostracized or in jail.

That thought just might carry me through the day. I could make this work. I just had to get my lucky charm from my car first. Which meant, I had to face the pretty and annoying mechanic.

The Jalopy was almost as infuriating as the mechanic had been. I had trouble with the clutch and it jerked all over the road, not to mention the eyesore factor. It was an old wooden-paneled SUV with chipping paint that probably used to be white but was a disgusting cream color now. The front seat was a bench all the way across. When I made a turn I felt like I was going to fly over the seat and out the passenger window.

But, despite the harrowing ride, it got me where I wanted to go: RxR Auto Shop. I wasn't sure if it was meant to be pronounced as R *and* R or RR or what. The sign was painted like a Railroad sign, which was a big red flag in my mind, but it wasn't like I had a choice if I wanted to get my stuff back.

I pulled into the parking lot, gripping the wheel with white knuckles, disbelieving I was about to enter a location that had anything to do with a railroad.

Sighing, I got out of the truck and made my way inside the shop. Charlie was sitting at the counter with his nose in a laptop, surrounded by car-related products, tires in every corner, about fourteen coffee mugs, and a 2-year out of date calendar hung on the wall behind him. The only thing missing was a pinup girl in a bikini on a motorcycle.

"Well hey there, Miss Doe. Good to see you again so soon."

"Hello, Charlie. I came to get some things out of my car. I was in such disarray this morning, that I forgot some important stuff. Would I be able to get it?"

"Sure, sure. Let me get the boss."

"Oh, no need to trouble Rex. I can just slip in and out. It won't take but a minute."

He scratched his head. "Well, yeah, see, I can't let civilians in the back without permission. There are codes and things. We may not look like a spiffy shop, but we do follow the law."

"I'm sure you do."

I wasn't that sure.

Especially since Rex was the owner/operator. He looked like he skirted the law on the regular.

"Just tell him, I need my bags. It truly won't take long."

He disappeared into the door that led to the workspace. I was afraid to sit on the chair in the corner, mainly because I was wearing a white skirt, but mostly because I still had no panties on, thanks to Uncle. I had no idea what kind of stains were on that thing. Grease, probably. Something heinous, most likely.

Charlie came back in quick time, opening the door and motioning me through. "Boss says come on back. Just be careful where you step. And white was not the best color to wear here." He chuckled, closing the door behind me.

I couldn't help but shout my response through the shut door, "Your boss was wearing a white shirt earlier."

"Glad you noticed."

Jerking my head in every direction, I failed to find Rex among the cars.

The place was packed with them, lining every nook and cranny in the large room. I had to turn a corner to locate my car. It was sitting in the middle of a workspace, away from the other cars.

For a garage, the place was eerily quiet.

Except for the music.

Coming from my car.

I approached, looking underneath, because that's where mechanics were supposed to be, right? Under the car. When I didn't find him there, I walked over to the driver's side and peeped inside. My entire steering wheel was gone. Tools were lying in my seat and that music? It wasn't mine. It was some kind of bluesy instrumental that seemed out of place in conjunction with what I thought a garage mechanic would listen to. I leaned down, stretching my neck so my head was inside, looking over at Rex who had his feet on my dash and a joint in his mouth. His eyes were closed, but I knew he'd been fully aware I was in the building before I found him. "What no heavy death metal?"

He smiled. "I'll take that as an insult, Tragedy. You assumed because I was a mechanic I'd listen to metal trash. That's about the same as someone slinging the g-word at you?"

I sighed, reaching in and trying to move the seat back so I could grab my stuff and go, but it wouldn't budge. He had some shit on the floor behind it, making it lodge in place. "Listening to heavy metal and being called a racial slur are not on the same level. Now, get that joint out of my car."

He slowly angled his head toward me before taking the joint out of his mouth and offering it to me. The dare was written all over his pretty face. I wanted to wipe that smug look off with my bare hands.

So, I took what he'd offered me, taking a slow drag and letting it out. "Maybe you're not such a Tragedy after all."

To bring home my point that I was in control of this little exchange, I took one more puff and then dropped the thing on the floor, putting it out with my ruined Jimmy Choo's.

"Hey, that was a perfectly good joint. You owe me."

"Whatever. I need to get things from my car."

"I'm not stopping you."

"Actually, you are. I can't get in through the driver's side because of whatever you've done to my seat and I can't get in the passenger side because you're in the way."

"Hm, I'd say you should've bought a car with four doors then."

Wishing I'd taken more than two hits, I marched around to the other side of the car. "What is wrong with you? You're the owner of this business. You're supposed to be nice to your customers, not get high in their vehicles and insult them."

"Am I? Shit, I've been doing it wrong all these years."

I clenched my fists, trying to let the frustration roll through me and out. The truth was, Rex was the cherry on top of a very bad sundae and I didn't want to deal with him. I wanted my stuff.

"You know who my Uncle is, right? He will kill you if he finds out you're treating me this way. I could tell him right now." I clutched my phone in my hand, making the idle threat with as much venom as I could.

"You think? Call him, let's find out."

I closed my eyes. I wasn't going to call him and somehow he knew it. "Yeah, called your bluff there, Tragedy. See, I know who your uncle and I know what a dirtbag he is and I have a sneaking suspicion if I called him now and told him about the packed suitcases in the back seat, he'd be madder about you leaving town than me getting lit in your car."

He was right. And the worst part was the smile that crept across his face when he knew I knew it too.

"Just get out of my car. You have no idea the kind of day I've had, shit, the kind of life I've had. Everything is crashing around me and if I don't get my stuff soon, I am going to lose control of my senses. Do you hear me?" I yanked the door open, giving him a chance to get out of the car, but he stayed right where he was, eyeing me with that dark hazel gaze that seemed to reach inside and pull something out of me.

"What's wrong with losing control now and then?" he asked, his voice barely a whisper.

"Let me see, if I lost control I'd be an embarrassment to my family, piss off my unpredictable and dangerous uncle, and potentially jeopardize the only chance I have to escape from here and put my demons to rest, as you so aptly noted by pointing out my suitcases, so losing control is out of the fucking option, Grease Monkey."

I was done waiting for him. If he wasn't going to move his ass from my vehicle, the only option I had was to crawl over him. I hiked my skirt up, just a little, then slung my leg over his lap, reaching for my bag behind him, but not quite able to make it. So, I pulled the other leg in, effectively straddling him, but I got my hand wrapped around the suitcase handle, so that's all I was thinking about.

The problem was that I failed to calculate the room and force needed to pull both bags out with me as I got off his lap. I tugged hard, trying to pick up the suitcase and exit at the same time, but it didn't work in the least. Not wanting to give up, I put my all into pulling that suitcase. I jerked and grunted and jerked some more, bucking against him and straining to break free from him at the same time. When that didn't work, I stretched my other hand over him, using both of them to try and get my suitcase out.

Over and over and over I pulled at that bag—for how long, I couldn't say—until I had to give up, screaming my frustration into the air with a loud wail that burst from the car and bounced all around the hard concrete surfaces of the garage. This scream wasn't just about the suitcases. It was about my entire life in one crippling wail, and when I was done, I panted, heaving in and out, my chest feeling like it would implode.

The sound that left Rex's mouth was primal. I'd never heard a man—certainly not Quinn—growl in that way. I looked up. His pupils were dilated, his chest heaving like mine. He grabbed my throat in his hand, dragging me to him before crashing—and I mean crashing—his mouth into mine.

Shock didn't begin to cover it.

What did cover it was lust. A pure, sharp, knife's edge of lust that danced on the thin edge of pleasure and pain.

I didn't want to want him, but I did. At that moment when everything was spinning around me, he was the steady calm in the storm. So, I let him kiss me. I let him thrust his tongue into my mouth and explore all he wanted.

His kiss was as rough as his fingers as they wrapped around the column of my throat. It took no longer than a second for me to realize I liked the feel of his calloused skin against my flesh. I liked the way he used his teeth and his tongue to turn my lips numb as he squeezed tighter around my throat.

This was beyond anything I'd ever known.

This was like opening my eyes and finding myself in someone else's life. As sad as it may have been, I longed to be this person, whoever she was.

He pulled away, searching my face for…something I probably couldn't or shouldn't give him. "I told you there was nothing wrong with losing control."

I didn't know what had happened to my phone. I dropped it somewhere in the car as I was trying to get my bags, but the sound of it buzzing brought me back to my senses. "That's probably my uncle. I should…"

Rex fished between the seats, finding my phone. We both glanced long enough to see Uncle on the caller screen, but instead of handing it to me to answer, he threw it out the open window. Hard.

It shattered against the concrete wall, plastic and metal raining down.

Something inside me snapped. Seeing the tattered remains of my phone and knowing I was in the process of disappointing Uncle unleashed a beast from the depths of me.

That beast was ravenous and wanted her prey.

I wanted Rex.

It didn't matter that he made no sense. I failed to care about anything except the feel of his hardness beneath me. I turned my head slowly, meeting his dark eyes. "What's it going to be, Tragedy? Are you getting out or getting off?"

My chest was heaving, pulse pounding, an ache like I'd never had before rose and did my thinking for me. "Get me off. Right now."

"Good choice." He ripped my shirt off, nearing pulling my arms out of the sockets with force, but I found that I liked the burn of it, the desperation of his moves.

Leaning forward, he bit at my nipples. They were already straining against the fabric of my bra the tingle I felt shot through me. As he nipped and moaned, I reached behind me to undo the clasp and he helped slide the bra off me. It landed on top of my shirt.

As he sucked on one nipple, then the next, he slid his hands up my thighs, making his way to my ass and squeezing. He looked up through his dark lashes. "No panties? You're a fucking naughty girl, aren't you?"

I wasn't.

Well, maybe I was a little. But I didn't want to tell him where my panties were. I just wanted him to make me feel something, anything, other than the way I'd been feeling. I wiggled against him, making like I was trying to get out of the door. "I guess you're not going to get me off after all then."

"Did you just use reverse psychology to make me to fuck you?"

"I don't know. Did it work?"

"No. I want to do that of my own free will." He kissed me, raking his tongue over my lower lip first, then flicking it along the roof of my mouth in a way that made chills erupt over my skin.

I yanked at his coveralls, trying to get them down, to free the hard cock that kept brushing against my pussy. "Fuck. Help me get these down."

"Raise your hips," he grunted. I lifted, thinking he was going to take a second to take his coveralls off his shoulders and hips, but he didn't. He took the coverall fabric in his hands and ripped it at the seam, exposing his underwear first, then opening those to expose himself.

Before I could say or do anything, he grabbed my ass and slammed me down on top of his cock. I moaned as he slid inside me and filled me up with his shaft, pumping in and out as we rocked the car.

It was insane the way we went at each other. He kept the pace quick and I reached behind him, gripping the long length of his hair as I rode his cock. I was certain I was pulling, but he didn't seem to mind. He just kept lifting his hips and groaning. "Yeah, that's it. Grind my cock with your wet pussy." He bit his lip and it looked so good on him. I just stared at him until he gave me a smirk.

I pulled off him, just for a second, stopping to get on my knees so I'd have more power, he let me adjust and then went right back to driving into me as I rocked against him. This way, I was in a little more control. He gave it up freely. Moving to kiss the spot between my neck and shoulder, he licked along my collarbone, before ducking down to my breasts. Those kisses were sweet, tender even, showing me a surprising side of this man whom I shouldn't have been with.

I tried to shake that thought because it might not have been the best idea to let go like this, it certainly felt better than anything had in a long time. No offense to Quinn.

He took one of my nipples in his mouth, swirling his tongue over the pebbled skin, then sucking it hard. I arched up, giving him room and encouragement to go after the other one and give it the same treatment. He alternated, sucking, nibbling, flicking his tongue over them while he squeezed the other with his rough hand.

I was lost in him.

"Oh god. I'm about to come. I want you with me, Tragedy. I want to feel you come on my cock." He hissed as he ground his hips in a circle, getting as far inside me as he could. His cock was long enough to reach that place inside me and I screeched in pleasure as his tip hit it over and over and over.

My legs began to shake in anticipation. That was the best part. Finding that high between the buildup and release. I wanted it to last as long as it could because when it was over, I didn't know what I'd feel. What he was doing to me had felt too good and I wanted to live in that feeling until I disappeared.

"Are you trying to fight me? Are you trying to keep from coming? Such a bad girl." He grabbed the nape of my neck, pulling me down so he could kiss me again, slipping his tongue inside and stroking slowly. It was so sensual, but also rough and needy, I nearly exploded, but I steadied my breathing, aching for release and denying myself at the same time. "No. I'm in control here and you'll come when I tell you to come. Now tighten that pussy. I want to feel you squeezing my cock."

He put his hand between us and toyed with my aching clit. I managed to tighten just a bit and we both lost it, moaning and cursing as he filled me and made me shudder with pleasure. "That's it. Your pussy feels so good. Come for me, Tragedy."

I couldn't say about that, but his cock seemed to be the perfect fit. All of it seemed to be perfect and feeling the pulse of his release almost sent me reeling again.

When it was over, we both panted, coming down as he touched me, running his hands over my face, in my hair, down my arms and back and thighs. We stayed connected like that for a few minutes. In those minutes, the train of regret barreled through me.

It felt good and it may have been the best sexual encounter of my life, but I wasn't sure what to say or do next.

"The real tragedy here, Tragedy, is if you get off my cock in a second and tell me that was a mistake. Don't do that."

"But—"

"No buts. No regrets. Just appreciation for the amazing lay we just gave each other. You needed it, I wanted it. Doesn't have to be anything more than that."

Finally finding my nerve somewhere within me, I lifted off of him and maneuvered out of the car, grabbing my shirt and throwing it on quickly. He followed me, pulling up his coveralls first—gaping hole included—then getting my bags out of the back seat. "What were you so pressed to get from your bags? I bet you have enough clothes and shoes to outfit a third-world country left in your closet."

"I do. I just have a memento that means a lot to me in my suitcase. It may seem silly to you, but I don't like going to sleep without having it near me."

"You'll get no flak from me. You have to do what you have to do to survive. I would know."

The way he said the words told me it wasn't just idle chatter. He'd been through something in the past.

Hadn't we all though?

He ran his hands through his hair. I'd never been attracted to guys with long hair, but it suited him. He played the strands, getting them to fall just right. There was something else he wanted to say. I could feel it bubbling from him. When he didn't immediately come out with it, I took a step back. "Um, do you know what time it is? I don't wear a watch and my phone…"

He glanced at his watch. "It's one-thirty. I'd say I'm sorry about your phone, but I'm not. You're better off without your Uncle keeping constant tabs on you. I've got an extra burner or two upstairs in my loft if you want one."

What kind of guy had burner phones lying around? Not the good kind. Yet, I couldn't shake the feeling that there was a lot more to Rex than a mechanic and garage owner. "Yeah, that would be great. I'll tell Uncle something happened to mine after the wreck."

"Good. Let's head upstairs. You probably want to wipe my cum off your legs, since it's dripping."

Mortified.

He wasn't wrong, but something about him just declaring it out loud made it feel…dirtier. I nodded and he grinned. He liked catching me off-guard. It was starting to be a habit for him.

Leading me to the other side of the large space, he yelled out to Charlie. "We're heading upstairs. You're in charge."

Jeez. I'd forgotten about Charlie. He could've come into the garage and found us.

What was beyond mortified?

Rex appeared to be completely nonplussed about it.

Climbing the stairs in the corner of the room, we landed on a narrow walkway that overlooked the entire garage. I hadn't even noticed it before. The walls—if you could call them that—were covered in strips of that clear heavy-duty plastic. I couldn't see through them, not really, but it was obvious there was something beyond them other than a solid wall. We traveled to the end of the walkway, where the plastic had been pulled back and held by a car door handle attached to the concrete wall. It was pretty cool looking for what it was.

Rex stood aside, holding out his arm for me to enter, so I passed through the open doorway, into his loft and couldn't believe what I saw. Two of the walls were made of normal concrete blocks, painted white, but there was a huge bank of windows built in toward the top, washing the space in light. The third was the plastic sheeting, and the last wall is what blew my mind. It faced the back of the property and it was made entirely of garage doors. The kind you find in regular homes. "Wow," I whispered. You took that garage aesthetic and ran with it, didn't you?"

He smirked, then sauntered over to his bed in the far corner. There was a huge light switch beside the bed. He pressed all six of the buttons on it and the garage doors all began creeping up.

They worked.

When they'd all climbed up, the entire wall space was open. His father must have paid a fortune for the land because the garage backed up to the only lake in Between.

Most of the landscape surrounding the town was sagebrush and desert land, but Lover's Lake had created a small oasis right on the outskirts of our city. I couldn't help but be drawn to its unusually blue waters. "This is a great view. It's been forever since I've been to the lake."

"Yeah, the only reason I have the doors down today is because of the heat. I sleep with them open every night, no matter the time of year."

I walked over to get a better view of the rocky shore dotted with trees. Rex grabbed my elbow to stop me. "Watch out. The drop is farther than it looks."

I looked down and found he was right. With the garage doors up, there was no barrier between us and the edge, and while it didn't feel like we'd climbed too far up, it had to be the equivalent of three stories by the looks of the ground below me. "So, you take a chance you won't roll off your bed every night, huh? Or do you just like living on the edge?"

"Both, I guess." He ran his hands through his hair. "My body is under my control, as you just experienced. I wouldn't roll off the bed. I sleep in one position all night."

That was something we had in common. When I did sleep anyway.

He took my hand, leading me over to the far corner, then glancing down at my legs with a pointed look. "Bathroom. I'll make us some tea."

Again, I'd forgotten about the *remains* of our encounter in my car. I rushed inside and closed the door. Well, I slammed the plastic sheeting down so he couldn't see me, clearly anyway. I'm not sure what he had against regular doors.

Inside, the bathroom was tidy and clean, with white tiles and towels, and his toothbrush holder was made of spark plugs or some other car part. I wasn't sure. His hamper was three tires on top of each other with more car door handles, and the mats around his toilet and shower were mats you'd find in vehicles, Ferrari, specifically. Though it wasn't the way I'd decorate my own space, it certainly was him and it made me feel comfortable. I liked that his personal space wasn't dirty or greasy like the garage itself and it was tidy and I would imagine frugal, in that he probably got all the stuff he used for free.

Shaking myself out of my stupor—who cared how he decorated—I grabbed a washcloth from the bar, made from another car part, and wet it. As I cleaned my legs and hooch, he called from outside. "What do you want in your tea or do you like it black? It's oolong. Hope that's okay."

I loved oolong. "Straight oolong is fine."

I stared at myself in the mirror trying to fix my hair. I ended up washing my face wetting the hair and staring longer than I'd liked to have. It's not that I was afraid to go out there with him. It was more like I didn't know what to do with myself when I did. I wasn't a one-night, or rather one-day, stand kind of girl. Especially not with someone like him. I was upset at myself for losing control and ending up riding his cock.

Although, it had been a fantastic ride.

I couldn't think about that though. It was a mistake and yeah, he didn't want me to admit that, but it was.

After I'd cleaned myself up, I washed my hands and joined him at a small table that was set against the plastic sheeting. He handed me a mug with my tea and I looked behind him to the kitchenette. It was small but tidy. The most obvious thing about it was a tea kettle on the stove and the lack of a coffee maker. "So, you drink tea then, not coffee?"

"Yes. Does that surprise you or do you think I'm just some uncivilized grease monkey?" He took a sip from his mug, but not before experiencing the aroma first, like a professional tea connoisseur.

"No, that's not it. I just…most people drink coffee is all."

"Yeah? Coffee gives me the shits, so there you go."

"Nice. Great manners."

"You asked."

"I didn't, but whatever. The tea is good."

I got a grunt and a nod from him.

We drank our tea in silence for a few minutes. That silence did a number on my head. I didn't care for the thoughts tumbling around in it. The curse, Uncle's panty raids, getting out of town, all of it was swimming in my head making a soup of things for me to deal with. I needed to focus on something besides my woes. "Hey, why the plastic sheet for a wall?"

"I can see any issues in the garage from up here when I'm taking breaks. Mostly, it gives me a way to open the space and let the air flow through. I don't like enclosed spaces."

"Same." We shared a look, an understanding, I guess. We were nothing alike, but we did have that in common too. "Something happened to me when I was a kid. Residual trauma, I suppose. I have it under control most of the time, but sometimes, I just want to be in the middle of a desert with nothing around me."

I think it was the first time I'd ever voiced that out loud to anyone in my life.

And I told my mechanic.

That I'd just fucked.

My head was a nightmare. If Uncle allowed me to go, I bet I would've paid for some therapist to have three vacation homes and a Lamborghini with my crazy.

"Mm. Is that where you were going? With all the suitcases."

I took another drink. Stalling. "I don't know where I was going. Just somewhere beyond Between."

He reached across the table and grabbed my hand. The tenderness in the gesture surprised me. "Between's not so bad."

I jerked my hand away, not wanting to give the wrong impression. What we'd done in my car was in the past. "Yeah, maybe for you, but for me…"

"Where you are doesn't matter. The demons that come in the night know your address."

"Well, that's comforting, thanks."

"It's true. You just have to know what to do to exorcise them."

"Yeah, like what?"

"I killed one of mine."

I stared at him, trying to discern if he was telling the truth or joking. I couldn't. I didn't know him well enough and I could see it going either way. It was funny that I realized if he was telling the truth, it didn't frighten me. I was oddly comforted if he had found a way to deal with his demons.

"Yeah, well I can't kill what happened to me, or my Uncle, or the curse, so I guess I'm screwed." I downed the rest of my tea and attempted to get up, to leave, but he grabbed my hand. Again.

"Don't go. Wait until I've finished my tea at least."

I glanced in his mug. He was about halfway through. I could stay a little longer. It wasn't like I had anywhere to go anyway. I was still banned from the Tea House until further notice, I didn't have Quinn anymore, and going home would feel like going to prison because I'd be locked away in my own room with my own thoughts and I didn't want that either.

So, I sat.

He took another sip of his tea. "Tell me about the curse. How did it get you?"

For the life of me, I didn't get why, but I told him. The dirty mechanic who had no business knowing. Something about him just felt trustworthy and he had a way of pulling things from me like a magnet. "I'm not one hundred percent on this, but earlier when I read my cousin's tea leaves, I saw something that happened in the past."

"Isn't that normal for people like you? That's what you do in the Tea House."

"How did you know that?"

"Everyone knows that. Your face is all over town and the internet in ads."

"Oh right. Well, for me, I've never been able to read the tea leaves. I'm not true Romani, I don't think. I was adopted when I was eight. With me, it's all an act.

"Anyway, when I looked into Selene's teacup, I saw our uncle taking her panties. She confirmed it had happened, so I'm making an educated guess and saying I see the past."

He raised an eyebrow. "Your uncle took her panties? Why?"

"We don't know. He just…asked for them and because he's the head of our family, we have to comply. I know that probably sounds strange to an outsider, but—"

"Wait. Is that why you weren't wearing panties? Did he take yours?" I didn't answer, but the way he looked at me told me I didn't have to. He assumed and he was correct. "What kind of asshole motherfucker is this guy and why do you do what he says?"

"What kind of person? A bad one. And we do what he says because it's our way. Like I said, I don't expect you to understand, but I do hope you can respect that it's the way of our family and I don't have a choice in it. You already know I was running away until the Wayward Warbler struck."

"Okay, so now you're cursed to see something from the past in your tea leaves?"

"Yeah. Please don't say anything about this. If Uncle knew I was telling people I was a fraud or if he knew I'd told you about the curse before him, let's just say I'd probably have more to be worried about than my underwear."

Rex cocked his eyebrow. "We'll circle back to your Uncle. But first…" He downed the rest of his tea, then swirled the leaves in it like he knew how we read them. Then he set the mug in front of me. "Read my tea leaves."

Alarms were going off in my head. This was a bad idea. I'd fucked him when I shouldn't have, I'd seen his personal space, and I'd even told him secrets I'd never told anyone else. Reading his tea leaves was one more act that would bring us closer together. I didn't need anyone close. Not with me getting out of town as soon as I could.

Yet. He was willingly opening himself up knowing I was cursed.

Finding out more about him might tell me if he was a killer like he claimed. Or just a guy with a bad-boy complex.

Did I even need to know that? Probably not.

Definitely not.

I wouldn't give him a second thought after he fixed my car.

"You're sure. I don't even know if it's accurate. I just did it the one time with my cousin."

"What better way to find out then, huh? Go ahead. I have nothing to hide." He paused for a second. "Well, I have plenty to hide. Just not from you."

I shook my head. "We aren't friends."

"Didn't say we were."

"Then why—"

He cut me off. "Would I trust you with the deepest, darkest secrets of my past? I don't fucking know. Maybe this will explain why I feel like I've known you forever. I felt it the moment I laid eyes on you, long before we fucked. You're sitting right here with me and haunting me at the same time."

I wasn't sure what to say. It wasn't that he seemed familiar to me—I definitely wouldn't forget a guy who looked like him, even if we'd met in passing—it was that he had a way of pulling me out of my head that I found comforting.

Bad idea or not, I wanted to know why.

"Take the cup in both hands and swirl what's left of your tea. Don't look at the leaves, just stop when you get the feeling you should, then place the cup on the table with the handle facing South. So, I guess, this wall behind you with the kitchen."

Thank goodness I had the lake to ground my directions. In the Tea House, it was always the same for us, but elsewhere I had to think about it.

Back when I was faking it.

I watched him intently as he moved his cup, never letting his eyes stray from mine. I was starting to get the feeling that I did know him, but I chalked that up to him saying that about me. And we'd been very close in the car, so it made sense I felt like I knew him better.

Finally, he set the cup down, angling the handle like I'd told him. Despite my misgivings, I reached for it.

Peering inside, the tea leaves seemed to jump up at me. This is the feeling Mama and Baba had mentioned when they read leaves. They said the leaves would speak to you and for the first time in my life, they did.

"Well?" Rex said, with a raspy grumble to his voice. He leaned forward looking at what I was seeing.

"No weird past vision, but I can tell you about these leaves. If I were reading this in my shop I'd show you this leaf here that looks a bit like a crocodile. Since it's near the handle, that signifies something happening in your life now. Most usually the crocodile is a warning. You have enemies and they mean to bring your destruction."

He looked up through his eyelashes. They were long for a guy, which only served to make him hotter. "Could it mean that I want to bring destruction to *my* enemies?"

"Yeah, it could. How many enemies does a garage mechanic have?"

"I'm not sure, but I'll let you know when I find out." He grinned, then pointed to the bottom of the cup. "Am I crazy or does it look like a piece of cake?"

"Not crazy. It is." I pressed my lips together, not wanting to divulge the meaning of that. "The teapot here on the side means that you're meant to share something with someone. Usually, when my family sees this they say that only you can interpret what the means and whom you need to share with."

"Okay. Got it. Already shared some of my secrets with you. What about the cake, Tragedy?"

I tore my gaze from the leaves, looking up at him and frowning. "Why do you keep calling me that?"

"Because tragedy is something I'm very comfortable with. I've dealt with more than my fair share of them, so much that I feel right at home inside one." His eyes were blazing, like he was trying to bore some sense into my head as he spoke. "And like I said when I picked up your car, everything about you is a tragedy. Like, it's a real fucking tragedy that we're not over in my bed right now. Cake?"

Feeling flushed, I closed my eyes. I didn't want to see him as I gave the information. "Cake means pleasure and commitment. It symbolizes taking care of someone and caring for them above your own well-being. It's near the top of the cup, so it's talking about your life as it is now or in the immediate future."

He leaned back on his chair and propped his feet on the table as he put his hands behind his head. Typical. "I like how that sounds. Do you think we have a future, Tragedy?"

"No. We don't have a future or a past and the only now we have is until you fix my car. Maybe you should get on with—"

I'd been in the process of standing up and walking right out of the plastic sheeting, but I was overcome with a chill I could not bear. I bent my legs, needing to sit and hoping the chair hadn't moved. As soon as my ass hit, adrenaline spiked and I froze in place, unable to move any part of my body as the cold cascaded through me.

Consciously, I heard the sound of Rex's feet hitting the floor and of his watch scratching across the table as he gripped my hand, but I couldn't feel his calloused fingers. Or his warmth. I was freezing and my vision was glued to the bottom of his cup when I saw something materialize that I had seen a million times over in my nightmares.

He was younger, twelvish. His eyes held the same intensity even though I couldn't see them inside the dark railway car. His body was mashed against a little girl's with long dark hair and a haunting expression. He gripped her hand like it was the only thing keeping her alive.

It was.

He was.

The girl was crying and he was using soothing tones as he stroked the back of her hand with his thumb. "What do we say?"

"We'll be okay if we stick together."

"Right. Do you feel my hand? Do you feel it?"

"Yes."

"I put super-glue in there and we're stuck. You and me. We will be okay. Say it."

"We'll be okay."

"Good."

He squeezed the girl's hand and she climbed into his lap. "I'm cold, Twenty-two."

"I know. I've got you. Close your eyes. We're due for another stop soon. I'll try to lift you a sweatshirt or something."

"If they don't take me to the next stop."

"Where you go, I go, remember? If they take you, I'll fight them so they take me too."

"Good. I'm not as afraid because you're with me."

"Me too, Twenty-three. Me too."

The vision, the memory faded, dying out like the light at dusk.

When I looked up, I was panting, and shaking, and tears were streaming down my face. I felt Rex's hand squeezing mine. Just like it had in the vision. I tried to speak, but my voice was hollow and weak. "You. It was you."

"What are you talking about? What did you see?"

I couldn't believe it.

I couldn't believe I'd forgotten his eyes. Even though I was eight years old when it happened.

Eight years old when I was taken, thrown into a van, and then pushed into a packed rail car of crying, screaming, frightened children.

He leaned against the opposite side of the car with his arms folded over his chest and his expression full of venom for the men who'd taken me. Him. The others.

The door to the car slammed shut and darkness engulfed us. The only light was streaming through the cracks of the door. I was frozen to the spot, too frightened to move speak, or even cry. The only sensation I had was utter, bone-breaking cold.

He—Rex—made his way over and took my hand, just like he had now, and led me to the wall, sitting me down and showing me the light coming from the bottom seam of the car. I looked at that light and treasured it like it was the most priceless thing in the universe. Because it was. Everything around me for the next month would be bitter darkness.

"Esme, you look pale. Tell me what you saw in my tea leaves." His voice was full of concern, but I knew then the concern wasn't over what I'd seen in his past or future or now, his concern was for me.

Several times, I tried to start the sentence and attempted to put everything into words, but nothing came out but an odd squeak.

I owed him the truth.

I owed us both the truth, but it was stuck somewhere inside my throat. Having no other way to express myself, I wrenched my hand from his and shoved my bracelets up, revealing my four-leaf clover tattoo. I turned my wrist and held it up for him to see. The only word that I could form was, "You."

His face turned to stone. It took a few very long seconds for him to register what I'd shown him. When he got it, he ate up the space between us, knocking the small table, mugs, teapot, and all over to get to me. Cupping my face in his hands, he took a shuddering breath. "You mean to tell me all this time you were right here in Between. Right where I could touch you, and I never knew."

As more hot tears fell, he smiled, then swiped them away.

It was him.

"I-I-I didn't recognize you. I was so young, and we were in the dark for long periods." My pulse fluttered and I would've sworn my heart was going to fly out of my chest. "I never knew your real name. Oh god, I should've recognized you."

"No. Don't say that. We were kids and we were traumatized by what had happened to us. I wanted you to leave it all behind, even if I couldn't. Esme, fuck, I can't believe I'm standing here with you. If you knew how many times I dreamed of finding you."

"Me too." He ran his fingers over my tattoo. "The thing in my bag that I came for? It was the bracelet you gave me that night when we escaped and I lost you."

"You've got that wrong. I lost you. It was my responsibility and I lost you. It is the one single regret I have in my life." He lifted my arm and pressed a soft kiss on my wrist. "I guess we're lukey we found each other now."

I burst into laughter. The cheap bracelet that he'd stolen from a gas station outside of Vegas was made in some country where the translation skills were lacking. It should've said 'lucky' but they botched it in the printing department. The night he gave it to me was the first time we'd laughed since we'd been taken. For hours we went around saying, "Oh lukey at that car' or 'lukey, my shoe's untied.' Stupid kid stuff.

That got me through an awful time.

"I can't believe it's you, "I sighed, then something clicked in my head like a shot being fired. "Oh god, I can't believe we fu—"

He captured my mouth in his, kissing me softly at first, then before I knew it we were groping each other and tangled in a heated match that seemed to want a winner.

When he pulled away, I was once again breathless and staring into the eyes of my savior. "Don't let the past fuck with the now. Please, I couldn't take that. More than any two people on this godforsaken earth, we know each other. No matter what the last ten years have done, we're together now, and you are full of fucking shit, Tragedy, if you think for one second I'm going to let you out of my sight again."

Now I was the breathless one.

He yanked his coveralls down and for a moment, I thought we might have sex again, but when he turned his back to me, I knew that could wait. He was showing me his reminder of our time together.

The tattoo on the upper part of his back was a beautiful railroad sign like his shop logo, but there was a train circling it, squeezing it into an elongated shape. In the middle of the X part, there was a number. My number: twenty-three. "See. You've always been a part of me, Esme. Always."

I traced my fingers over the middle of the tattoo, the lines of my number he had placed on his back, disbelieving it was there. I pulled away, overwhelmed with so many emotions I couldn't name them all. "Don't stop," he whispered. "I love the feel of you on my skin."

Stepping forward, I kissed the twenty-three, then made my way around the rest, feeling the ripple of his muscles as they reacted to my touch. His skin was smooth and when I wrapped my hands around the front of him, grazing his pecs, and his abs, he sucked in a sharp breath.

Without letting go of each other, he walked us over to the bed, and then climbed on his stomach, bringing me with him so that I was laying on him directly.

It was how we slept in that train car. There were others with us, a lot of them, but the two of us gravitated toward each other and we took care of each other. Well, he took care of me. I don't know what he got out of it. I, for one, got a softer bed than the cold rusty, dirty floor of a train car.

He sighed as I lay against him, drawing on his heat and his strength. "Sometimes, I wake up and I'm so cold. It doesn't matter if I have on sweats and three blankets, I'm still shivering. I think the cold got into my bones somehow and is trapped there forever."

"I know. I did everything I could to keep you warm. You know that, right?"

"Yes, I do." I turned, looking out at Lover's Lake. "I get why you don't like enclosed spaces now."

"Yeah." He let a few moments hang between us, enough time for us to feel each other's heart beating, to appreciate the raw feeling this vision had brought us. His voice was so soft I nearly missed it. "I killed him Twenty-three. I killed god."

At the mention of his name, my mind reeled backward. It was the night I'd been taken from my home. We'd been riding for hours but stopped in a nearly deserted train station in some state I couldn't name. The man had made us all file out of the car and line up in number order. Thankfully, I'd been given the number after Rex.

"I am your master on this little journey. You can call me God because everything I say comes to pass. Do you understand me?"

When none of us answered, he shouted. "Do you understand me?"

"Yes, god."

"Good. Now some of you will be with us for a while, and some of you will be stepping off here. Numbers one through five to be exact. Y'all get out of line and go with my friend, Mickey Mouse over there.

The rest of you will have fifteen minutes to eat the food inside and make your potty breaks, then we will be on the way again. If any of you step out of line and try to escape," he said before whipping out a gun and swirling around his finger like an outlaw on an old western. "I will shoot you and you will die. Amen."

"I used to wonder what happened to the ones they took."

"You know what happened to them. Maybe not then, but now."

"Yeah. Did you really kill him?"

He managed to turn over without bucking me off his back, leaving us face to face again. He brushed my hair from my face. "Once you know, you can't un-know it. I don't want you to suffer any more scars than you already have. I couldn't take the thought of that."

"Tell me. I don't think it could hurt me. Maybe it would help."

Rex grabbed me back the nape of my neck, pulling me in for another heated kiss before taking my lower lip in his and sucking it until it popped out. The sound was…arousing. "In that case, I'll show you."

He insisted we take the Jalopy and told me he'd explain why on the way. So, after we changed clothes—and I strung my Lukey bracelet around my wrist—we left the garage. Before he would even pull out though, he pulled me over, cradling me against him instead of all the way across the bench. "I want you close. Always."

I didn't mind. I was getting over the fact that I shouldn't want to be close to him. He'd morphed from one person to another within a heartbeat. I trusted him, and cared for him even, just by seeing who he truly was. "How did you find god?"

"It was a lucky—I mean lukey—break. He strolled into my shop one day. I couldn't believe it. I was struck speechless, but there he was, nineteen years later with that same nasty toothpick hanging out of his mouth. His hair had some gray streaks in it, and there were a couple of wrinkles on his face, but it was him and he was standing on my property looking down on me and asking me to fix his car."

"What did you do?"

"I fixed his car. But not before looking up everything I could about him. I would love to go after all the buyers that sold kids to, but even if I had their names, it would be too many. But thanks to whatever divine intervention it was, I've put together there were three main players in the trafficking ring: the railroad guy, the transporter, and the money man. God was the railroad guy.

"All railroads are federally operated in the States, but he owned several freight train companies across the U.S., with his main location being Vegas. The beauty of his operation was that there were so many freight lines and companies coming and going with very little oversight as far as cargo-checks, that we were able to slip us through the cracks on actual real freight deliveries. All those times we had to be quiet when we stopped was them unloading freight."

It made sick sense. That turned my stomach.

"After I fixed his car, I followed him to Vegas and I staked out his office, trying to get proof that he was trafficking, but after several months, I discovered he was out of the business."

I experienced immediate guilt for being disappointed. It wasn't. It meant all the kids who would've been trafficked were safe at home.

Rex bit his lower lip. "Since I couldn't do the right thing and go to the police with nothing but the word of a kid who'd been taken ten years prior, I decided to take the law into my own hands."

We turned off the main road onto a road that was mostly dirt. "Where are we going? I've never been out here."

"Yeah, not many people come this way. Cinderella Loveridge owns all this property for about ten miles, I'd say."

The mention of her name sent shivers up my spine. "Are we safe coming out here? The last thing I want is a second curse on top of the one I already have."

"Yep. We're perfectly fine. I wouldn't bring you otherwise. Let me just go a few more miles and we'll stop."

We passed by a field of flowers that seemed to sprout up in the middle of a deadland. They were orange and had little springs of purplish blue mingled in between them. Pretty, but the vibe they were giving off was to not go near them.

Pulling off onto yet a smaller dirt road, Rex swerved to the side, parking the car next to a field of dead brown weeds. With the flowers behind us, there was nothing but grassy nothingness as far as I could see.

Except for the small orange flag whipping the breeze about a hundred yards in the field. "That's my mark." He grabbed my hand and pulled me through the weedy grass, apologizing when I yelped about the scratchy, prickling weeds brushing my calves. Within the next heartbeat, he'd bent over. "Get on my back. I'll keep you above the bristles."

Finding myself right at home on his back—we'd traveled that way a lot when we escaped—I jumped up and he ate the short distance between us and the flag. It had been planted in a small clearing next to some ancient-looking tombstones. Though there was no tombstone where the flag was. He wouldn't have bothered and neither would I if I were him.

When I slipped off his back, he put his hands on my shoulders. "Okay, Tragedy, this is your last chance. What I say next will make you culpable after the fact."

I didn't care about that. If he ever got caught by the police, I would be there for him, lying if I needed to. It was the least I could do after what he'd done for me. "Tell me everything."

He plopped on the ground, next to the flag, so I joined him, folding my legs underneath me. Unsatisfied with that, he pulled me onto his lap, keeping my legs off the itchy grass on the ground. "When I realized he'd retired from the business, I had a choice to make. I could forget it and move on or I could do something myself. Please don't take this the wrong way when I say this, but all I could do was picture you shivering in that railcar, whimpering against my back as you tried to sleep, and I couldn't let it go.

"So, I used a guy I know from a motorcycle club here in town to get me an untraceable gun and I followed god home one night.

"He had a bigass house, no doubt from the money he made trafficking, but the thing is, he was alone in it. There were no pictures of a wife or kids of his own, no personal things. It looked like he'd bought all of the furnishings straight out of a showroom or catalog. It made me feel better about putting the gun to his head."

Rex stopped, turning my chin with his finger, gauging my reaction. I looked him square in his pretty eyes and did nothing. Not even a blink.

"Before I shot him, I asked if he remembered me. Or you. I told him exactly who I was and you know what he did? He fucking laughed. He called me 'the one who got away;' he said that after you, the other one who got away, I was going to bring the highest price."

His body tensed under me. "I couldn't take him talking about you like that, so I shot him. Then I rolled him up in his designer rug, threw him in the back of my Dad's old truck, and drove him out here where no one would find him."

"I don't know what to say. I can't believe you did that. I'm fucking *glad* you did that."

He nestled into the crook of my neck. "I'm fucking glad you don't hate me for it."

"How could I hate you, Rex?" I laughed. "It's weird to call you Rex now. I want to say Twenty-three."

"Yeah, well you can call me anything you like as long as you're talking to me. I hope this doesn't sound too, I don't know, pedo, but I want you more now that I know who you are."

I went to kiss him, but a voice beyond the brush stopped me. "Is that you, boy?"

"Yeah, it's me Cinderella. I've brought a friend."

An old lady—heaven help me, Cinderella—pushed through the brush with a cane. She stopped right in front of us and smiled at Rex. "I see what kind of friend you brought. It's bad luck to fuck over a grave boy, even if it's the grave of someone who deserved death. I would know."

"Oh, my word, "I whispered.

"What? I'm just saying. Anyway, I thought I'd take a stroll about. Some folks got me stirred up by asking about the Wayward Warbler and his curse. I had to walk it out."

I sighed. "Man, that was probably Quinn and Fallon. She struck me as someone who would try to logic or force the info out and Quinn would never turn down an opportunity to get more research."

Rex squeezed me. "Esme got the other half of the curse. That's partly why we're here. I mean, other than showing her ole' Clyde Higginbotham, here."

"Ew. That was his name?" He nodded. "Well, Ms. Loveridge, any help you could give me would be appreciated. It's a bit of an issue for me to be cursed."

She took a few steps toward me, then bent down, squinting. "Ah, you're a Doe. Ha, that's a good one, but I can't help you. That curse has a mind of its own. It's what I was trying to tell the other ones. If you're cursed, there's a reason. It's up to you and yours to figure it out. Now, I'm going to get. This old lady needs her food and rest. Bye boy, like I said before, feel free to use my cemetery anytime as long as the bodies laid here deserve it."

"Will do, Cinderella."

She shuffled back into the weeds and all I could do was laugh. "You're friends with Cinderella Loveridge? That's insane."

"Yeah, well, she caught me digging a grave on her property so it was either make friends or join Clyde. I chose to make friends. She's not a bad old lady, totally misunderstood, I think. And she's lonely without her other half, which is what she calls him. I feel bad for her."

I took his face in my hands, giving him a sweet kiss. "You amaze me, but I think it's time to go. I don't want to be near this man ever again and I'm sure Uncle is ballistic right now."

He smirked. "Yeah, fuck him. I'm the only one who gets your panties from now on."

My mind was going a thousand miles an hour. Much faster than we were traveling down the bumpy road back to civilization. "Is there a reason you're driving so slowly or are you trying to piss my Uncle off by keeping me out of reach?"

"Maybe."

"Well, don't. I'll have to pay for it later if I don't get in touch with him soon. You don't understand."

"I'm pretty sure I do, but if you want me to drive faster, you're going to have to give me an incentive." He cocked that eyebrow in just the right way and I knew what he meant. I wasn't opposed to it.

"What? Promise you a blow job when we get back?"

Without taking his eyes off the road, he unzipped his blue jeans and opened the crotch of his underwear. "Why wait until we get back?"

"Are you serious? I can't just go down on you when you're driving!" I screeched.

"You can. There's no one else on this road."

"Yeah, but I don't…"

Because he'd insisted I sit glued to him in the truck, I was close enough for him to grab my throat, wrapping his fingers around it and yanking me to him. "Don't sit there pretending to be a good girl. I know what's inside you. I've felt your darkness and pain like it was my own. Leave what the world thinks you should do and be behind in that grave, Tragedy. You and I both know you're in charge of your own life and if you want to suck me off right now, do it."

I'd never been spoken to in that way before. The fierce determination in his gaze, the feel of his fingers squeezing, the knowledge that this man was not only my savior in the past but maybe my savior in the present too.

I wanted to do what he said. To shuck the expectations of my family and uncle behind, to not give a fuck about what the world thought.

Maybe it was a little step, but it was a step all the same.

"Tell me. What are you going to do, Tragedy?"

"I'm going to suck your cock until you come in my mouth."

"That's what I'm talking about, bad girl."

He shifted, throwing his right leg up on the seat and switching to his left to drive. Serving himself to me on a platter, so to speak.

I brushed my hair out of the way and went down on my knees in the passenger side, angling to get closer.

His cock was already hard when I grasped it in my hand. He smirked as I flicked my tongue over the tip and began sliding my hand up and down as he moaned. "Fuck yes, take it all."

I did as he asked, sucking as I pushed him to the back of my throat, then pulling him slowly out again, keeping my eyes trained on his beautiful face.

My head bobbed up and down to the soundtrack of his moaning. His fingers tugged on my hair, showing me how fast and how far he wanted me to go. Knowing I was making him gasp and groan was everything. I loved the taste of him, but I loved the sound of him even more.

When my jaw got tired—he was bigger than the last penis I had between my lips—I pulled him out of my mouth, and then licked from the base to the tip and back again. Over and over until he was squirming and throwing his head back against the headrest.

He was so beautiful like that. I wished I could take a picture of us, me on my knees with his hands in my hair and him with his head thrown back, both of us grunting and getting hotter. It felt like a moment that should've been painted on a canvas and hung on the wall.

Screeching tires broke through our sex sounds. The truck swerved and bumped over the side of the road. I raised my head. "What happened?"

Smiling, he pressed my head down, feeding me his cock. "Nothing. Just don't stop."

I wouldn't have dared. I wanted his release more than I wanted anything. Just thinking about him shooting 'God' on behalf of all of us who'd been taken, getting justice when there was none, got me even hotter.

Picking up my pace, I sucked, moaning into his cock, letting him know how much I wanted him. His pelvis shook and as he thrust his ass came off the seat. "Fuck. Fuuuuck, I'm going to give you what you want soon, Bad Girl. I love how my dick feels in your hot mouth."

"Mm-hm," I said as best as I could with the width of him in my mouth. That small noise seemed to be the magic ingredient because he took his other hand off the wheel and grabbed more of my hair, pulling and grasping it tightly as he came.

I swallowed, again and again, taking every bit of his release down my throat with the heady satisfaction that I'd done that to him. When he was finished, I sat up and my head reeled with dizziness.

He smirked, then used his thumb to wipe the corner of my mouth. "You're a dream, Tragedy."

"Those two things don't sound like they go together. Am I a dream or a tragedy?"

"You're both, which is exactly what I like. Now let me return the favor." He skimmed my thigh with his calloused fingers, eliciting chills as he made his way up. "Spread your legs."

It would've been hard to refuse him, though I didn't want to. I wanted him to touch me. Ached for it in a way that scared me. We had this dark history, but there was a lightness about being with him. It exploded through me as soon as I realized who he was. It was probably messed up and this was probably a mistake, but I didn't care at that moment.

So, I spread my legs and leaned my head against the seat as he skated under my skirt, reaching my clit and circling it with his fingers. "Is this what you want, me playing with that hot cunt of yours?"

"Yeah."

"Good. I want to watch you come apart for me."

He pushed his finger inside me. I was already so wet for him that he didn't have to work hard at it. He groaned nearly as loud as I did but then went back to telling me what to do. "Tilt your hips. Give me more."

Angling toward him, I tilted, giving him more access. He drove a second finger inside me and I yelped. I didn't know how he was managing it because his arm was twisted, but he stroked his thumb over my clit at the same time, sending waves of heat through my body.

I moaned. "God, yes."

"God has nothing to do with it. Neither of them. This is all me."

I hadn't even realized what I'd said. I was so into the pleasure, that I was going loopy. "Yeah, I know. It feels so good. I haven't felt this great in a long time."

He didn't stop, he doubled down, pinching my clit, then driving inside me harder. "What about your boyfriend? He doesn't make you feel like this?"

This was not a conversation we should've had with his fingers between my legs, but there we were. Panting between the words, I told him, "Broke. Up."

He chuckled. "If I were a better man, I'd feel bad about that, but you and I both know you were mine long before you were his, even if we didn't know it yet."

The stark reality of his words hit me like lightning. We'd forged a bond that no one would ever be able to break. It was a miracle we'd found each other again.

Or a curse, I guess.

I bucked against his fingers. I was getting close.

"Say it, Tragedy. Say you're mine."

"Rex, I—"

"Say it."

This was as dangerous as it was insane. It had been less than a day, but as my legs shook and I gripped his shoulder, I embraced the insanity. "I'm yours."

He let go of the steering wheel, taking my face in his hand and diving for my mouth, kissing me like he was trying to seal my words inside both our hearts. The sensual sweep of his tongue, his moans, and his heat sent me right over the edge. My orgasm exploded right as the truck lurched off the road into the grassy ditch.

He never stopped kissing me.

Vaguely, I was aware we'd stopped moving, which was a great thing considering Rex's eyes were not anywhere near the road.

When he finally pulled away, I was breathless. His expression was so warm and he was so focused on me, that I felt safe.

Even though we just had a minor accident. "We really should try a bed next time."

He laughed. "Oh, I've got a long list in my head of places we will try, but before we get to that, I'm going to find out what the fuck your bastard uncle is doing with your underwear."

"Rex, I don't think this is a good idea." It wasn't. Not at all.

"It'll be fine. I know what I'm doing."

"I don't doubt that, but if Uncle or any of his crew catch you, they will make you disappear. I'm sure of it."

He kissed the tip of my nose. "Then I'll make sure they don't catch me. Come on, I need some tea."

It had been his idea to go to the Tea House near closing time and pose as a regular customer. We were going in separately and wouldn't acknowledge each other so no one would notice he was with me. I tried to tell him he *would* be noticed, especially by my horny cousin Charity, but he didn't care. He had a mission.

As much as I wanted to know what was going on and as much as I loved him trying to find out, I was nervous about the whole thing.

Watching him enter the dining room first, I went around back and entered through the kitchen, finding everyone, including Uncle. He gave me a smarmy smile and I had to force myself not to react. "Hello, Uncle. Everyone."

"Why aren't you answering my calls, Esme? I've been trying to reach you for hours. It doesn't bode well that you're dismissing me so easily after your screw-up."

"The wreck wasn't my fault and my phone has died and won't hold a charge. I think it was damaged in the wreck. I'm here now. What do you want?"

Mama's head swung around. I hadn't spoken to Uncle like that since I was a child and didn't know better. What could I say? My hackles were raised and I was nervous about Rex being feet away.

"What I want is to see you in action. I've been told you're seeing visions now so I need to know how this works before I decide on how to deal with this fiasco. Come, let's go. We'll offer a free reading to someone now."

Thanks for nothing, Selene. I thought she was on my side, but she'd also succumbed to the family position of delegating everything to Uncle.

He pushed through the swinging kitchen door, tugging on my sleeve to pull me along with him. The rustling behind us told me the whole family was coming out to see too.

I scanned the room. Two old women were sitting at one table, chatting as they dug in their purses to pay their bills and Rex was across the room at another table. He was on his phone, casually scrolling when Charity walked over with his tea. He thanked her and went back to his phone.

Uncle approached Rex's table, clearing his throat. "Excuse me. We're having a special this evening. We'd love to provide you with a free tea leaf reading in thanks for being our customer."

Rex looked up and scanned Uncle's face, then his gaze shifted to me and the entire family around me. I wished I could've sent him a telepathic message of some kind, but that wasn't possible. I was forced to stand there and smile like everything was normal with this request. He took a sip of his tea. "Sure, that's cool. I need to finish it, right? That's how it works?"

Uncle nodded. "Yes, just wave at one of us when you've got a sip or two left in your cup. Thanks."

While Uncle answered his phone, the rest of us shuffled to the back of the room so we wouldn't crowd Rex. Charity came running over, grabbing me by the shoulders. "I think he's into me."

"What? All you did was serve him tea and he said thanks. Don't be absurd."

"It was the way he smiled at me. God, he's so hot. What do you think he's like in bed?"

Good. Great. Fantastic. Zero to orgasm in sixty seconds.

"How would I know?"

"Look at him. I bet he's sweet and gentle in the sack. He has kind eyes."

I sighed. She needed to get a better feel for men if she was going to survive. While his eyes could be kind, he definitely wasn't sweet and gentle in the bed department.

He was brutally honest, rough, and had a way of knowing exactly what I needed before I did.

"I don't know, Charity. Some people will surprise you."

"Yeah, well I'm shooting my shot right now."

I wanted to stop her, but I couldn't very well explain why, so I watched her hit on him, cringing the entire time, including the part where he simply said, "No thanks, but I'm ready for my reading."

Ouch.

She shuffled back over to me, whispering, "I think he's gay."

Nope. Un-uh. Not even a little.

I waited for Uncle to end his call before walking over to Rex's table and sitting in the seat across from him. He shot me a smirk, the one I was starting to swoon over, and picked up his teacup, swirling it like I'd taught him before.

Uncle's presence loomed over me as he leaned in. "If you don't mind, Sir, I'll watch. I'm the owner and I want to make sure my niece gives the best experience possible."

"No problem." Rex's face was calm, steady. "I'm sure she'll give me a perfect experience."

He bit his lip so he'd keep his smirk on the inside so no one would know.

Making sure to pretend for Uncle's purpose, I launched into our scripted speech. "Place the cup with the handle facing the door. I'll look inside and tell you what shapes I see and their meanings. I might have clues from your past and, or your future. It's up to the leaves to tell me what they want you to know. It'll be up to you to interpret them. Are you ready?" He nodded. "Okay, focus on what you want to show me."

I peered into the cup, nerves shooting through me. Every other time I'd done this—before the one I'd read for him earlier— the tea leaves never looked like anything other than lumps of tea leaves to me. This time, I saw many things.

"I see a horse at the top of your cup. The horse means you have the power within you to make whatever is important to you a positive thing. If something is troubling you or someone you love, you can turn it around for them." I swallowed, knowing exactly what he was thinking, but following the script. "Does this make sense to you?"

He slid his foot across the floor, rubbing it against my shoe. "It does. I know exactly whose life I can make positive. I've already started."

I pressed my lips together, trying to suppress the smile he was putting on them. "This one is a mask. A mask in the middle of your cup signifies that you are always true to yourself. Your natural state is not to hide things."

"A mask means I *don't* hide myself? Interesting."

"A mask in the middle does, yes. It's showing me, um, us, you are who you are with no apologies."

"Hm, okay, that's true. I always said that life is too short, and too precious, to waste on anything other than what's real." He slid his foot up my leg and back down again. Goosebumps erupted over my arms.

I took a deep breath to keep from jumping up and kissing him right there in front of Uncle.

Focusing on his cup, avoiding his hazel eyes, I leaned forward. Before I could tell him about the fire I saw at the bottom, my vision blurred, and frigid cold flooded my veins with a thickness that made it hard to get oxygen to my lungs. The vision was coming.

I saw myself as a child, inside that gas station. Twenty-two had fastened the lukey bracelet around my wrist, then grabbed my hand.

I hadn't realized it at the time, but he glanced up and saw someone coming in the door. 'God.' We'd been safe for hours and thought we'd lost them, but we hadn't.

He sprinted between the aisles, dragging me along with him, pulling my arm to the point where it hurt. It was so unlike him that it baffled me. Until we turned a corner and ran right into the people we'd escaped from.

'Mickey Mouse' jerked me away from Twenty-two, easily throwing his arms around me and subduing me with his strength.

'God' punched Twenty-two, knocking him to the ground. He was still just a kid, so he wasn't able to fight back when 'God' hauled him up and wrapped his arm around his neck. He whispered, "We're all going to be calm and quiet. If you try to run or act like anything is out of the ordinary, I will kill the girl right here in front of you. Do you feel me?"

Twenty-three nodded.

I'd had no idea what he'd said. I was crying about having been caught again, knowing I was going right back to that train.

A voice from the front of the station called out. "Everything okay back there?"

'God responded, "Yep. Sorry about that. Kids are being unruly."

They started walking us to the door, but a man stepped in front of them, blocking the path. The man that would come to be my Uncle. "What's going on?"

"Nothing. We're just taking the kids back to the truck. No treats for them when they behave like this."

Uncle put his hand on 'God's' shoulder. "No. I don't think so." He leaned down to get eye-to-eye with me. "Honey, are either of these men your dad? Your family?"

Mickey squeezed my shoulder until I was certain it would bleed. A warning. I glanced up at Twenty-two and his eyes were full of fire. He shook his head up and down, telling me to go ahead, so I did. "No."

The rest happened in a blur.

At least it did then. But my vision was about to clear it up for me.

Twenty-two—Rex—elbowed 'God' knocking the wind out of him long enough for him to escape out the door. At the same time, Uncle took me from 'Mickey Mouse' and ushered me out the back door and into his car where the people who'd become Mama and Papa were waiting. Meanwhile, Rex had sprinted around the corner and out of sight, while I wailed for him in the car.

I'd always thought, assumed—hoped—he'd gotten away, but I was strapped into a vision that was telling me otherwise.

While Uncle drove the car slowly, looking for Rex at my demand, he'd scrambled up and over a sandy hill dotted with sagebrush. He slid down the other side, landing on a service road.

He'd sprinted as fast and as far as he could, but it was a few minutes later when 'God' and 'Mickey' caught up with him. He was knocked out, thrown into their truck, and driven away.

When my vision cleared, I looked up at Rex. He was studying me, checking that I was okay.

I was not okay.

His voice was quiet. "Did you see?"

I nodded, knowing my face was going pale.

He'd been recaptured. He hadn't escaped at all.

Uncle's voice boomed above us. "See what? Esme?"

I opened my mouth, but I couldn't speak. I couldn't tell Uncle that Rex had been the boy with me that day. I had no idea how he'd react to that. I couldn't ask Rex the questions that swirled in my mind. I couldn't say anything.

I didn't have to.

"I think she just saw my tragic past. Both parents were killed, the grandpa that I lived with died of cancer, shipped to a foster home, you know, the usual sad stuff that some people have to deal with. I could see the pain of my past in her expression. That's how I knew."

My shuddering breaths were getting worse, so Rex leaned across the table and took my hand. The familiar feel of his fingers threading through mine calmed me. "It's okay. It was a long time ago and I'm over it."

"Is this what you saw, Esme?"

I shut my eyes tight. The last thing I wanted to deal with was Uncle. He was an intrusion on this thing between us. "Yes, Uncle. I saw those things. His childhood was a tragedy."

Rex squeezed my hand, then dropped it, for pretense's sake I was sure. "Life goes on, Esme. I'm the man I am today because of my past."

Uncle patted him on the back. "Wise words for such a young man. I hope you'll come back and visit with us soon."

"Don't worry. I will."

"Oh my, did you just see his past?" One of the old ladies was up and also intruding. Of course, Uncle was ready to take any advantage of any situation.

"What do you think about that, ma'am? Would you like for you to read your past too?"

"Oh my, not today. If I had more tea, my bladder would keep me up all night, but you can bet I'll be back tomorrow. I never gave much credence to reading leaves, but what I just saw convinced me it was real. There was no way she was faking. Her face was pale she was trembling. You'll see me and my friends in the morning."

Uncle beamed, and I knew he'd decided my fate. He was going to work on this. "Of course. Esme will be here in the morning. Tell everyone you know. She's been blessed by the Wayward Warbler, the first blessing ever known. That's how special she is. We'll see you tomorrow."

He started dialing his phone, no doubt getting the PR department on this dramatic announcement. My mother, grandmother, and cousins started their nightly clean-up, but I couldn't move from the chair.

"Mama, is it okay if I take this customer up to the sitting room so we can discuss this? I want to offer him my support."

"Sure, my love, take your time. If we're gone when you finish, just lock up behind you. You know how your Uncle gets."

I nodded and gave her a quick kiss on the cheek. Seeing her in my vision and how loving she'd been when Uncle threw me in the car made me appreciate her more.

Rex was already walking toward the stairs when I caught up to him. I touched his arm, stopping him and trying to tell him everything I was feeling, but again, my words failed. He put his finger on my lips. "Don't say anything. Not here."

Nodding, I followed him, even though he had no idea where he was going. I was too numb to do anything else.

He stopped at the top of the stairs and I fumbled my way around him, opening the door to the private sitting area we had set up for special customers. It was two doors down the hall from Uncle's office and although I knew he was itching to get in there for my panties, I wasn't going to let him do anything until he told me the rest that I didn't see in the vision.

Stepping into the room, I flicked on the lamps next to the blue velvet Victorian-style lounge and flopped down, needing to sit before my legs gave away. He sat beside me, taking my hand in his. "You're in shock, but it's not as bad as you're imagining. Talk to me, Tragedy."

"How dare you call *me* Tragedy. They took you back and you didn't say anything all day long. Why, Rex?"

"Because I knew you'd be upset. Yeah, they got me. And they took the escape out on me too, but they didn't do permanent damage. I had to look good and be fully functional when I reached my destination."

My stomach lurched. Even as kids we knew what there would be someone waiting for us, someone who'd paid. "Did you get, I mean, did they, oh, god, Rex, I don't even know how to ask you."

He took my face in his hands, stroking my cheeks. "You use the words. Don't let them have power over you. Did I get sold and abused? Yes. Just once. I was old enough to know what was happening when that man jerked off in front of me, but I was lukey." He paused to laugh at our joke, but I didn't find any of this funny.

"The guy liked the way I looked, so he didn't make me suck him or fuck him. He just wanted to stare at me until he busted a nut. After he came, I grabbed the screwdriver—he was planning on keeping me in his tool shed—and stabbed his limp dick, and took off. No one has ever had possession of me since. Other than you."

He *was* mine. Had been from the beginning.

"I don't know what to say. It's all so awful. I just want to forget everything and get as far away as I can. It's too much to think about."

"Far away from *me*?"

He searched my eyes, looking for confirmation. "No. I mean, I don't know. I was so determined to leave, but I just found you again and we've changed our relationship and you're saying all these amazing things, but my head is full of this curse and that determination I had to leave." A silent sob wafted through me as I felt the blood rushing in my ears. "It was so haunting to see you get caught."

"I'm sure it was, but it's over." He wrapped his arms around me, pulling me in and nuzzling me against his chest. "I will support you, but you should know I'm not going to lose you again, not now that I've had a taste of what you've become."

The door creaked open and I jumped. Rex kept his arms tight around me as Uncle stepped into the room. "What's going on here?"

Shit. I pulled back as fast as I could. "Uncle."

Rex stood calmly. "She was upset about what she'd seen in my vision, so we came up here to talk about it. I was just leaving." He turned to me. "Thanks for your sympathy. I appreciate it more than you know. I'll be back soon."

Uncle frowned. "Yes, of course." He nodded at me. "Esme will walk you out. I've got some work to do."

We had no choice but to go back downstairs after Uncle left for his office. Luckily, he'd bought our story, but I could tell by the way Rex's body was coiled and tight as he stepped outside he was mad that he wasn't getting in that office that night. "What if you text me when he gets home and I'll come break in. I've got the tools."

"No. First of all, his security is tight here. You won't get through it. Some men patrol our whole compound all the time. Secondly, you never gave me a phone."

He cocked his head. "I gave you something else. Real good, if I recall."

"Good grief. Yes, you did. Still don't have a phone."

"Okay, let's do this. You go home and play good little girl for your Uncle—nope I don't like the sound of what I just said. You go home and go to bed. I'll come tomorrow night, same time, slip you a phone with my number in it, then execute the plan. Simple."

"None of this is simple, but okay. I guess I need to take you home."

"Nah. I don't want to alert your family that I'm anything more than a nice guy with a depressing past. I'll get Charlie to come get me. You just get some rest." He pulled me in for a long hug. "I had no idea when I saw you this morning how this day was going to go, but I couldn't have imagined it better. I'm so glad we found each other again." He kissed my forehead, then walked down the sidewalk, turning the corner and disappearing into the night.

Within moments, I realized how alone I had really been before him.

The next morning, Uncle hovered, as well as the reporters he'd bribed to come by, as I read tea leaves and gave out visions. Within the first four hours, I'd seen more sweaty sex, bitter goodbyes, weddings, kids playing, and now-dead dogs playing fetch than I ever thought possible.

My head was killing me, my voice was hoarse from all the talking, and most of all, I missed Rex.

I'd spent the whole night sleeping on my stomach, just like I'd been accustomed to when I was in that train car. I swore I could feel his body underneath me. However, I woke myself up screaming as the vision of him being punched and thrown into the truck played back through my mind.

Was that the curse trying to tell me something? Trying to show me I should've tried harder to find him? Once it was clear that I was not going back to my real home because the trauma had made me forget my real name and where I lived, I begged Mama and Father to help me find him, but they had no information to go on. All I knew was Twenty-two.

So, with that being a closed subject, I locked who I was away and became Esme, Romani daughter and granddaughter who knew about tea leaves and loved the family who adopted her.

Sometimes though, in the depths of my mind, I almost remembered my real name. It was like a shadow and when I grasped at it, my hand came back empty.

None of that mattered though. What mattered at the moment was making it through the day.

After Uncle had pulled me into his office and taken yet another pair of panties from me, griping at me to hurry and saying, "It's not a big deal, Esme."

It was a big deal and even though I'd given them up, I hated myself for it, not that I had time to think about it because he'd ushered me downstairs and made me start reading right away.

The woman in front of me set down her cup, smiling. "I hope you can tell me something about my nephew. He was hurt last night."

Great. Another weeper.

I wanted to feel sorry for these people, but my sympathy was running low after going through traumatic thing after traumatic thing all day.

"A loop like this at the top of your cup means you are about to face reality in a situation."

"Is that good or bad?"

"I'm unsure. As I said you'll have to interpret the meanings."

"Tell me about my nephew then. Does that mean his reality?"

"Ma'am," I started, but I cut myself off when the telltale chill of my vision washed over me.

I was at a football game. It looked like young kids, not college or high school. Maybe junior high. One of the kids with the white jersey and purple pants caught a ball and flew down the field, zig-zagging between players and leaving them in the dust. He scored the touchdown and did a silly dance to celebrate. I saw the same thing over and over, in different games.

He was a good player even at a young age.

Then the vision just stopped abruptly. It was so jarring, that I had to grab the table to keep from falling. It reminded me of the way Fallon looked when she had her vision in her coffee shop. Unstable.

"Are you okay?"

"Yes ma'am. I'm just getting tired."

"What did you see?"

Right. We were here for her, not me. "Does your nephew play football? I saw a young kid making touchdown after touchdown. He was always wearing number twenty-one." Saying a number so close to my own sent a bead of sweat down my back.

The woman in front of me wailed. Literally. "Not anymore he doesn't. He broke his neck last night. He'll never walk again, much less play football." She took out a hankie and blew her nose.

"I'm so sorry to hear that. What I can say from my vision is that he was always happy on the field. I felt it, coming off of him. It's hard to explain, but even though he won't play again, he has those memories that make him happy."

"What do you know? How could football memories make him happy now? You silly girl." The woman stomped away, slamming the door behind her.

"That's it. I'm calling it." Baba said, wrapping her arms around me. "You need a break. Get out of here while your Uncle is distracted. I'll handle him this afternoon."

She did not have to tell me twice. I wanted to be anywhere other than where I was, so I kissed her, grabbed a thermos of my favorite tea, and shot out the kitchen door like a bullet.

I was in the Jalopy, remembering what Rex and I had done in it the night before, on my way to his shop when I passed by UNB. Taking the shortcut through the back of the campus, I noticed Quinn's car in his reserved TA parking space.

It wasn't like I was dying to see him, but I was curious if Fallon had any luck deciphering the curse. So, I parked and went in, taking my tea with me.

I found him in his professor's office, head down at the computer, papers everywhere. "Hey."

"Esme? What are you doing here?"

"Would you believe it was a force of habit?"

"No. Esme Doe doesn't succumb to force of any kind. I would know."

I laughed. "Nice try. You never forced anything on me, Quinn. You're too good for that."

"Maybe. What's up? You look tired."

"I am. This curse has brought up a lot of demons and I didn't sleep well last night. This morning I was reading people's pasts in their leaves and seeing such sad things, Q. It was bad."

He walked over, pulling me into a hug that felt familiar and distant at the same time. "I'm sorry. That sounds dreadful. You said you're seeing the past? Fallon sees the future."

I pulled away, sitting on the edge of the desk. "Really? Opposites. Makes sense. Has she figured out what it all means and how to stop it?"

"Not yet. You?"

"No. Would you be willing to let me try reading your leaves? I figure since I know you well it might give me a hint. Maybe it'll show you and me together and I can figure it out because right now I've got nothing."

"Sure. Anything to help, as long as I can tell Fallon what you say about it."

"If it helps, go for it."

I took a mug from the cabinet where the professor kept them and poured him some tea. It might not be as accurate if I were going for a real reading, but that's not what I was after. I was chasing down clues to my past as well as his.

He drank the tea quickly, did the correct swirling, and even pointed out south to me. He truly was a great guy.

Not the one for me, though. Even if I hadn't found Rex again.

I looked in Quinn's cup, seeing a couple of formations that told me he was going to have a streak of luck and happiness, but that wasn't what I was waiting to find out.

When the frigid waves overwhelmed me, I leaned back in the chair, looking in his direction, but not seeing the office in front of me or him either.

Well, not exactly.

I saw him standing on the side of a road, washed with orange and blue flowers. I knew that place. It was Cinderella's land, not far from where 'god' was buried.

Quinn had Fallon clutched to his chest, whispering in her ear. The intimacy between them was obvious. They'd just met yesterday, but the two of them looked like they'd been together much longer than that, just by the way they looked at each other and their body language.

Fallon suddenly climbed into the front seat of the car and Quinn went to the back, digging out his rugby ball and throwing it at the Wayward Warbler in the tree next to the car.

That was not the way to get rid of the curse.

The bird flew off and then managed to get inside the truck with Fallon, but she climbed out at just the right time, locking him in.

Okay, maybe it was the right way to get rid of the curse. Or at least the bird.

I guess to celebrate, Fallon wrapped her legs around Quinn's waist and they kissed until the Warbler busted the window with his beak, escaping without looking back.

I thought the vision would be over, but it wasn't. I sat there in horror watching as Fallon got on her knees and started to suck Quinn's cock right there next to the car.

I *knew* he was into her, but for them to go from meeting to blowjobs in one day was a lot. He was *really* into her. He wouldn't have been with her in that way if he didn't want a relationship. I don't think he knew the meaning of a one-night stand.

The vision faded and I sat there gaping at him.

"What? What did you see from my past? That awful haircut I had in third grade? Please say you didn't see that. My mother tried hairdressing for one week and I was the casualty."

"Um, no. I saw you getting your bell rung by Fallon's mouth. On Cinderella Loveridge's property. *Yesterday.* The very day we broke up."

"Oh. That. I hope you're not jealous."

"I'm not. Just surprised it happened so fast. I knew you liked her."

"She's amazing, no offense. Everything is easy with her. I think…we get each other if that makes sense." It did. Lots of sense. "Do you think the curse is trying to tell you to get over me?"

I reached out and patted his arm before moving toward the door. "No, the curse is about me and as much I still care for you, I don't think you're a pivotal part of my life, no offense." He grinned and I was glad we still got along like we did.

"I think the message is in the Warbler. I saw you two trap it in your truck, and then it escaped."

"Okay, so what's the thing the curse wants you to do?"

"I don't know. Maybe you and your girlfriend should try to figure it out."

"Or maybe you should help us with that. You might be able to save yourself in the process."

I imagined the four of us sitting around a table trying to get to the bottom of the curse and it made a bubble of laughter form in my mouth, but I shut it down. Until further notice, I was Esme Doe and I needed my mask in place, even if I didn't want it there. Quinn had been nothing but good to me and I didn't want to bring him or Fallon into the nightmare of my past. I wasn't ready for that.

"Listen, I have so much shit going on in my head right now, I'm going crazy. But it was good to see you, Quinn. Give me a call if you get any great ideas about this. I'm sure you and your girlfriend will figure it out. See you around."

I hurried out of his office and back to the Jalopy, certain that I knew what the curse was saying to me anyway.

It was all about escape.

Rex and I had escaped when we were kids. The Wayward Warbler had escaped from Quinn's car. I needed to escape again.

It made little sense though because the curse had kept me from doing just that.

I spent almost an hour with Rex and we'd wasted none of the time talking about things. He'd simply thrown me against the concrete wall with my hands up as soon as he saw me, hiking my leg up and giving his cock to me over and over until I was screaming his name and making the car we stood bedside's alarm go off.

He barely got my skirt down before Charlie came running in to see if he needed help. He'd informed me he loved the blush of my cheeks when I was embarrassed and I'd told him he needed to think about getting Charlie a set of noise-canceling headphones.

Sadly, knowing Uncle was hovering around the Tea House had made me go back sooner than I wanted and I spent another four hours reading pasts under Uncle's watchful eye.

When read the past of a man who'd watched his Dad confess his affair to his Mom and her subsequent breakdown, I thought I was going to lose it.

Then Rex shuffled in the door and I felt more at ease.

He was out of his garage attire, wearing black jeans and a tee, complete with black sneakers and a blue jean jacket that he didn't need in the weather. He had his hair all pulled back, which made his eyes shine brighter. It wasn't the time to ogle him, but boy was it hard to avoid it.

He dipped his head in my direction and I hurried over to 'take his order,' handing him a menu. Smirking, he looked up at me. "You know what I want. Take the menu carefully." He folded it up, then handed it to me with his hands on top and bottom. "My number's programmed already. Under Twenty-two in case your Uncle gets nosy."

Smart.

Though I didn't intend to let Uncle get anywhere near my burner phone.

After I'd taken his oolong back, we spent the last hour of my shift carefully avoiding, but not really avoiding each other. I learned he could speak a thousand words with his eyes alone. So, when Uncle came down from his office, heading for the kitchen, I knew he was slipping upstairs to figure out the underwear issue.

My skin started to tingle as nerves flittered through me.

I couldn't watch, so I trounced in behind Uncle, needing to make sure he was heading home instead of back upstairs.

"Good evening Uncle. What are you up to tonight?"

I could hear the lie in my voice but hoped he couldn't. "Well, for one thing, I will be trying to contact your mechanic. He isn't answering my calls and that doesn't bode well."

"When I was there, I noticed it was only him and one other guy. Maybe they're too busy fixing my car to answer the phone."

"Maybe. You did well today. Our receipts have doubled in one day. Whatever you do, keep this curse until I say to stop. Do you understand?"

"Yes, Uncle. It takes a lot out of me to do it all day though. Maybe tomorrow I could have a few more breaks."

"Don't think I don't know you were off galivanting around all day. You'll work all day tomorrow. That's final." He called over his shoulder as he was walking through the door. "Baba—I'm in the mood for that special blend I like. Where have you hidden it?"

She turned toward him. "I haven't hidden it anywhere. I stored it in the cupboard away from the inventory." She tsk-tsked him, then went about making him a cup.

Rex was safe, at least for a little bit.

I hovered, telling Uncle that none of the patrons in the serving room were interested in readings. The truth was I didn't know that for sure. I just needed a break. And I needed to make sure Rex was going to be alright.

He made a couple of calls while his tea steeped and when he was finished with them, I slid on the stool beside him. "You look tired Uncle. Why don't you go on home and I'll come make you some supper."

He cocked his head. "You've never offered to cook before. What is going on with you? What do you want?"

"Nothing. I was just being nice. Never mind."

Sipping first, he shook his head. "You're not nice, Esme. It doesn't fit you. I'm going up to finish my work." He waved in the general direction of Baba and headed back to the stairs.

I got my phone out as quickly as I could and texted Rex, telling him to get out immediately, then I parked myself on the bottom step to wait for him.

After twenty minutes, he still hadn't come down or replied to my text.

The only consolation I had was that I didn't hear anything from Uncle's office, so I didn't think he'd been caught.

Though I didn't know for certain.

Baba distracted me, calling for me to help her clean and close up the shop since it was time. I had no choice, so I did what I could, keeping one eye on the stairs the entire time as my heart almost catapulted out of my chest.

I hadn't felt that level of fear since I was eight years old.

What if he did something to Rex?

Finally, after another fifteen minutes, Uncle came downstairs and told us he was going home. I offered to set the alarm and do the lights and, thankfully, they agreed to let me.

Of course, I headed upstairs, bumping into Rex as he came out of the bathroom down the hall.

He hadn't gotten caught.

But he was not alright.

The best word I could think of to describe the look on his face was enraged. Incensed maybe. It was so far beyond mad that I had trouble pinning it down. "What happened?"

"He almost caught me, but I had the sense to duck into the bathroom because I knew there was no way to get downstairs and I worried he'd go into the sitting room. I got some information for you."

He pulled me inside the office, closing the door quietly and beginning to pace as I stood there wondering what he'd found. It was only when I stepped in front of him, taking his face in my hands that he stopped. "What is it?"

Wrapping his arms around me, he buried his face in the hair falling over my shoulder. "Your Uncle is a bad seed."

It was more of a confirmation than a surprise. "Did you find my underwear?"

He stepped back, shaking his head first, then pulling the baby pink lace ones he'd gotten that morning from his jacket pocket. "Yep. They're mine now, by the way. I found them in the top drawer in a manila envelope like you said. The whole drawer was full of the same kind of envelopes, so who knows what other women he'd been stealing undies from?"

It sickened me to think about it. Did his twisted game involve more than us younger family members? Was it Mama and Rhoda too? The wives of his sons and cousins that worked for us in one way or another?

I still didn't understand. "What else?"

Rex bit his lower lip. "The envelopes were addressed to men all over the country, but he had your name on the return address on two of them. The rest had other girls' names.

"Your panties were going to a Mr. Brent Jordan in Norman, Oklahoma. According to the receipt I found with the panties, he'd paid a thousand dollars for them. They came with pictures of you from what I assume is your bedroom. You were half-dressed or getting out of the shower, all sorts of images some dirty old fuck would want to jerk off to."

I thought my lungs were going to implode. I couldn't believe it. Rather, I could and it made me ill.

"It gets worse. He had a ledger in there. Your sick Uncle has been doing this for years. Your cousins, other women. He made a thousand dollars for each transaction and there were at least fifty pages of numbers and names. The best I could tell was he'd never sent anything from you until today. The name on the ledger was Henry Hurst, but I couldn't find his envelope, so it's probably already gone."

Sitting on the desk, I rubbed my temple. "He's been spying on me, taking pictures and selling them to strangers over the internet? That's just…obscene."

"Well, Mr. Brent Jordan of Norman, Oklahoma is going to be in for a big surprise when he opens his envelope and finds crude stick drawings and some black boxer briefs in there." He pulled back the waist of his jeans, showing me he had no underwear.

So, he'd replaced mine with his.

I was shaking, unsure whether to laugh or cry. Finally, released a sob because even though I knew it now, there was no way I could stop it. If I removed the camera, he'd know. If I told him I knew, he'd say he didn't care. I was making him money. We all were.

I had no escape. None.

I had to get out of Between.

When I'd finally recovered, at least a little, Rex let go of me. "Look at me, Tragedy." I wiped my tears away and stared up into his beautiful eyes. "I think there's more, but it's just a suspicion. I know a way we could find out though."

Sniffing, I steeled myself. "How?"

He pointed to the desk where Uncle had left his teacup. "If you don't want to do it, I'd understand, but if he's doing this, what else could he be into? Maybe…"

His voice trailed off and I had an inkling of what he was implying, but I wasn't ready to know that yet.

On the other hand, if I was to get away from Uncle, then maybe reading his tea leaves would give me the clue to the curse or proof that I could take to the police. The fact that we'd willingly given him our underwear made it difficult to turn him in. If we'd said no and he still did it, maybe we'd have a case against him, but we hadn't said no.

Sucking in a big breath, I walked around to the desk and sat in Uncle's chair. "Okay. I think I need to do this."

Rex held out his hand and I took it. "Do you feel it?"

"Yes. Always."

"Good. You are the strongest person I know, Tragedy. No matter what you see, you and I will get you through it."

I nodded, then faced the handle South, and peered into the cup.

The chill seemed deeper this time, like my bones were breaking from cold, but I held tight to Rex's hands as I succumbed to the vision of Uncle's past.

He was walking into the office at the railyard on the outskirts of town. My stomach clenched just seeing the place and remembering it was there. No matter where I had to go, I always avoided that place, even though it was closed down now. Just seeing it clearly in the vision was enough to make the blood in my head pound with voracity.

Uncle was younger in the vision, with more hair on his head and a lot leaner. He strolled into the office whistling. "Boys," he said. "Are you here yet?"

From the corner of the office a door swung open and out strolled 'god' and 'Mickey Mouse.'

Nausea overwhelmed me. I tried to move, to squeeze Rex's hand, to hurl my guts up, but I was frozen in the vision.

Uncle pulled two envelopes from his pocket, giving one to each of these men who'd abducted Rex and me. "Here's your spoils from the last run, minus the one girl, of course. I should charge you more for letting those two escape though."

'God' was quick to shake his head. "We would'a had her back if you didn't stop us, Boss. Why did you stop us at the gas station?"

"I saw a simple solution to a growing problem. My younger brother has been making strides with the relatives and he has a lot of support and goodwill among the other families in the state too.

"I was afraid he was going to usurp me when the old man dies. His wife is anxious for a child, but they've come up empty so far, so I figured giving them a child on a silver platter would help me in two ways: one, it'll garner me goodwill with him, and two, she'll take up his time and he won't want to run the family when the old man kicks it."

He reached around the counter and retrieved a bottle of bourbon, taking a long swig then handed it to 'Mickey' who took a drink and passed it to 'god.' Once they all had a drink, Uncle leaned forward, pressing his hands on the counter. "If you two lose another child, I won't hesitate to kill you. I have planned and honed this operation to run perfectly for years and now that we're in motion, nothing should keep us from delivering every order we get. Do you understand?"

They both nodded, but 'god' gave him a loud yessir.

"I'm sorry, I didn't hear you, Mr. Weathers."
Mickey bowed his head. "Yes, you've got it, boss."

The vision faded and I'd never been colder in my life.

194

I don't know how I made it back to my room.

No, that's not true. I know that Rex helped me turn on the security system and sneak up the back stairs of our house with only Selene seeing us. I knew she wouldn't rat us out. Especially when I told her what I now knew.

Sampson Doe was a sex trafficker.

Sampson Doe had knowingly brought me into his own home after he knew—*knew*—I'd been abducted. He'd planned and executed that abduction.

Sampson Doe was going to pay.

Rex shut the door behind us, locking it and laying me on my bed, then he got to work, scouring everywhere in the room a camera might have been. "You can't take it out," I whispered. "He'll know. He might be watching now."

He ignored me, searching and searching around my vanity, using his hands to skim every surface, open every drawer, and look all around. Finally whispering "Ah-ha, you sick fucker, I've got you." He stood to the side of my vanity, blocking the view of the camera I guessed. After looking at everything in my room, he went over and moved the clothes rack I had where all of my scarves and purses were hanging over near the vanity, then crawled next to me on the bed.

"I'm not taking it out now. That'll come, but that painting of the Eiffel Tower over there is where the camera is. Keep something in front of it and maybe it'll stop him for now." I nodded. It was all I could do. I couldn't speak or move or breathe.

The blood started to rush into my ears and before I could do anything else, the wretched gasping started. My heart pounded against my chest and my body was jerking with unbidden sobs.

Through it all, Rex held my hand. "Do you feel my hand?"

"I can't. Rex, no."

Louder this time, not giving a shit if Uncle was standing outside my door. "Do you feel my hand?" Choking, I nodded. "And what do we say?"

"We'll be okay if we stick together."

"Right. We will make sure he pays, but we have to play it right or nothing will stick. All we have now are panties that were given to him and a vision due to a curse. We need more."

"Yeah, I know."

"This is going to be the hard part." He squeezed my hand, and I finally looked into his eyes, ready, knowing what he was going to say. "You have to act like everything is normal while I play this through in my head. I have no problem walking in there and killing him right now, fuck knows I want to, but I can't."

I sniffed, finally feeling my heart slow down. "I know. I don't want you to get caught. I couldn't make it without you, Rex. I couldn't."

"You won't have to, Tragedy. We are going to figure this out, but right now, even though I want to get on top of you and drill that nightmare out of your head with my cock, I want you to sleep. Lay here in my arms and sleep." I opened my mouth to argue and tell him it was dangerous, but he put his finger over it. "Don't argue. This is what we both need right now. I'll be right here. Rest. There's nothing more to say right now."

Waking up with Rex was the best feeling. Despite the damning evidence we'd found and no idea what to do with it, I was happy.

It wouldn't last long if anyone caught Rex in my room. I was a grown adult and could make my own choices, but that's not how our family operated. The women would fawn over him and tease us relentlessly and Sampson or the other male members would kick his ass or worse. I shoved and ran my hand over his arm softly. "Wake up. You have to get out of here."

"Beg to differ, Tragedy. *We* have to get out of here." His voice was sleepy and it seemed even sexier than normal. I wanted to hear him like that every day.

"You're the one who said I had to do things business as usual."

"A man has a right to change his mind. I've thought about it all night and I don't want you here with him."

"I don't want to be here, but we have to be smart about this. I thought about it as I went to sleep too. Just because you killed Clyde Higginbotham doesn't mean they stopped trafficking."

He rolled over and stretched and I wanted his body close to mine again. I was in deep and I had no idea if it was because of who he used to be to me or who he'd become to me. I couldn't think of that though. "I agree, but I think I have a solution. What if good ole' Brent Jordan of Norman, Oklahoma were to ask for something more than pictures? If your Uncle is still trafficking, then he'll be more than happy to accommodate him for enough money."

"Yeah, sure. All you have to do is get Brent to cough up some money and suddenly be into children. I don't want to dampen your enthusiasm for catching them, but that seems unlikely."

He kissed me on the cheek, then jumped up. "Not when you have a Charlie like I do. He's a hacker extraordinaire. I've got Brent's address from the envelope. Charlie will be able to set it all up, even make a money transfer that looks real. Once your uncle takes the bait, we can follow him and get evidence. Charlie can even help deliver it to the police without us being involved."

"Charlie? The guy in your shop?"

"Yep, you don't think I hired him for his good looks and mechanical skills, do you? He doesn't know shit about carburetors, but he can work the computerized stuff in modern cars like nobody's business. He can do this, no sweat." Hope bubbled in my chest. "You just have to hang on a couple of days, three tops. It takes a little time."

I sat up. I could do three days. Especially if I knew Rex was with me. "Okay, let's do it."

He swung around. "Okay, if you insist."

Diving on the bed and throwing me back in the process, he kissed my neck, making chills erupt over my skin as he went straight for my panties. Just as he got them down to my ankles and had his fly undone, Sampson banged on my door. "Why is this door locked, Esme? You know the rules of this house."

Rex froze for a second, glaring at the door, then jumping off the bed and heading straight for it with his undone fly. He had murder in his eyes and I knew if I didn't stop him, he'd be in jail before the hour was up.

I hobbled over to the door with my panties around my ankles, putting myself between him and the door, whispering, "You can't. It'll ruin the plan."

"I don't care. I want to kill that motherfucker with my bare hands. He doesn't even let you lock your door?"

Sampson was still beating on the door. So hard, it rattled against the hinges. I took a steadying breath. "Give me a second, Uncle. I'm getting dressed." Lowering my voice, I focused on the man about to explode through that door and ruin the rest of his life. "I know you want to end him, but look at me, Rex." He was seething, air flowing in and out of his clenched teeth. His fists were so tight, his knuckles were white. He wasn't hearing me at all. "Look at me, Twenty-two."

The number snapped him out of it. He lowered his gaze, glancing through eyelashes. I put my hand on his chest. "Do you feel my hand here over your heart?" He nodded. "The heart I feel beating so fast right now belongs to me. And as much as I'd like to watch you tear him apart, I can't let you because if I do, we will lose each other again. I can't live through that. Please don't leave me again."

I was trying to be the calm rational one, but unexpected emotions flooded through me. A tear fell and it nearly broke him.

Throwing his arms around me, he buried his face in my hair. "You're right. I'm never going to leave you. I'll back off."

"Okay, I have to get out there fast. You hide. I'll text you when everyone is out of the house." I grabbed a skirt from the floor, throwing it on with the T-shirt I'd slept in. Then I waited until Rex had hidden himself in my closet and shut the door.

I ran my hand through my hair and yanked the door open, ready for Sampson's tirade. "Good morning, Uncle. What has you so upset?"

"I couldn't get in your room. You know there's no lock policy in this house."

"I do know that, Uncle. What I don't know is why a fifty-something-year-old man needs to go inside his single female niece's bedroom at six in the morning. It makes no sense. I lock the door when I shower and dress so that no one can invade my privacy. If you don't like that, you can kick me out."

I marched out the door and left him standing there dumbfounded. I knew for certain he wouldn't kick me out, not if he wanted to keep sending my panties all over the world and he wanted me to keep reading tea leaves of the past. I had him, he just didn't know I knew that.

Suffering through another three long days of past visions was excruciating. Suffering them in the absence of Rex was even worse.

We'd agreed that it was best for him to stay away as Charlie worked his magic, but it was tough for both of us. We ended up burning up the text lines most nights until the wee hours of the morning. We talked a lot about what had happened to us.

I learned that his "adopted father" wasn't official. Rex had walked into his shop when he was fourteen and asked for a job. The guy took pity on him and they became close. He knew everything that had happened to Rex and he loved him like a son. It made me feel so much better about what had happened to him. Not that anything could erase the black hole our abductions left inside us, but it was a comfort to know he'd been loved afterward. So had I.

I got another text from him just before I went to bed.

I have a question for you.

Ask me anything.

You know you're always going to be my Tragedy, but you've never mentioned your real name. Why?

I don't remember it. I know I should because it wasn't like I was a baby, but every time I try to remember, I can't. I'm not sure I want to know.

Why not?

I think I'm afraid to meet yet another version of myself. Sometimes I want to know, but other times I think that Twenty-three, Esme, and Tragedy are enough for one woman.

They're all the same to me.

Maybe. And maybe when this is over, I will find out, but for now, I'll just be me. You should know it's cold without you here.

My whole life has been cold without you.

Why do you say such amazing things?

Easy, I'm an amazing guy.
Shut up.
Goodnight Tragedy. Sleep well.

Goodnight Rex. <3

He called me the next morning. "Charlie got it done. Your uncle responded just now. Asked what kind of special package he was looking for, so I responded with 'grade A certified veal, if you get my meaning. I'm coming to Vegas for a business trip and I can swing by and pick her up. Can you handle that or do I need to find another supplier?'"

"Ew. That made me throw up in my mouth."

"No kidding. I wanted to make sure it sounded like code and he understood he meant a young person."

"And?"

"And, your Uncle responded to give him two days to make the arrangements. Told him to wire the twenty-five thousand first and once it was confirmed they'd have a deal."

"Will Charlie be able to fake wire that much?"

"Yep, he said he could. We set it all up. He's going to approach in the car and pretend to be Brent Jordan of Norman,

Oklahoma. We just have to be there when they make the exchange to get any footage we need."

I laid back down in the bed, pulling the blanket over me. "I don't like putting a child in danger."

"I don't either, but she won't be because I'll be there. I promise you, you're the only Tragedy in my life. If I have to forfeit letting them get away with it over making sure she's safe, I will, but I believe this will work."

"I want to come with you."

"No, you don't."

"Yeah, I do. Please, Rex. I have to see this through."

"Let's talk about it later, okay? I don't want either of us to make rash decisions."

"Okay, but I won't change my mind."

"I know."

Two days later I was pulling into Rex's garage. Uncle had gotten a bug up his ass about my car repairs, so he'd sent me to go check on my car. I laughed all the way over. Dumb fuck.

I went inside the office, spying Charlie on the computer. He waved. "You won't believe how stupid your Uncle is. His password is his birthday. I've got all his email right here at my fingertips. When the operation is over, I could erase what I did and he'd still go to prison for the rest of his life."

He really was a dumb, egotistical fuck.

I went inside the garage, finding Rex underneath my car. The hood had been replaced and from the outside, it looked pristine. It made me sad to think about it. I'd kind of gotten used to the Jalopy.

I kicked his foot.

He came sliding out and cursing. "How many times have I told you, Charlie—"

I waved. "Not Charlie."

"I see that. I've never wanted to fuck Charlie like I do the vision in front of me."

Laughing, I put my hands on my hips. "Sampson is mad that you haven't fixed my car yet. What gives? It's not like you have anything better to do."

"Oh, I have something better to do, but I am almost finished. Want to take a look underneath?"

"I have always thought it looked fun to slide around on one of those slider things, so why not?"

He helped me lay down on the creeper, I'd learned, and scoot under the car, pointing out all the things he'd fixed. It was nearly cute how excited he got to show me the suspension system and talk about differential timing or something like that. His enthusiasm was such a welcome lightness to my day, I turned over and kissed him, hard and rough, just like he liked.

He groaned. Though it was a tight squeeze, he pulled me on top of him and grabbed my ass as he nipped at my lips with his teeth and I moaned against him.

"Good lord, I should've called first."

I froze. "Quinn?"

I got back on my creeper and slid out with Rex right behind me. Sure enough, Quinn was standing there looking down at us with his eyebrow cocked. "Sorry to interrupt your…sex under the car session, but I need your help, Esme. Right now."

The concern in his voice was worrying. "What's wrong?"

Fallon is having bad headaches and losing her memory. Has that happened to you?"

"No, I have headaches, but I haven't lost my memory yet." It was troubling to think the curse was becoming physical. If she was that bad off, how much longer would it be for me to get there? "I don't t know, Quinn, maybe it has something to do with her seeing the future. What if it's erasing her past when she uses her ability?"

If that were the case, and I hoped it wasn't, but it if were, it would mean with every look into the past, I was losing some part of my future.

The curse was taking years off my life I looked at Rex, then Quinn. It was obvious we'd all come to the same conclusion. It was killing us. "What should we do?"

"I want you to come with me and we can sit down and figure this curse out and get rid of it. You can read her past and she can read your future and maybe it'll be enough."

Rex was already shoving his coveralls over his shoulders. when we started walking to the cars. 'Um, Esme, you might want to change clothes. His greasy handprints are all over your ass."

Rex smirked, not embarrassed by his handiwork. "There are some sweats upstairs. Use anything you want."

Dying of embarrassment, I hurried up the stairs and left the two of them to introduce themselves and deal with any awkwardness. I was back down in one of Rex's hoodies and some of his sweats with my hair up in a messy bun. We were on the way moments later.

"Esme? What are you doing here?"

"I was kidnapped by your boyfriend."

Quinn shook his head. "You were not. You want this over as badly as we do. Sit down and let's figure it out."

He made the introductions and I was floored at how Fallon looked. She was pale and sickly, with dark circles under her eyes. I wanted to help her. I was just hoping I could and that we could end this.

I held out my hand to Fallon. "It helps me read better."

She took my hand and her vision came on fast. I squeezed as a bedroom materialized in her cup.

A woman was sitting on the bed with a laptop, ledgers, and all kinds of papers. Her brow was furrowed in concentration as a young Fallon with short hair bounced into her room and asked if she wanted to get ice cream.

Her mom. She wasn't annoyed by the question, but something was eating at her. I could see it in her face. "You're so much like me, Fallon. You know that, right? Always thinking and trying to figure things out. Always the one to solve everyone's problems and issues. You're even the one trying to plan a family night. I know your Dad wants to go, but it was you who asked him first, right?"

Fallon nodded. "I like planning and organizing everything. I guess I am like you, Mom."

"I'm so proud of you, Dear. I hope you see that, but because you're so much like me I want you to remember there are other things in life. Do you understand?"

"I don't know."

"I'm afraid our similarities will lead you down the wrong path. Don't get me wrong, I love taking care of your father and you girls, I love running the business for our family. I wouldn't change any of that, but at the same time, I think there is more for you than the kind of life I've led. I've missed out on so much and I want your life to be as full and vibrant as you are, my love. Don't forget to see beyond your responsible nature and your need to organize. It will make you unhappy in the end."

The vision ended and after I told Fallon what I'd seen, I let her know what I thought. "Fallon, I think you're seeing it from the perspective of a person who has lost their parents, not from the perspective of a young girl who didn't know what was coming.

"I'm sure your mom was happy in her life and I could see she loved your family, but I took what she was saying as a warning. She didn't want you to be like her and have to miss out on family ice cream runs. She wanted more for you. She wanted you to use your brain and abilities to seek more than she had. To enjoy life and ice cream and chase dogs down the hallway. She was warning you about balance."

She had a hard time believing me. I think she'd spent her whole life trying to live up to the model her mother was without knowing her mother had regrets. It wasn't up to me to force these new ideas on her, but I truly hoped in my heart that she understood and learned to have that balance. She certainly would have a great partner in her life to help her find the world outside her shop.

Right before Fallon was to tell my future, Quinn picked her up and carried her over to the counter by the register, setting her down and having a conversation out of our earshot.

He was concerned. I was too. She hadn't taken the news about her mother very well and I couldn't blame her. Rex leaned over. "Do you think she can get an accurate read when she's pissed like that?"

"I'm not sure."

"I hope so but look at this. I just got a text from Charlie. It's happening tonight at midnight."

I nodded, hoping my nerves would last through this reading and what we had to do later. My pulse sounded in my ears and that familiar feeling of dizzy nausea overtook me. I fisted my hands to gain control over my impending panic attack. "Hey, look at me. You're in control. Don't let this change your outlook on any of this, do you hear me?"

I nodded as Fallon approached, picking up my mug and looking into it. With determination. She zoned out for a few minutes—longer than my visions usually felt—but it forced me to keep my breath calm and steady as I waited for a response. Finally, she was ready to tell me.

"In the future, I don't know when exactly, but you both looked the same as you do now, so I'd guess soonish, I saw you curled up in an abandoned rail car. Esme, does that make sense to you?"

I gasped at the mention of the railway car, but Rex slung his arm around me I nodded for her to continue. "You were alone at first, sitting in the corner in the darkness. I couldn't tell if you were sad or what, but as soon as Rex opened the door, you both looked pleased to see each other."

Rex smirked. "Of fucking course, she was pleased to see me."

I touched his jaw, then pushed him away. It was not the time for joking. Not to be pushed around, he grabbed my throat and pulled me, biting my bottom lip and leaving a steaming kiss for me to remember forever.

I'm sure Fallon and Quinn were dismayed, to say the least. I didn't care. This was us, Rex and me, and the others didn't matter in the equation.

Fallon cleared her throat and carried on. "Rex said something about finding you, so I don't know if you were hiding from him or someone else, but he said some sweet things to you. I don't want to repeat them now because I think you should hear them from his mouth in the future, not mine." Rex agreed by shaking his head. "He asked if you'd made a decision. I think you'd decided something but I don't know what your options were or what the final choice was because my vision faded before you could tell him."

I glanced at Rex. Obviously, the decision to leave or not was weighing between us. He was quietly simmering as he listened to everything.

As much as I liked being with him, as important as he was to me, I still had no idea what I'd do when this was all over. Especially knowing what Sampson had done. The thought of staying anywhere near where he'd been made me ill. It was still a fight or flight situation and I'd gotten nowhere with silently fighting him all these years.

Fallon sighed. "I'm sorry. I didn't give you as much to go on as you did for me."

I touched the bracelets on my arm, twisting them in such a way that both Rex and I could see the lukey tattoo. "No, you did. In a way, it's exactly the opposite of what I told you. My vision said that you should re-examine the path you were taking. Your vision told me I should stay the course." I stood. "If only either of those things were easy."

Rex pushed away from the table. His simmer had turned to a full-on boil. "What do you think I am? Or Quinn for that matter? I've been telling you that you're not alone. Neither of you are. Both of you should stop wringing your hands over this shit and do what you need to do to end this fucking curse and get on with your fucking lives."

Quinn tried to suppress a laugh and failed. "Couldn't have said it better myself."

They were right, of course. I just had to make myself believe them.

I'd searched everywhere I could think of, looking for the feather, the symbol that told us the curse was fulfilled. Even though I didn't believe it would appear until we got rid of Sampson and I made my decision about leaving or not.

Rex was quiet as we drove to the rendezvous point for the exchange. The very railyard I'd seen in my vision of Sampson's past.

It was closed now, but I guess they still had access to it. Of course, he would pick that place to do his dirty exchange.

We were both armed with our phones to get footage if needed. Rex was armed with a gun, which didn't bother me in the least. If I had to go to jail for this unknown kid they were likely abducting at that moment, I would do it and not think twice about it. Knowing what she would be subjected to if we didn't stop this made that an easy decision. Rex felt the same way, but the plan was to do this without using the gun. Or harming the child.

We pulled in across the vacant lot of the railyard. Rex turned off the ignition and swiveled to face me. "I don't like us splitting up."

"Me either, but we have the best chance to get all the information we need this way. I know the plan is for Charlie to call the police, turn in a tip to get them here at midnight on the dot, but anything can go wrong. We need proof and if we're in two different places, it's more likely we get it."

He wrapped his hands around the nape of my neck and kissed me, hard and turbulent, like he was forcing everything he wanted to go right into being just by kissing me. I'd never experienced anything like his kiss. The depth of it was dizzying and when he pulled away we were both breathless. "You're right. Just promise me you'll be careful."

"Same goes for you."

We sealed our promises with our lips, tongues, and hands, our entire bodies as we tangled up in each other. When he tried to lay me down on the seat, I pulled away from him. "We don't have time for that."

He groaned, pulling me upright again. "You're right. But after, you should be prepared for all the twisted things I will do to wring as many orgasms out of you as I can."

Sounded good to me.

I moved to get out of the car, but he stopped me. "Let me pull up closer, so you don't have to walk." He angled the car through the parking lot, past the main building, veering for a spot past it, so I could get out unseen. We were an hour early, but neither of us wanted to leave anything to chance.

As he turned the truck to the left, to the side of the building, I gasped. There were a dozen rail cars parked on one of the old tracks. The building had been obstructing our view of them, but as soon as I saw the rusty brick red car with the word 'Blisstake" scrawled in graffiti on the side, my entire body went limp. "Rex. Look."

My hand shook as I pointed to the car.

The car.

They'd kept it at the rundown railway station like a twisted souvenir.

Rex, took my shaking arm, threading his fingers through mine. "It can't hurt you anymore. You're safe."

My chin trembled as I spoke. "Then why do I feel so cold right now? It's like I'm back inside it again."

"You're not. You're with me. And when you get out of this truck to go do what we have to do, you are still not alone. You can do this, Tragedy. I know it."

I nodded. "Okay. You're right, It's just a railway car. It's the men who hurt us."

He kissed the back of my hand. "Right. And we're about to make sure they don't hurt anyone again."

After steeling myself by clutching his hand so hard it probably cut out his circulation, I swiveled, ready to get out of the car, but he stopped me again.

For the first time since we'd left to come do this, I noted uncertainty in his expression. He was being strong for me and I appreciated it more than I could express, but his furrowed brow told me he was concerned about something. "What is it?"

"I wasn't going to bring this up, but I don't know if I can focus on what I have to do if I don't." I nodded, another wave of nausea churning in my gut. "When we found each other again, just a week ago, you were leaving Between. Once this is over, is that still your plan?"

I didn't know how to answer him because I didn't know myself. "I can't tell you."

"Because you don't want to hurt me or because you don't want me to know?"

"Both. Neither. I'm not sure. If Fallon hadn't read my future, then maybe I'd know, but it feels like the curse is telling me to keep going the way I was, and if that's the case—"

"You leave me behind."

"I didn't say that. I'm sorry, I don't know what I'll do. Without knowing exactly what the curse wants from me, I don't know how to answer you."

He bit his lower lip and I wanted so badly to kiss his pain away. Pain that I'd caused. "If you're so convinced the curse is telling you to stay the course, have you considered it means to stay where you are?"

I hadn't had time to consider anything. Not with this plan in motion. "Maybe."

"You should go."

"Rex, we can talk—"

"Go. If they see us, it's all for nothing. I'll park. Meet me back here at the car when it's over." He got out, slamming the door, and walking in the other direction.

All I could do was watch him go.

A half-hour later, I'd crept my way around the front of the building, pulling over a rotten wood bench that I could hide behind as we waited for the exchange.

I knew Rex wouldn't let me down even though I knew I'd already let *him* down.

He wanted me to tell him I was staying. With him.

I couldn't.

Not yet.

Maybe not ever.

I had come too far to make the wrong decision now.

As much as I wanted him, needed him, as much as I felt like our connection was made of bone and tissue and flesh, not the awful circumstances that brought us together, I was torn.

My heart hammered against my chest as the anticipation rang through me. I'd lost sight of Rex as we took up our positions. I knew he was going to get close to Mickey, but I didn't know how or where exactly.

We should've made more specific plans.

It was too late for that.

The gravel crunched as a truck approached. I ducked down so the headlights wouldn't catch me. A door closed and when I peeked up to see what was going on, I nearly crawled out of my own skin due to the nerves.

Sampson had gotten out of the truck to unlock the gate. Once he'd done that, he piled back in the truck and it crept through the open gates.

I hit record and raised my phone. In the moonlight, I caught a glimpse of Rex slinking in the gate behind the truck. He darted away, taking a spot behind a pile of old oil barrels near the tracks.

The two men got out of the truck. Mickey lit a cigarette while Sampson left his door open, leaning in and speaking to someone inside. It had to be the girl they'd abducted.

Another car approached, inching through the gate and parking in the middle of it. There'd be no way for Mickey's truck to get out.

Charlie was smart. He would be able to get away fast when the cops come. He got out of his car, walking toward Sampson and Mickey with purpose. "Have you got my veal?"

Uncle stepped forward. "I may have something for you. I just need some assurance this transaction stays between us."

Charlie shook his head, approaching him with heavy footsteps. "Are you a fucking fool, Man. I just bought a minor for purposes of sexual gratification and you're worried about me telling the cops? Dumbass."

My stomach turned.

I checked my phone. The cops should've arrived, but there was no sign of them. If we didn't get them there to witness the girl who'd been abducted, we'd have nothing concrete.

Realizing this at the same time, Charlie scratched his chin. "Tell you what, I want to check my merchandise. Make sure it suits my needs before we shake on this."

I angled my phone, making sure to keep Charlie's face out of frame.

Mickey and Sampson shared a look. Sampson didn't look inclined to do it, but knowing him like I did, I knew he'd give in when he started counting dollar signs in his head.

Sure enough, after a few seconds, he went back to the truck and yanked the girl out of the cab, pulling the hood off her head. She was in her pre-teen years, but crying, shaking, looking from one man to the other, wondering what was about to happen to her.

I stood up, not concerned with staying hidden any longer. My body was on high alert. It was like my muscles were going to burst.

Charlie approached the girl, pretending to check her out from every angle.

God, where were the cops?

Having no choice, Charlie nodded. Sampson pushed the girl into his arms and began to walk back to the truck.

No cops.

No exchange.

No punishment.

No hope.

Even though I knew the girl was safe with Charlie, I couldn't let Sampson and Mickey get away.

I couldn't.

So, I marched over to the men, holding out my phone. "I've got you, *Uncle*."

Sampson turned around. The moment he realized who I was, he began laughing. "What do you think you have on me, Esme?"

"I have you abducting and selling a child, something you both have been doing for years." I pressed my lips together tightly, trying to keep myself in check. "It's over."

"Ha. It's over when I say it's over. You've always been so petulant. You should've thanked me for taking you in all those years ago, but no, you continued to live in my house and reap the rewards of being a Doe." He shook his head, walking toward me, then backing away, like he was gearing up for battle. "You know, before you look too far down your nose, these abductions that you're so offended by paid for your pretty red sports car, your shoe obsession, for everything you've ever had. It's all because of this revenue stream."

I swallowed, but there was nothing there. My mouth was dry and my limbs shaking, but I kept walking, using my phone like a shield. "It's not a revenue stream, they are children. *Children!* You are a sick bastard and both of you are going to pay."

Charlie kept his arm around the girl protectively. "It's over. Just give it up. We've got everything on camera. You're going down."

Mickey shouted. "Never," before whipping a pistol from his waistband. I'd been so focused on Sampson and the girl, I hadn't noticed it there. The silver gleam of the barrel in the moonlight made the girl scream. Charlie, pushed her down to the ground, just as Mickey fired the shot.

Charlie went down.

He didn't get up.

Oh, God.

Again, the girl screamed in terror. Mickey aimed his gun at her, but a loud shot went off before he took his.

Rex.

He'd fired in the air to get Mickey's attention as he walked out from behind the barrels. They faced off, their guns aimed at each other.

I didn't know what to do to help. Or to stop it.

The girl was on the ground now, trying to wake Charlie up.

"Stop this, Uncle. You've done enough damage. No one else has to get hurt tonight."

He laughed at me.

"You don't understand how the world works, Esme. It's a matter of supply and demand. If you want to be angry about what happens to these children, be angry at the men and women who buy them from me.

"It's like being mad at the waiter who brings you raw chicken. The waiter didn't cook it. He just brought it to you. The fault lies with the chef."

He was sick. Disgustingly sick and I wanted to strangle him with my bare hands.

The sound of sirens blared in the distance. We all glanced to the south and saw the blue flickering lights.

Thank God. They were on their way.

"Mick, get in the truck," he barked.

Rex took another step. "I don't think so, Mickey Mouse."

"Who are you to tell me what to do, Boy?"

The look of fire on Rex's face was as beautiful as it was scary. He wasn't going to back down. I could be moments away from losing him. My entire body went rigid like my veins were full of ice.

"Who am I? Take a good look in my eyes, Mickey Mouse. You might not remember me, but you know me. Twenty-two. The one who got away. Then got away again."

Mickey squinted, keeping his gun trained on Rex. "I'll be damned. Small world."

The sirens were closer now. Sampson was smart enough to know they needed to leave. He walked over to Mickey, taking the gun from his hand. "Get in the truck, Mick."

Mickey did as he was told, climbing in the truck and starting the ignition. As Rex and Sampson stared each other down, my pulse rocketed. Sweat ran down my back as I slowly headed toward them.

"Uncle," I whispered. He turned his head, just for a second, and in that moment, Rex cocked his gun. "Don't, Rex. Don't shoot him. I can't lose you. I can't."

Rex lowered his gun, this time his arm trembled. He wanted to kill him, but he stopped himself.

For me.

Sampson took advantage, cocking him in the head with the barrel of the gun. Rex fell and I screamed as loudly as the girl on the ground did. Sampson shot at the girl as Mickey turned the truck, slamming on the brakes long enough to pick up Sampson.

He fired two more shots in the direction of the bodies on the ground, then hit the accelerator, ramming into Charlie's car and moving it a few feet until it slammed into the gate. The truck tires spun, trying to punch through, but it didn't work. The car was at just the right angle to keep the truck from moving.

I ran over to the girl, checking to make sure she was alright. She was trembling and crying, but I didn't see any blood on her. She threw her arms around me and I held her tight, rubbing circles on her back and telling her it would be okay.

Gravel spun behind us when Mickey put it in reverse and punched it, aiming for the fence a few yards away from the gate. The weaker chain gave way, allowing for easy access.

I spun around, needing to check on Rex, but he wasn't lying on the ground anymore. Panicked, I called out. "Rex, where are you?"

He whistled and I turned my head in that direction.

I screamed until I had nothing left inside me.

He'd climbed into the back of Mickey's truck and was speeding away aiming the gun at the cab.

The girl, Samantha, was unharmed. The police had taken her back to her parents after the EMTs checked her out. They insisted on checking me over too, though I told them I was fine.

Charlie had been rushed to the hospital for emergency surgery. The bullet had struck him in the shoulder, missing anything major, but he had a long road of recovery ahead of him. Or so I was told.

Officer Simmons had taken my statement and he'd believed every word I said. They'd suspected Sampson of illegal activities for years but couldn't get any dirt on him by legal means. I guess we'd helped them in their investigation.

He'd assured me they were working on finding Rex and making sure he was okay, but I wondered if finding him would be the right thing.

If he'd killed either one of them or both, he was going to jail.

Or if they'd killed him, I was never going to be the same.

It might have been better to leave it up in the air so I'd never have to hear the devastating news.

But I knew better.

After I assured Officer Simmons I would be fine to take myself home and the police left, I did what I already knew I would do. I climbed into the railway car, closing the door behind me.

I tucked myself in the corner, like I had done so many years ago. It was cold. It was dark. But I was no longer scared.

I stayed there for hours, thinking, wishing, replaying everything that had happened since I was cursed, trying to figure out what it was saying to me.

Fallon's seemed so much easier to decipher.

The door creaked open, allowing a beam of moonlight to stream in and highlight Rex's beautiful face as he looked at me and smiled. I knew I'd find you here."

"Yeah, well I knew if I went here, you'd come. You always do."

"And I always will."

"I know."

He came over to me, pulling me into his lap and wrapping his warm body around me. I wanted to ask him what happened, needed to know if the police were after him or if Sampson was alive, but I knew that would have to wait. He needed to know something else first.

I would've known that from the look in his eyes even if Fallon hadn't predicted it. He picked up the end of my hair, wrapping it around his finger. Just like he had my heart. "Have you made a decision?"

"Yes."

"And?"

"The past is the past. The cold won't hurt me anymore."

He kissed the back of my hand, playfully biting it in the process. "No one will hurt you ever again. I would pull the fucking sun from the sky if it would warm you, T. You and I. Always."

"Yeah, well..."

"Yeah, well, what?"

"You know how the curse was telling me to stay the course and we both assumed that maybe that meant continuing my trek out of Between?" He nodded, squeezing my hand like he needed it for support. "Twenty years ago, our course started in this car. Together. I think this is the only course I've ever needed to be on. You and I. Always. Twenty-two and Twenty-three."

He laughed. "I'm partial to calling you Tragedy."

"And I'm partial to hearing it, but I don't feel like a tragedy anymore."

"You're my Tragedy."

"Yeah. I am and I'm glad you made it back to me."

"I have you to thank for that. Pretty damn smart to put the whole thing on Livestream."

I laughed. "I hoped it wouldn't backfire."

"It didn't. We got a couple of miles up the road, aiming guns at each other. He tried to destabilize me by slamming on his brakes at one point, but I had used a bungee cord to lash my ankle to the truck.

"Sampson took the gun away from him so he could drive and when he pointed it at me, I knew I was a goner. I did the whole life flashing before your eyes thing and all I saw was you."

I ran my hand over his jaw, hoping he could feel what I wanted, needed him to feel. "Before he could get a shot off, a convoy of motorcycles appeared. The Labradors Motorcycle Club. Some of them had seen the Livestream and mobilized from the bar up the street, knowing the cops weren't there yet.

"They knew your Uncle was shady before this, so they came with guns and shot out the tires and had them at gunpoint before I could blink. It was crazy. Their president gave me a ride back and made both of us honorary Labs if we want," he said through laughter. "That was quick thinking and now all of Between knows what kind of man Sampson Doe is."

"I'm just glad it worked. Can we get out of this car now? I want to put it behind me."

"Behind us."

"Yeah."

We got up and went over to the door. He hopped out first, then caught me as I jumped down into his arms. The sun was just cresting over the horizon, giving us a beautiful sunrise to start—no, to continue—our journey.

He took my hand and before we could take one step, a black feather drifted between our clasped hands. He bent over and picked it up, tucking it behind my ear, then he pulled me to the Jalopy and drove me to the garage and we celebrated the end of the curse in as many ways as he could imagine.

KEEP READING FOR THE EPILOGUE

EPILOGUE

Wayward Warbler
Two years later

I don't drink coffee and I don't drink tea
I don't drink blood unless it's made for meeee.
If you think you know me, you best think again,
As soon as you figure me out, you'll see I'm not your friend.
This Wayward Warbler used his magic one more time,
And now he thinks it's time for him to end this little rhyme.

A lot can change in two years. A lot can stay the same too, but that's not what occurred in this tale. No, the ending of this story is one I predicted, if I do say so myself.

As I do crow myself, I guess would be the technical term since I can't speak.

After Fallon and Esme successfully ended the curse and I delivered my feathers to them, they thought they were done with me. They weren't. I always check in on my victims from time to time, just to make sure they fully got the lesson.

I swooped down over the garage, flying low enough to peek inside the open door. Rex was finishing up under the hood of a black sedan while Esme was out in the back in her converted railcar.

Rex had personally towed the car from the abandoned railyard to the back of the garage, as a gift for Esme. I figured she'd want to help him destroy it in some way, but she managed to surprise him by asking him to help her turn it into something better, something she could use.

So, with Fallon and Quinn's help—along with the muscles of some rugby players—they cleaned it up, painted a nice calming shade of blue, and set it up as a lounge for Esme to use when she counseled young girls who'd been abducted.

And here you were thinking the curse was all about her and Fallon. Shame on you for underestimating my power.

Driven by what transpired, Esme went back to school, took classes online and in person to finish faster, and got her counseling degree. She used the car to set up a safe space for kids to come and talk. In the few months she'd been operating, she'd helped more than one girl come to terms with what happened. Her first client had been Samantha, the girl she'd inadvertently put in harm's way by setting that trap for Sampson.

Never you mind that either. I was always watching. That girl was never to come to harm. I was there that night and had my eyes trained on the situation.

Like I do.

But this part of the story isn't about Samantha.

Nor is it about Sampson who'd hung himself in his jail cell a week after he landed there. Or Mickey who was still trading cigarettes for sexual favors.

While most of the people in this tale were too polite to cheer the day they landed in jail with life sentences, you best believe I whooped and hollered as best as I could with a beak instead of a mouth.

This story is about Fallon and Esme.

Just as Esme was locking up the door, Rex came ambling out of the garage, wiping his hands on a rag, then tossing it on the ground. The path between the two spaces was littered with his rags because Esme insisted he not grope her with dirty hands.

Dirty mind and dirty mouth were completely different stories though.

"Don't lock up yet, Tragedy," he drawled as he liked to do with her. She loved the slow churn of his voice and when it included that sexy rasp, she was molten in his hands. "I want to rail you good."

For his part, Rex enjoyed getting physical in the rail car. It was his way of erasing the stain of what happened to them, christening the space with love and light.

And sex.

Lots of sex.

Watching them was always a treat for me. Thank the good goddess they usually left the door open.

He wrestled the keys from her hand and pushed her back inside as she giggled, knowing what was coming. Specifically, her. "We'll be late," she offered, but she didn't really care, not when he'd already dropped his coveralls before she could turn around.

Kissing her to the point where she was delirious, he backed her against the wall, wrapping his hand around her throat.

She loved that too. Not just the sensation of his hand, but the idea that her life was his in those moments when he squeezed. She'd never known trust like that before and she reveled in the idea that he brought her to the brink and back again. Always her savior.

He snuck his hand under her skirt, pulling her panties down to her ankles, then helped her step out of them with his foot. Before she could even look up, he'd hiked her leg over his hip and rammed his hard shaft into her wetness. Gentle ease was not his style. He wanted her to feel how much he desired her and she did.

Moaning, she wrapped her hands in his hair, loosening his binding so she could dig her fingers into it. "Pull it," he barked. So she did. His groans were music to her, set to the beat of his thrusts.

It didn't take long for her legs to shake, for her breath to come quickly. Knowing she was close, he put his hand between them, pinching and tweaking her swollen clit as he rammed into her pussy. She broke seconds later, bringing Rex with her as they crested the euphoria that was uniquely theirs.

When their hearts stopped pounding, he pushed her hair away, kissing her temple. "Always."

"Always."

Staying where they were, he mumbled against her skin. "It came today. Whenever you're ready, say the word."

Sighing, she nodded. "Not yet."

He understood and knew she'd get there one day. Maybe sooner than later.

~~

As they readied themselves for their appointment, I flew across Between, keeping a watchful eye on its residents, always searching for the next two to suffer my curse along the way.

Not today. Soon though. I felt it coming like an itch that couldn't be scratched.

As I approached my mark, I settled myself on a branch in a tree near the rugby field. I couldn't very well be seen, now could I? Wasn't time for that, no sir. Like I said, soon.

Fallon sat in the stands with her new full-time employee North, and her sister Zoey, leaving Oscar to mind the shop with the new part-time employee. She hadn't texted him once since she'd left the shop hours ago.

She was wearing the very same Rugby shirt Quinn had given her that first night, cheering her lungs out as he coached the team to the finals.

All the way to the championship in the second year was a huge feat, but nothing he couldn't do. He'd been the rightful coach all along. I just had to find a way to get that cheater gone.

I did not abide by cheaters. Couldn't. Shouldn't. Wouldn't.

Yeah, that was all me.

Of course, I wasn't going to get my name on the trophy, but I'd always know I set those events in motion.

As the timer counted down, Fallon and company made their way to the side of the field.

Five, four, three, two, one.

UNB wins! Let the celebration begin!

Fallon threw her arms around Quinn just as the team was executing that strange custom by throwing a keg of something cold over their coach. The two of them got drenched in the process.

It reminded both of them of the first day.

"Congrats Coach! You did remarkable."

"Couldn't have done it without you, Suds."

They shared a sweet kiss, then Fallon stepped aside, giving Quinn the opportunity to do the after-game process—interviews, pats on the back, locker room hi-jinks. When he was done with all that and he'd cleared the locker room out, he called for her to join him.

She, naturally, went running to his side, heading into the locker room like she owned it. In a way she did, because that was where part of his heart was and she owned that outright.

Me? I was perched on the windowsill, poking my face inside.

Quinn grabbed her hand. "Come with me."

"I'm soaked in Gatorade. I need to change before we—"

He captured her mouth in a blistering kiss. Whatever she would say next was gone from her brain, never to return. The feel of his lips on hers was her favorite thing in the world.

It would soon be the second, but I'm getting ahead of myself.

After locking the door first, he started the shower, pulling her in with him, clothes and all. As his hands roamed her body and removed her clothes, alternately, he muttered against her skin. "I didn't think this kind of happiness existed in the world."

She laughed. "I did. I knew the moment I saw you. I know that's cheesy, but it's true. I love you, you know."

"I do. Right back at you, Suds."

He was fast with his own clothes. Even faster to take her hand and place it right where he wanted it. As she pumped his stiff cock, she peppered his neck, his chest, his abdomen with kisses that gave them both chills, even under the hot spray of the water.

Needing more, he leaned down to kiss her, using his tongue to explore her mouth. Even though it was not new to them, the kisses always seemed to bring about a fresh feel every time. They never tired of it.

Pulling back, he bent to nip the shell of her ear. "Turn around. Hands on the wall."

She complied, throwing up her hands and baring herself to him. He grabbed her hips and pulled her to him, thrusting his hardness inside her and moaning at the feel of her pussy. "Fuck, you feel good," he grunted as he pushed into her.

"So do you."

He increased his pace, pulling her hips and loving the sound of their wet skin slapping together as he fucked her. "I love this tight pussy so much." She turned to look at him and smile, but he cocked an eyebrow. "I said hands up, Suds."

"Yes, sir." She slapped her hands against the tile again, knowing she'd be rewarded for that term. Sure enough, he reached around to the front and toyed with her, bringing her into the same state as he was.

If anyone had heard the sounds they were making, well, they would've known these two had it bad for each other.

Look at what I did. Such love and such lust. The two go together if you didn't know.

Nearing his release, he went harder, giving her just what she wanted, purring in her ear. "I'm going to come in that wet pussy and I want to feel you coming too."

She made a sound that I couldn't interrupt. I assume it was an agreement because they came together in the next instant. He never stopped playing with her, giving her all he could as she squeezed his cock until he was dry. When it was done, he brought her to his chest and they stood there together until the shower went cold.

~~

Esme and Rex entered the coffee shop. They were late because they'd stopped again in the car on the way over, but Fallon and Quinn didn't care. They were too busy deciding how to break the news.

Quinn wanted to pop open the champagne first, but Fallon insisted they act normal so they could spring their surprise on them.

She had truly embraced her new life, looking for ways to add laughter and joy into the lives of everyone, not just her friends and family. The balance she'd acquired after stepping away from her shop now and again was a benefit to all around her.

She set Esme's coffee and Rex's tea in front of them. Quinn got his regular Nora Roberts and she took a bottle of water from the fridge. They sat at the same table they'd been at when they figured out my curse. It had become a regular occurrence for the four of them. Sometimes they even played that silly card game or got drunk. And sometimes Esme and Rex would talk about what happened to them, or Fallon would share stories from her childhood or Quinn would describe some new urban legend he'd discovered.

This night was different though.

Esme was the first to notice. "My Romani intuition is telling me something is going on."

Quinn raised his eyebrow. "You're not Romani."

Rex added, "That we know of."

"Mm, yeah, but I can tell something is up. What is it?" She turned to Fallon. "Oh my—"

"I'm pregnant!"

There were a lot of woman squawking and men nodding and the celebration went on well into the night.

Finally, just before they were to leave, Esme cocked her head. "Have you thought of any names yet?"

Quinn laughed. "No, we haven't talked about it yet, but I would wager my next year's salary that Fallon has a list written down somewhere."

She calmly went over to the counter where the register sat and pulled out a notebook, showing them a list of handwritten names divided by gender, ranking, ease of pronunciation, and initial potential.

Mine was nowhere on the list, sadly.

Rex slung his arm around Esme. "I didn't realize there was so much involved in picking names."

"A rose by any other name, am I right?" Fallon quipped, looking at Quinn.

As the expectant parents beamed at each other, Esme quietly leaned to Rex. "I think it's time."

Smirking, which he knew she loved, so he did it quite often, he pulled a piece of paper from his jacket pocket, handing it over to her without any ceremony whatsoever.

Fallon, who missed very little, asked her, "What's that?"

"It's me. My birth certificate. My actual birth certificate. The police helped me find my birth parents and Rex has communicated with them some, letting them know I'm not ready to meet them just yet, but I will one day. They've been understanding and sent this to me in case I needed it. I wasn't going to look, but now knowing that the family is growing, I have a desire to know…how I started."

Rex squeezed her. "I only care about where you're going. I would find never knowing your birth name. You know that, right?"

"Yes, but it's time to get on with the rest of my life. Once I know this, I'll know I'm fully healed. I'm the person I'm meant to be."

She opened the envelope with trembling hands. It wasn't so much nerves, as it was anxiousness to put it in her rearview. Like she said, once she knew she'd close the gap in her life.

"My birth name is Temperance Holland."

Rex chuckled. "Another T, Tragedy."

Fallon quietly scribbled another name on her list as Quinn finally got to open the champagne.

The rest, as they say, will be history or future or some gray area in between.

ACKNOWLEDGEMENTS & A WORD FROM THE AUTHOR

This book hit different for me and I really enjoyed writing it for you. The inspiration just struck me one day and what I thought was going to be a novella ended up being a full novel (or very close to it.) You can thank my barista son for some of the content. Also, he makes a great cup of coffee, I'm told.

I'd like to start by thanking the massive snowstorm that came our way right after Christmas. I got six days off from work, so I did the bulk of the writing in that time. Without it, this book would not be finished yet.

Next, I was serious when I thanked the coffee shop employees in the dedication. Not only did I get the inspiration from their actual shop, but the employees were and are instrumental in my career and things having to do with it. It's the best coffee shop in the world.

Side note: I don't drink coffee! What?!?

Thank you to all of my ARC readers and everyone who has picked up this book because you thought it sounded interesting. Seriously, THANKS. As always, I ask you to please leave a review. For your convenience, please use this QR code for your Amazon review. And I always appreciated your GoodReads and any other sites you post reviews on. It really does make a difference.

Don't forget to follow on socials. Post your thoughts and tag me in positive reviews and say hey!

Last & never least, I want to shout out to my partner in writing crime, Mandy O'Dell. Love you, woman. I don't know what else to say, but you know I appreciate your encouragement and help.

This will not be the last story from the THE CURSE OF BETWEEN world. I will be finishing up my DIMINISHING MAGIC series first. The final book comes out this Spring, then I'll be onto the next story in the Between, Nevada universe.

If you liked this story, check out my Diminishing Magic series. It's a paranormal romance with a hotttt werewolf and a gnome with a problem and a feisty personality. It has horny fae, found family, lots of chemistry & banter between the leads, and "sexual tension that simmers off the page." That's a direct quote from a review.

Following is the blurb & the first chapter starts right after. Check it out on Kindle Unlimited /Amazon, Barnes & Noble, or check your fave indie bookstore.

JEWELS OF CLAY Blurb:
Desperation drove me to insanity. It's the only reason I can give for my quest to be admitted into the magic Conclave. If I hadn't been facing the repossession of my grandmother's home, with zero career prospects on the horizon, and flat broke, I wouldn't have ended up in a werewolf camp facing my almost-assured destruction.

Yet here we are.

In order to prove my—and my species'—worth to the Conclave, I entered into a magic Perception contract with the surliest and frustratingly hot of the pack's beta wolves. He wants me to complete some specially designed—ahem, impossible— trials to prove my worth, and if I fall short? Well, let's just say, I don't get to go back to my life knowing I tried my best. Nope. He gets to kill me the second he perceives me unworthy.

Outlook not so good.

If I can't use my gnome craftiness—yeah, I said gnome, and no, I don't have a pointy red hat. It's a beanie—my epitaph will read HERE LIES TERRA. SHE DIED DROOLING OVER A WOLFHOLE WITH PURPLE EYES AND INSANE ABS. AT LEAST THE VIEW WAS GOOD ON THE WAY OUT.

This is a steamy, slow-burn romance with enemies to lovers and a pack of hot shifters, full of humor, heart, and heat. It's perfect for fans of Kelly St. Clare or Leia Stone. Or anyone who ever used a Magic 8-ball.

CRITICAL REVIEW:
READERS' FAVORITE 5-STAR REVIEW

Cat Collins' writing shines in Jewels of Clay as she skillfully weaves a narrative that balances plot, pace, action, characters, and themes with finesse. The plot is engaging, offering a unique twist on the classic fantasy journey, and the pace keeps readers hooked from start to finish.
--Jacqueline Neves (Readers' Favorite)

DIMINISHING MAGIC BOOK ONE, FIRST CHAPTER

I couldn't believe I'd done it: cash-apped a sketchy leprechaun two-hundred bucks for intel on the location of the closest fairy ring. In my defense, I was running out of time, and catching fae wasn't illegal by definition; just frowned upon by most Magicals.

Good thing I was *half* magical.

I laid my oversized purse onto the kitchen counter, careful not to jostle the contents inside the small carved trunk or scatter the cooking utensils I'd laid out in preparation for this. The food was in the fridge, the recipes picked. I'd even grown and picked the vegetables with my Earth magic that morning and pre-rinsed them for good measure. Rinsing veggies was easy. It was the fairy's job to do the hard stuff.

Taking a deep breath, I removed the box, eager to see if giving up the last of my savings account for the ride-share it took to get to the ring and back was worth it. I didn't have a choice. Not if I wanted a roof over my head. Throw in months of bank notices, unopened letters from bill collectors, and stacks of Gram's unpaid medical bills, and my situation added up to be one big pile of suck.

Nabbing a fairy was the only way I could see out of it.

The lid creaked as the fairy burst out, cerulean wings fluttering as he sailed around the kitchen. He was easy to track because he wore what had to be Polly Pocket clothes from the eighties—bright pink shorts and a neon yellow and green tank. He whizzed by, almost colliding into the antique rack full of banged-up pots and pans before passing behind Gram's lace curtains that were now more cream-colored than their original white.

He finally flapped toward me and hovered a few inches from my face, coughing in the most exaggerated way as his shaggy mess of blonde hair flopped. "What in the name of the Mage did you let die in that bag? It smells like pig's feet and donkey ass!"

I stuck my nose inside the purse, picking up the scent of leather and breath mints. "No, it doesn't."

He pointed toward his nose. "Trust me. You'll appreciate my overdeveloped sense of smell after you taste what I make for you. That's what you said when you ripped me from my home: I'm here to cook. Right?" His voice was pleading and hopeful, and a nugget of guilt lodged in my gut. I quickly assured myself that Magicals had probably captured fae for much worse things than cooking. "Yes, I need this meal to be perfect." Mage knew I wasn't going to chance this very important meal on my culinary skills or lack thereof. I could barely make toast.

"Well, you nabbed the right fairy, Babycakes." I raised an eyebrow at the nickname, but it didn't slow him down a bit. "In Aetheria I was known for my skill with the culinary arts. Have you tried roasted strix? I know it's hard for some to stomach eating something that eats human flesh, but once you get past that, they're delicious. Though, I guess I'd have to pop over to the Mediterranean to get some. I could be back in a day, maybe two. Where are we, anyway? I was in that trunk for a few hours. Are we still in Oregon?"

"We're in Eugene. My deceased Gram's house. In a retirement village." I checked my phone, nervous titters swirling through me. Six hours and counting. No time for strix hunting. "I need you to understand: an entire species of Magicals is at stake here."

Not to mention my accommodations, living expenses, food on my table. Or, again, lack thereof. I couldn't survive on tomatoes and carrots I'd grown in my garden. Vegan was more of a dirty word than way of life for me. And I'd had enough ramen noodles for two lifetimes already.

I kept mum about how I was about to be kicked out of my home and had no real job outside of a seasonal gig at the garden center and part-time meal delivery service driver, where I'd skimmed a few fries off the top now and then. He didn't need to know how desperate I was.

"A whole species? Sounds ominous." He dropped to a lounging position on the counter, crossing his legs and throwing his muscled arms behind his head. "As the humans say, spill the coffee."

Already, he was getting under my skin, and he'd been there less than five minutes.

I shook my head. "Spill the *tea*, not coffee."

"What-the-fuck-ever. I try to steer clear of humans as much as possible."

Same. Which was weird considering I was half human. But truth be told, I stayed away from just about everyone, human or magical. If I'd had a middle name, it would've been hermit. That was mostly due to circumstance. It was hard to form relationships, friend or otherwise, when you spent all your time caring for an ill, unstable person. Once my Gram died, I didn't even know where to start to look for people to socialize with outside of work, so I didn't.

I took a deep breath. It seemed like a point of no return moment, but I needed the fairy to fall in line. "We're petitioning to join the Conclave."

I'd sold Gram's car to Liam for information on the leader and how the petition process worked. Which meant I was no longer going to make food deliveries. Another gamble that could've left me homeless if it didn't play out as I'd planned.

Even at his small size, the fairy's deep throaty laugh filled the entire kitchen. "I'm impressed you got anything on the Conclave, but they haven't let a species join in hundreds of years. The last one was gargoyles. That ended *so* well for them."

Thanks for the reminder about how high the odds were stacked against me.

I grabbed a dish towel and threw it at him, which he dodged like a professional…dodger.

Douchehead.

"We've got more to offer than gargoyles and we wouldn't let being in the Conclave go to our heads like they did." I sounded lame, even to myself. I was more worried about my personal stake in this than getting my species in the Conclave. They'd managed millennia without the protection and privileges the Conclave offered. Me? I had another week or two, tops before I was out on my ass.

Helping gnomes into the Conclave was the only way to get to Aetheria, the birthplace of magic—my true purpose for all of this nonsense. In Aetheria, there would be no hiding from humans, no taxes or monetary system to worry about, and oceans of ambient magic, free for the taking. It sounded like the perfect place to be. Besides, I had no ties keeping me in this realm since Gram had died two years ago, leaving me a house I couldn't pay for and no inheritance whatsoever. I couldn't even afford to change the old-lady lace curtains or, Mage help me, the wall-to-wall gold shag carpet.

The fairy took me in with his crystalline blue eyes, which matched his flittering wings. "So, what species are you? No, don't tell me." He surveyed me, trying to pinpoint my species.

My pulse raced under his scrutiny because being in the spotlight was not my thing. It unnerved me. Enough that I went straight to goading him. "What? Your super sniffer failing you now?"

I folded my arms across my chest. Not my most mature moment, but he was wasting my time and frying the last remnants of my nerves. Again, he laughed. Then, he sailed off the counter and made swirling circles around my neck. I didn't have to hear or see him to know he was sniffing me.

Sniffing. Me.

Though, in all fairness, I basically invited him to take a whiff.

In response, he grunted. Not sure if it was a good or a bad kind. I almost grabbed the fly swatter, but I stopped short.

Slow your roll, Terra. You need him.

He flitted around my head, picking up a strand of hair before he nearly landed on my nose. "Plain brown hair, so you aren't a pixie; dark eyes instead of gold, so gryphon's out…too small to be Valkyrie…Who else isn't in the Conclave like us lowly fae?" He said with a hint of bitterness in his voice, then landed back on the counter, cocking his head. "You smell of buttery gold and rich soil after a rain. And there's something else, but maybe just your own personal aroma."

"Can we just get—"

"Wait. Oh, my Mage. Are you…no way, you can't be!"

There it was.

He slapped his own knee laughing and nearly rolled into the jar of flour he should've been using to cook my meal. "You're a gnome, aren't you? An elusive gnome. This just keeps getting better."

Among Magicals, not even trolls got the amount of ridicule that gnomes did. We didn't deserve that but having so little magic made a difference in our world. I released a slow breath. I didn't have time for his nonsense.

I slammed my hand on the counter for emphasis, setting my features into a cold stare. Letting him know I meant business. "Yes, I'm half-gnome. You've got three seconds to stop laughing and get busy. Or did you forget? I captured you, so I own your ass."

At least I thought so. Liam was a little loose with the details on that.

"Yes ma'am." He managed to pick himself and assemble what resembled a serious expression, then ruined it by turning and slapping his own butt. "This ass is yours."

What had I done?

I'd gambled the remnants of my savings, not to mention my future, on a flippant, smartass fairy.

To his credit, he didn't even blink at the half-gnome comment. Being half-blood had cursed my entire life. Most Magicals did a one-eighty when they found out about it. And, of course, I couldn't tell any human friends about my magical half. If I'd had any. I guess if you counted co-workers who occasionally ate in the same breakroom and had conversations about last night's TV shows count as friends, I did.

Yup. Terra Hermit Youngblood had a nice ring to it.

I turned my back on the fairy. The pressure was getting to me, and I didn't want to lose my shit in front of him. There was too much riding on this.

He pricked my shoulder with his tiny finger. "Oh good, I thought you were turning into a statue. You know, like a garden gnome. Get it? Garden gnome!"

Anger rocketed through me. I grabbed a dirty glass containing the remains of my breakfast milk from the sink and slapped it down over the fairy, capturing him in one swift motion. Droplets of souring milk dripped onto his head, splashing on his shiny hair. He did not like that.

As he flapped and gagged and made a fool of himself trying to escape, I tapped my foot. "I'm sorry, what? I can't quite hear you. Did you need something?"

Juvenile behavior — two. Maturity — zero.

I was overreacting. But Gram's gnome pride was ingrained deep. I even refused to sell the garden gnome statues at work. I let my co-workers think I was freaked out by them, so I didn't have to face the insult head-on.

When the fairy quieted down and sat cross-legged on the counter, I let him free. He raced to the sink, hit the nozzle, and took a little fairy shower. When he had the milk removed, he shook his head like a dog.

I could've sworn the ancient cuckoo clock hanging in the dining room ramped the volume up to eleven.

Tick. Tick. Tick.

If he didn't start cooking soon, it would all be for nothing.

"Sorry about the milk. I'm just nervous," I admitted.

Not that I owed him an apology because from where I stood, he started the whole mess, but I was desperate and anxious. Though, I understood the big question mark that accompanied the word, gnome. I may have forgotten all about that part of my lineage if not for my frantic need to provide for myself.

To appease some of his questions and get his ass in gear, I went with the simple explanation my dear ole gnome-proud Gram gave me when she told me what I was. "Yes, the cheesy garden gnomes are based on our species. No, we don't all have pointy red hats." Though my favorite beanie was red, but that didn't count. "We're an ancient, cunning, and noble guardian species formed by the Mage to guard the palace jewels for the Fae Kings of Court. We're experts at hiding and protecting valuables."

If it was someone else's, not our own, but he didn't need to know that part. There were other things too, but I wasn't going to share them with a fairy. Before she went loco and died of some unknown disease no human or Magical doctor could pinpoint, Gram had told me fae couldn't be trusted.

She also said trolls were the best lovers and she'd spoken to the Mage many times and he replied because he was her bestie. She was full cuckoo at the end, my Gram. I'd filled an entire journal with her harebrained ramblings because they made me laugh. *Gramisms*, I called it.

"Gnome. Okay." He side-eyed me like he was trying to make sense of my existence. Been doing that for twenty-two years and hadn't come up with much yet, so good luck, Bud. He sailed off the counter, buzzing around my head. "Gnomes are alchemists, right? So, you could make some edible gold leaf for the meal if I asked?"

If only.

Most gnomes were great at alchemy, but I sucked at it.

I assumed I didn't have enough magic in me, thanks to my human mother. Not that I could've kept the gold for myself anyway. Magical rules and all that B.S. I *did* have some that Gram had made tucked away though. I nodded at the fairy. "Yeah. How much will you need?"

He rifled through the pile of recipe cards and clapped his hands. "A quarter-cup should work. Now, I have dishes to prepare. Go somewhere else and deal with your nerves, get laid or something."

Not an abysmal idea, but I didn't have the time to dedicate to that endeavor. Besides, who was I going to sleep with? I had no prospects on the horizon. My life had been about prepping for that night, not Terra's personal plan to hook up with the hottest guy I could dig up.

Which was usually how my encounters were. One-night stands or occasional sexy liaisons that lasted a few days or weeks. Because even though I was a solitary soul by nature and by circumstance, I still had…needs. Though getting laid would have to take a back seat, at least until I got into the Conclave. Maybe then I'd find a sexy elf or gryphon in Aetheria that caught my eye. Until then, ix-nay on the ex-say for me.

I tromped down the stairs to my basement suite. The rich brown walls reminded me of the soil when I tunneled. It was dark, cool, and enveloped me like a hug. I was safe there. Protected. Throwing myself down on my comfy and unmade bed, I wrapped my homemade green comforter around me and glanced at my bedside table.

Out of instinct, I reached for my Gram's Magic 8-Ball. It was a silly human toy she'd bought for my father when he was young, but after her mind started to go, she used it every day when she wanted to *consult the Mage.*

I had to swallow down the lump in my throat. I missed her so much. So much that I made a point to ask the thing at least one question a day, just to keep her memory alive. Since the fairy had put the thought in my head, I went with the obvious question. "Magic 8-Ball, will I get laid anytime soon?"

Reply hazy, please try again.

That's what I figured. I needed to stay the course and see my plans through. There would be time for all the hook-ups in Aetheria as soon as I got gnomes into the Conclave. Obviously, Magic 8-ball agreed.

Reluctantly, I set the 8-ball back in its place and pulled myself off the bed. There was work to do. I went over to the tiny water closet where my ever-so-seventies gold tub and toilet were located and started the shower. Thanks to the practically-prehistoric water heater, it would take about ten minutes for the water to heat to a bearable level, so while it warmed, I pulled my Gram's battered old trunk from under my bed.

Inside were the last fragments of my Gram's gold stash. She hadn't made gold in quite some time before her passing, but I'd kept the last of her supply just in case I needed to sell it. Turned out I had exactly a quarter-cup.

I swore when I died and went to Netheria—that is, if a half-magical person's soul were even permitted in the resting place of Magicals—I'd ask the Mage why he'd made gnomes incapable of keeping any treasures or riches for ourselves. That sick trick of nature was responsible for a lot of pain. Though, in fairness, my human side didn't seem to be that great at holding on to my own money either.

After I showered, I dressed in my black dress pants and fitted black sweater, attempting to look as put-together and professional as I could. Out of habit, I reached for the vial that contained soil from my birthplace. It hung from a black cord, and I only took it off to shower. I even slept in it.

Gram was too deep into her delusions to ask where the soil was from when I discovered the vial tucked in her jewelry box with a note saying *"Terra, this is the soil from where you were born. It will ground you and guide you."*

It didn't matter where I was born. What was important was that I had something that connected me to who I was, to Gram. I put it on, feeling the familiar silk cord, the weight of the vial against my chest, and stared at myself in the mirror. I instantly calmed. The vial *did* ground me. But I was still waiting for the guide part to kick in. Maybe it and the Magic 8-Ball needed to get together.

The cord looked fine with my outfit, but something about having dirt hanging from your neck screamed weak and desperate. Okay, I was weak and desperate, but they didn't have to know that, so I pulled the vial off and hung it over my mirror.

I poured the last sprinkles of Gram's gold into a bowl, then headed upstairs, where the fairy forbade me from helping him. Great idea on his part. I almost burned my whole house down making French fries in the oven.

Teach me to try and be healthy.

I set the table as best I could, using gold-plated utensils that I hoped wouldn't be too obvious because it was all I had. The tablecloth and napkins were made of gold silk I picked up at a thrift store and I added a sprinkling of gold leaf down the center of the table. It looked majestic and elegant. That's what I was going for. The Conclave was all about formality, tradition, and sticking to magic rules. It's how Magicals had survived undetected by humans for so long, according to Liam the leprechaun.

I gathered the rest of the gold leaf in a bowl and pushed the swinging kitchen door open. "Here's your go—" The glass bowl slipped from my hands and tumbled to the floor. "Oh, my Mage!"

The fairy was standing at the sink with his back turned. He didn't even react to the shattering glass. "Oh, my Mage, what?"

He'd turned into a full adult-sized man—no wings.
Also, no clothes.

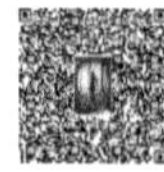

Continue to Ch. 2 by purchasing or reading on KU here:

AUTHOR BIO:

Cat Collins is the #1 bestselling author in her home. No really, her husband wrote a training manual for work once. He sold one copy to his boss. She writes what she likes to read: swoony alphas, witty dialogue, and steamy scenes that make your heart (and various other parts) flutter.

Her Diminishing Magic series has garnered a Readers' Favorite 5-Star critical review and praise from reviewers for its hilarious banter, sexual tension between characters, and turns you never see coming. Described as a "twisty bundle of fun," the series includes elemental magic, wolf shifters, and a main character who's full of sass.

A reading interventionist by day, a reader and binge-watcher by night, Cat lives in the Southern US with her husband as mentioned above, two kids, and two cats who like to help her edit by jumping on the keyboard randomly. Any stray typos must surely be the work of Raven or Poe.

She loves connecting with readers on social media. @CatCollinsBooks on TikTok, Instagram, Facebook. Join her reader group "Cat Tales" too.

Subscribe to her monthly newsletter at catcollinsbooks.com for behind-the-scenes exclusives, news, book recs, and more. Click or scan the QR code to see the subscribe link.